OLD **MAN**

OLD MAN

David A. Poulsen

DUNDURN
TORONTO

Editor: Sylvia McConnell
Design: Laura Boyle
Printer: Webcom

Library and Archives Canada Cataloguing in Publication

Poulsen, David A., 1946-
          Old man / David A. Poulsen.

Issued also in electronic formats.
ISBN 978-1-4597-0547-0

          I. Title.

PS8581.O848O54 2012   jC813'.54   C2012-903216-6

1   2   3   4   5   17   16   15   14   13

Conseil des Arts   Canada Council
du Canada   for the Arts

Canadä

ONTARIO ARTS COUNCIL
CONSEIL DES ARTS DE L'ONTARIO

We acknowledge the support of the **Canada Council for the Arts** and the **Ontario Arts Council** for our publishing program. We also acknowledge the financial support of the **Government of Canada** through the **Canada Book Fund** and **Livres Canada Books**, and the **Government of Ontario** through the **Ontario Book Publishing Tax Credit** and the **Ontario Media Development Corporation.**

Care has been taken to trace the ownership of copyright material used in this book. The author and the publisher welcome any information enabling them to rectify any references or credits in subsequent editions.

                                                                    J. Kirk Howard, President

Printed and bound in Canada.

Visit us at
Dundurn.com
Definingcanada.ca
@dundurnpress
Facebook.com/dundurnpress

Dundurn
3 Church Street, Suite 500
Toronto, Ontario, Canada
M5E 1M2

Gazelle Book Services Limited
White Cross Mills
High Town, Lancaster, England
LA1 4XS

Dundurn
2250 Military Road
Tonawanda, NY
U.S.A. 14150

For my children and their children
and for Glen Huser.

Author's Note

This book is not for everyone. It is, in part, about war and the savagery that is a product of countries sending their citizens into battle against one another. The results are often horrific, frequently tragic beyond our imaginations. For that reason the book is hard-hitting with scenes of violence and coarse language. Those scenes are not intended to shock readers or to celebrate what, in some cases, may be seen as the less admirable human behaviours, nor is the coarse language gratuitous. The author realizes there will be those who will be concerned about those elements of this work, particularly since *Old Man* is a novel for young readers. I understand those concerns and offer this advisory for that reason.

Old man, look at my life, I'm a lot like you were.

—"Old Man" by Neil Young

Fair is foul, and foul is fair:
Hover through the fog and filthy air.

—*Macbeth* by William Shakespeare

1

My old man ran off with a college student who was studying to be a dental hygienist. He was fifty-two. She was nineteen. I was five.

I never called him "Dad" again.

2

There were three days left. Three days to summer holidays. Three days to two months of freedom. And a summer vacation that was to be like no other. At least not one I'd ever had. Two months of getting important stuff done.

I'd even written out all the things I planned to accomplish. Had them recorded in one of my school folders. I'd be like this totally new me in just sixty days.

Maybe some people wouldn't have found my list all that impressive, but I was pretty pumped about it. This summer wasn't going to be wasted on hanging out at the 7-Eleven, practising skateboard moves, spewing one-liners like a comedy volcano, getting acne from eating fast food and looking at every girl with a nice chest that passed by, wishing that once, just once, I could get my hands on them ... uh ... her.

Those had been my last two summer holidays. And at the time they didn't seem that bad — especially the girls with nice chests part. I was sixteen, and I could do some pretty awesome skateboard stuff; I knew where to get the best fries, the best cheeseburgers and the best Dr Pepper slurpees; and I got off a ton of one-liners that had every 7-Eleven kid thinking I was one hilarious guy.

I also got horny. Pretty much every day. Tried out some of the *really* funny lines on girls as they went in and out of the store. Unfortunately I also perfected the art of the opposite sex strikeout. I went 0 for July and August. Two years in a row. Apparently people who didn't hang out at the 7-Eleven didn't think I was nearly as funny as the ones who did. Actually, a couple of the girls that I treated to some of my Huffmanian humour had a few lines of their own. Not real funny. Not funny at all really, but they definitely let a guy know what they were thinking. And, of course, we all laughed like it was all killer-funny. That way it looks like they're laughing *with* you not at you. Except these girls weren't laughing with me.

By the way, how does a guy get all the way through grade ten without ever having placed a hand on a lovely lady bump? Not one freaking time. Which is a fact known to no one. All of my guy friends think I'm a fondling ma-chine. Because that's what I've told them.

Anyway, this time was going to be different. I'd even given it a name. I called it The Summer of the Huffman. A summer with a *name*. Okay, so here's the list:

1. Win the War against Acne. Wash face twice a day and apply the cream. (I'd bought a bunch of

products and had them all lined up on my dresser in my room.)

2. Gain five pounds of muscle. (This is a two-parter.) a) drink a milkshake every day and b) actually use the weights that have been rotting (does metal rot?) in the basement since about four days after I talked my mom into buying them at a garage sale two streets over. The reason for this one is football — I got cut last year because I was too light. I'm five pounds heavier since then, and I figure another five should turn me into the Defensive Back from Hell.

3. Read two novels, good ones, one each month. I figured I'd start with *Catch-22*. (My ninth grade English teacher, who also happened to be my *best* teacher, said it was one of his top ten novels of the twentieth century). It's about some crazy guys in the war ... or maybe it's about how war is crazy, I'm not sure. Guess I'll find out. Decide on the second novel a little closer to August.

4. Work three nights a week at the grocery plaza. Maybe Saturdays too if I can stand my boss, Helen, "Bitch" Boyes, that many times in a seven-day period.

5. This is the big one. Take out Jen Wertz. This has been a goal since the first term of ninth grade when I sat across the aisle from her in social. All of the first four points on the list are tied to Point #5. Get rid of the acne, get bigger for football, get smarter, get richer and bingo — get Jen.

So there it is. The carefully crafted plan for one amazing summer. End result — the new improved Nate Huffman. Oh, and that was new too. No more *Nathan*, skinny kid with pimples who hasn't read anything that wasn't a graphic novel in two maybe three years. Soon it would be the clear-complexioned, almost brainy, football stud with money — *Nate* Huffman.

And the plan might have actually worked too. But we'll never know. Because three days before the start of summer holidays — The Summer of the Huffman … my old man phoned.

3

When most people refer to their old man, they're talking about their dad. I'm talking about my *old man*. Larry Huffman is sixty-two years old. Which means he was forty-seven when I was born and forty-six when he, you know, got me started. That seems ridiculously old to me, but, to be honest, I figure everyone over about forty should be settling back in a rocking chair with their own monogrammed clicker and staying the hell out of the way of younger people — the segment of society that really makes stuff happen. *My* segment.

So my mom was twenty-seven at the time she got pregnant — which seems a little more normal for that whole making-babies thing. The nineteen-year difference between her age and my old man's — hard to figure that one. But I guess it made more sense than the thing with the teeth-babe.

And now he's sixty-two. Sixty-two years old is something that I don't get — like sines, cosines, and tangents. What the hell do you *do* when you're sixty-two? Your kids are out working and having families, you're about to retire from whatever it is you've been doing for the last forty years, you hurt all over, and you can't find your glasses.

Memo to self — die before sixty-two.

The other thing about my old man is that since he left — eleven years ago — he's never been back. I hear from him about three times a year: Christmas — you'd expect that, Father's Day, (I don't get that at all, it would make more sense if *I* phoned *him* that day, which I wouldn't since the guy sucks at being a dad) ... and my birthday, I guess phoning is cheaper than sending a gift ... so, a phone call. Except that he doesn't very often phone right *on* my birthday, he's usually three or four days or even a week late. And a couple of times he missed the phone call altogether — which was actually a bonus since a) I didn't have to talk to him and b) I did get a gift, even though it was a couple of weeks later after I'd pretty much forgotten I'd even *had* a birthday.

Never has one of his three phone calls a year been at the end of the school year — which made this one special. No, bad word choice. None of his calls is *special*; let's just call it different. The other thing that was different about this call was that he spent a fair amount of time talking to Mom before he got on the phone with me.

Usually, it's a quick "hi, how are things" with Mom, and then it's my turn. There's a lot of small talk ... what's the weather like, what do you think of the Broncos this year (he knows I'm a big Denver Broncos fan), have you got a girlfriend ... that kind of stuff. And silence, there tends to be a lot of silence. Mostly because my answers are pretty short, and he runs out of small talk material fairly fast. But it's like he thinks the conversation has to go a certain amount of time to qualify as a dad-kid moment, so there we are in the silence. I'm usually waiting for the thing to end, and I sometimes get the feeling that he is too.

This time, no small talk. First, he talked to my mom. Like I said, for a long time. Mom wasn't saying much, and the look on her face was serious through the whole phone call, so I figured the old man was phoning from jail or something. I was knocking back a Dr Pepper and pretending to be reading the crap out of an Edgar Allan Poe short story for English, but since I was only maybe six feet from Mom, I could totally listen in on the call — at least her part of it.

Which, as I said, wasn't much. A few one-syllable responses and two longer ones. "Yes, he has a passport," and "No, he doesn't have asthma."

Great, the old man is sending me to Greenland or somewhere that you shouldn't go with asthma, and my totally amazing summer of intensive self-improvement is about to become a totally un-amazing two months of intensive boredom.

4

I was wrong about Greenland.

5

Mom handed me the phone. I shook my head *no*, but she passed it to me anyway.

"Hi." I didn't say *hi Dad* for the simple reason that I didn't call him Dad. Ever. I know I said that before, but you're supposed to repeat important stuff, so I'm repeating it.

I was also wrong about the small talk. One question, that was all. "How's school?"

"Yeah, fine."

Then it was straight to the big stuff. Big stuff for him.

Crap for me.

"I want us to spend some time together, Nathan."

"What do you mean by 'some'?"

"I guess it'll take a few weeks."

It'll take? What does that mean? What'll take?

"I have some plans — some stuff I wanted to kind of … do."

I heard him inhale, then exhale on the other end of the line. Like the doctor tells you to do when he's got the stethoscope on your back. "Deep breath, then let it out slow." You wanna piss him off, you let it out fast, all in one whoosh. I've done that a couple of times. To see what he'd say. But our family doctor, Dr. Phillip Lam, has no sense of humour. He just moves the stethoscope to another part of my back and says it again, "Deep breath, then let it out slowly." I always do it right the second time. No sense messing with the guy if he doesn't get that he's being messed with.

"I can promise you a summer you'll never forget."

"This blows."

"You can't know that until we've done it."

"Done what?" I looked over at Mom, who was avoiding eye contact.

"Several things. You might learn something and you might even … like it. If you let yourself."

He was using the same argument Mom makes when she wants me to try some really gross zucchini concoction.

"What exactly is a kid my age going to do with someone … your age … that is going to make this summer
something I'll never forget?"

"What's age got to do with it?" His voice had a little
edge to it. *Good. I'm pissing him off.*

I took a swallow of Dr Pepper. "What's your favourite
TV show?"

There was a pause. I guess he didn't expect *that* question. "I
don't know, I guess *LA Law* or maybe *Law and Order*. Why?"

"Mine's *The Simpsons*. Doesn't that tell you something?"

Another pause. "Tells me we shouldn't watch a lot of
television this summer."

Yeah, the old man's hilarious sometimes. A million
laughs. Except I didn't laugh. And that was it. End of conversation. He said he'd call me the next day, and he hung up.

I was still holding the phone in my hand as I looked over
at my mom. "Feel like telling me what that was all about?"

She turned, wiped her hands on her apron, and
looked at the chair across from me. But she changed her
mind and didn't sit down.

"I think it's better coming from him."

"I got *nothing* from him."

"You will. He'll tell you about it in his own way."

I opened my mouth to argue, but I could tell from the
way she was shaking her head that she wasn't going to tell me
what the old man had in mind for my summer. I went back
to Poe and re-read the same three-line paragraph four times.

I looked over at her and she was cutting up an onion.
I figured that was a good time to ask her. If she started to
cry, she could pass it off as that whole onion-tears thing.

"What's he like?"

She didn't answer.

"I guess the better question is what *was* he like?" In all the years since the old man had left, I'd never asked Mom about him. Guess I didn't care to know. And she'd never talked much about him.

Sometimes I wondered if she missed him or was pissed off at him or still loved him or what, but she never said, and I didn't ask, mostly because I didn't want to have any part in a conversation that had the old man as a topic. I was sure of one thing. I was pissed off at him *for* her. A dental freaking hygienist.

Mom gathered up the outer skin of the onion and stepped on the pedal thingy that lifts the lid on the trash can. Green metal job with a silver lid. Been sitting in that corner of the kitchen as long as I can remember. I figure that lid has been up and down a few thousand times. She dropped the onion skin into the can and let the lid back down.

"He played professional baseball."

"You're kidding." Definitely not the first thing I expected to hear. Not a ball player. A *professional* ball player.

Mom was back at the counter chopping the onion. I closed the Poe book.

"He only played one year, somewhere in Florida. Of course it was before I met him. Just the one year, then he got hurt. Quit baseball to … do other things."

"What other things?"

"It would be better if all this came from your dad."

I noticed she was chopping faster than usual. "Why?"

Mom shrugged and scooped the chopped onion into

a casserole dish. "It just would, Nathan, you'll have to believe me on that."

"What's the guy like — a spy or something?" It was a pretty lame joke, but I wasn't trying very hard.

Mom smiled and shook her head. "No, and I'm not trying to be all secretive. I just think he'd like to be the one to tell you about himself. Maybe he'll do some of that this summer."

"Maybe?"

"I don't know for sure. I think he will."

"But you're okay with me going away with him for the summer."

Mom turned to look at me. "He's not an evil man."

"Well, he sure as hell ain't no saint. He left you for a teenager."

"No, he's not a saint."

She was sort of defending him. That made no sense to me. Why couldn't she throw stuff around the house, cut his face out of all their photos, hang up on him? She'd never done any of those things. And now she seemed okay with him and me spending a bunch of the summer together. In a place you needed a passport to get to.

Parents are hard to figure.

Later, while we ate the casserole — she had added carrots, tomato, celery, and cheese (but not zucchini) to the onion — I studied my mom's face. I did that every once in a while. She was an okay-looking woman in a forties-looking kind of way. (What I said before about people over forty doesn't apply to Mom.) It's not like she seems younger than she is; in fact, sometimes she seems older, but she always kind of *gets* people younger than her.

Her eyes had wrinkles at the corners, but they weren't laugh wrinkles. Mom's not a big laugher. She smiles some, and sometimes there's this little throaty chuckle that's cool, but I've never heard her laugh real hard or real loud. Ever. I couldn't see any grey in her hair. I didn't know if that was because she coloured it. I didn't think so. Mom wasn't into her appearance very much. I was pretty sure she'd never gone out with a guy since the old man left. Too bad.

And she didn't yell either. It was like the laughing thing. Mom could make you know she was mad with her voice and with the looks she'd give you. But she wasn't much for yelling.

I worked the casserole for a while. "I had plans for this summer," I told her between bites.

"Your dad said he thought three weeks or a month. That still leaves a lot of time."

"I had some stuff I wanted to do."

She nodded. "Stuff you could do next summer?"

"Stuff I wanted to do *this* summer."

"But could be done next summer."

I shrugged. "Maybe, I guess."

"I know this isn't the way you'd like to spend this time, but I think you should do it, and I think you should give your dad a chance."

"A chance for what? It's a little late for him to be a dad."

"Yes, it's too ... no it isn't, not really. Maybe not a dad as in raising you, but —"

"What other kind of dad is there?"

"I guess ... I guess the kind who wants to be with you for a while, maybe be your friend as you get older."

A couple of times before, Mom had said she wished I knew him better. She didn't make a big deal of it, just mentioned it. I guess maybe that's why she was thinking this was all okay.

"He send you money?"

She looked at me, raised an eyebrow.

"You know, alimony, child support? He send money for that stuff?"

"He sends money."

"He send enough?" I'd never thought of us as struggling financially, but we weren't exactly the rich people on the block either.

"He sends money."

She reached for a little more casserole and asked me something about school, so I figured she was finished talking about the old man.

6

If you are going to read this, there are things about me you need to know. One of the things you need to know is that I don't like dogs. Pretty much hate them all. Including Jen Wertz's golden retriever. I've only seen the dog a couple of times and everybody says it's a real nice dog, but I figure once I'm in solid with Jen, like real solid, I'll just quietly mention to her that either the dog goes, or I do.

Yeah, that should work.

7

When I was four years old, I had a bad experience. Scary bad. My mom and I were visiting my aunt and uncle and their kid in Regina, Saskatchewan. I can't remember if the old man was there or not. He could have been because he didn't take off with the college student until a year later.

My cousin and I were playing outside. Her name was Sandra. I didn't like her much, I can't remember why, probably because she was two and I was four, and two-year-olds can be a giant pain in the ass to four-year-olds. I remember that it was a big deal if you called her Sandy.

"Her name is Sandra, S-a-n-d-r-a." I heard that a few times from Aunt Meg. She was okay as long as you didn't call the kid Sandy. Or swear. I remember one time I committed the worst of sins when I said "Sandy is a poop ass." Four-year-old swearing. I got a couple of whuppings for that, the first one from Aunt Meg for "Sandy" and the second one from my mom, who hardly ever laid a hand on me. I guess she figured "poop ass" was a little over the line.

Anyway, we were outside in the front yard and a dog, a big dog, got in the yard and went after my cousin. Attacked her. I don't remember the details all that well, but I think she tried to pet the dog, and it just went for her.

I jumped in to try to get the dog off her. I yelled at it, and I tried to hit it to make it go away. It stopped attacking my cousin and turned on me. I heard my cousin screaming. I don't know if I was screaming or not. The next thing I remember was being in the hospital, with my mom and my aunt standing beside my bed telling me what a brave little hero I was, and how I had saved Sandra.

I wound up getting sixty stitches, most of them on my arm but some on a leg too. Some cuts on my face, but those weren't major. The worst part was the needles for rabies. The dog was a stray, and he was gone by the time the adults got outside.

I was in the hospital overnight and the next day when I got home, they had a party for me … like a birthday party. There was a cake and some of Aunt Meg's neighbours were there and some little kids from around the neighbourhood. I didn't even know most of them. Sandy the poop ass was there too. I mean she would be. I saved her, didn't I?

My mom carried me in from the car and set me in this big soft chair in the living room of my aunt's house. I liked that chair. There was more of the "brave little soldier" talk, and people I'd never seen before were taking my picture and smiling big smiles at me and touching me on the face.

It was okay for a while, but then I started crying and couldn't stop, which pretty much wrecked the party. My mom finally carried me upstairs to bed and read me a story. I don't remember which one.

I think maybe the reason I was crying was that I knew they were wrong. I wasn't brave at all. I was scared to death. Long after it happened, if I thought about it, I'd start shaking, and I'd clench my eyes shut to try not to see that dog.

But it didn't work. For a really long time I'd see that dog's face right in front of me, the huge jaws, the terrible teeth, always coming back at me, even though I was already hurt and not doing anything to him anymore.

I don't see the dog's face anymore. Haven't for a few years now. But I'm still scared of dogs, especially big ones. Little dogs don't scare me as much, but I don't like them. We've never had a dog. I'm probably the only kid I know who doesn't bug his parent to get a dog.

8

Another thing about me you should know is that I get headaches. Mom even had me checked out a couple of times to see if there was something wrong with me, like *really* wrong with me, but nothing showed up. "Tension headaches," the doctor said. When he said that, I was like, *Come on, I'm fifteen years old. You can do better than playing the stress card.* But maybe he was right. Sometimes I get pretty wound up, I guess.

So, no surprise — the night after the old man's call, I woke up with a headache. The pounding kind … like there's somebody chopping wood, and they're using your head for a chopping block. This time I could definitely see stress as the cause. I got out of bed and crunched a toe trying to get to the bathroom in the dark.

I swore, fumbled for the light switch, turned it on and made it the rest of the way to the bathroom. I took a Tylenol, drank a glass of water, and stumbled back to bed, pain now throbbing at both ends of my body. Terrific. I hoped the painkiller would kick in real soon.

Meanwhile, I lay in bed thinking about the old man's phone call and my mom talking about him and sort of defending him, but all that did was make my head feel worse, so I tried thinking about something else.

When I was little, if I had a headache or an earache or a fever, all I had to do was let out one squeak and Mom was in my room like a shot. Then it would be a hot towel or ear drops or ground up baby Aspirin, whatever she figured I needed. Usually worked too. And she'd stay there until I fell asleep again.

She told me once she'd wanted to be a nurse. Couldn't afford to go to school to become one. Sometimes I think it must suck to have this thing you really want to do with your life, and you don't get the chance. She doesn't complain or even talk about it except that once, but I sometimes see her staring off out the window, not really looking at anything, and I wonder what she's thinking about.

I figure Mom would have been an awesome nurse — she loves to do things to help people, and if anybody we know gets sick, she's the first one over there with a casserole and a magazine for the sick person to read. Same kind of stuff that she did for me when I was younger.

Mom works for an accounting firm. Does some bookkeeping and receptionist stuff. She goes crazy at tax time. Gets home late pretty well every night for about a month, and I get to practise my cooking skills. I make killer Pizza Pops, chicken noodle soup, and peanut butter and banana sandwiches. Most of my meal preparation doesn't involve actually turning on the stove. Even the soup is a microwave creation.

It's weird but she never watches any of the doctor shows on TV. No *ER* reruns, none of them. I don't either, but with me it's because I hate watching shows about sick and dying people. I figured the way Mom likes to look after sick people, she'd be into every medical show on television, but it's just the opposite.

Maybe it starts her thinking about how she wanted to be a nurse and never got to be one.

9

The rest of that school year was pretty forgettable. I'd kind of lost interest after the phone call from the old man and the change to my summer plans. I did pretty good in English, social, and French. Okay in math and science. Kicked in phys ed. And that was it. End of tenth grade.

I tore up my list for the Summer of the Huffman. And gave up on Jen Wertz.

Shit.

Summer Part One

1

The old man pulled up to the house in a Dodge pickup. Black, dually crew cab. Not a bad truck except that it looked like he washed it every three, four years at the most. We wouldn't be picking up any girls in this tub. Not that we would've done any better in a Maserati. *My* girl, the lovely Jen, wasn't actually aware I was alive, and my summer wasn't likely to change that. And the old man, last time I checked, likes 'em young. The only dental hygienist in town was like fifty and wielded that cleaning thingy like a pickaxe.

So, no, I didn't need a fortune cookie to tell me babes weren't in my future. Which meant it didn't matter that the Dodge had little "Wash me" notes finger-scribbled into the dirt that was layered up on all four doors.

I was sitting on the front step holding a copy of *Catch-22*. I hadn't actually opened it and wasn't sure I would since it didn't fit in with the summer this one had become.

The old man didn't try to hug me, so at least he wasn't stupid. Didn't shake my hand either or even say much. Climbed out of the truck, nodded to me on the way to the front door of the house, and said, "Throw your stuff in the back seat."

I did that. My "stuff" was the duffle bag I'd found in the basement and my school backpack. Then I went back up the sidewalk, put *Catch-22* in the mailbox (I'd let Mom figure that one out) and sat back down on the front step. Mom had made blueberry muffins, so I figured he'd be a while talking to her, drinking coffee, and eating muffins. I liked where I was — outside, far from all of that. *Far from him.*

I thought about my first impression of him. Pretty well all of it was a surprise since I really didn't know what he'd look like. He was pretty tall. And skinny. See, right away I was wrong. I guess I expected a bald, fat, slobby-looking guy, dirty T-shirt, ass crack showing over his jeans whenever he bent over. The only part I had right was the T-shirt, and it wasn't dirty.

If he'd shaved that morning, he hadn't done a very good job of it, but his hair was neat, no Hank's Auto Parts ball cap, a little grey but not much. He was wearing jeans, but they were clean and new-looking, crease down the front of each pant leg. Looked younger than sixty-two. Maybe *fifty*-two. Still, no kid.

That's about all I had time to notice in the time it took him to get from the Dodge to the house.

I was right. He was in the house for quite a while. When he came out he was carrying a pretty good-sized brown paper bag. "Lunch," he said. "Your mom's looking after us."

I stood up as Mom came out onto the steps right behind him. She was smiling, but her eyes were wet. I wondered if he'd said something to make her feel bad. Or maybe she was just sad because I was going away. It popped into my head that the longest I'd ever been away from my mom was day camp. A couple of times we'd camped out overnight, which made it two days and a night that I wasn't home. So this was a big deal, I guess.

She hugged me like it *was* a big deal and said a couple of things in a squeaky voice. *Be good, look after yourself* kind of stuff. *Eat lots of zucchini.* Trying to lighten things up. We'd already done all the reminders — don't lose the passport, don't let the old man pay for everything (I wasn't sure about that part — the whole thing was his idea), and try to look like I was enjoying myself. (I wasn't sure about that part either.)

I held onto the hug a couple of seconds longer than usual. "You take care too. I'll phone, okay?"

She stepped back, but kept her hands on my arms. "Okay? You *better* phone, mister." She smiled again. I smiled back at her and turned to go down the steps. The old man sort of waved and started down the sidewalk toward the truck. His boots clicked on the pavement like there was something metal on the bottom. I thought about calling, *What are you — fourteen?* But I kept my mouth shut, probably the better idea.

He went around to the driver side of the truck, climbed in, and started it up as I was getting in the passenger side. I looked back at the house, and Mom was waving. I nodded at her, hoping I was letting her know that everything would be okay. And then we moved out — ready to get my summer started.

"They got car washes where you live?" I guess I wanted him to know right from the get-go that I wasn't happy. I don't think he got that, though. He just laughed and floored it. "They got 'em, but ol' Betsy's allergic to water."

The truck has a nickname. I'm about to spend half my summer holidays with the old man and Betsy the pickup. Can't get better than that.

2

"Think of it as a buddy movie." That's what the old man said about an hour into what turned out to be the most boring drive in the history of the automobile.

I didn't bother to tell him that we weren't buddies and that this wasn't a movie, but I did mention that it was the most boring drive in the history of the automobile. I mentioned that a few times.

Country music, a thousand miles of bald-ass, dick-all prairie, and rain that starred about an hour into the journey. What buddy movies had he been watching?

I figured out real quick that the old man wasn't a big conversationalist. Which was okay for the first while since I was working on what Mom calls the teenager pout. The teenager pout doesn't come with sound effects. In fact, silence is a big part of the pout. It's designed to make any thinking, feeling adult within several city blocks feel like crap.

If the old man felt like crap, he was amazing at hiding his pain. He sang along to some of the songs, chuckled a couple of times like he'd just thought of something funny, and ate sunflower seeds, spitting the shells out his side window, which he kept half open, even in the rain.

After what felt like three days but was probably three hours, I changed tactics. "I think we ought to have some rules," I said.

"Sure, rules are a good idea," he nodded. "Hungry? Feel like a sandwich? Your mom made up a bunch."

Actually, I did feel like a sandwich. "Sure."

"Okay, rule number one, you're in charge of the sandwiches."

I reached into the back seat and grabbed the bag Mom had sent. It was heavy. I pulled it into the front seat and opened it. There had to be six or seven of those see-through baggies things in there. That's a lot of sandwiches. Plus fruit and a couple of juice boxes.

I studied the baggies. "Looks like roast beef, cheese with jam, and maybe tuna. What do you want?"

"Roast beef … unless you want it."

I shook my head and passed him a baggie. "Want a juice box?"

"Not right now."

"Rule number two," I said.

He opened the baggie, pulled out the sandwich and took a bite the size of a small town. Then he looked over at me, chewing and nodding like he was ready to hear the rule. "We switch up on the music every couple of hours. If I have to listen to that shit all the way to wherever we're going, my brain will turn into Cream of Wheat."

"Not a bad rule. You say 'shit' in front of your mom?"

I shook my head and bit into the sandwich.

"Then maybe you shouldn't say it in front of me."

"Is that a rule?"

"Not a rule. A suggestion. Don't talk with your mouth full. That's a rule."

30

"You asked me a question."

"Good point."

"And your mouth is full."

"*Was* full." He opened it and showed me, which was about as mega-gross as you can get.

"When are you going to tell me where we're going?"

"Why don't you switch up the music? You remember, rule number two?"

I messed with the radio for a while until I found a rock station. I listened to a couple of songs — one oldie, Fleewood Mac, I think, and "Rock Star" — Nickelback. I wasn't a big Nickelback guy, but it was way better than what we had been listening to. I looked at my watch. "Twenty after one. You can change it back at twenty after three. I'm giving you a break. We had country a lot more than two hours."

"Gettin' more like a buddy movie all the time."

"No, it isn't, you know why?"

He looked in the rear-view mirror and shrugged.

"Because in a buddy movie both buddies know where they're going. I don't know sh—crap."

"Fair enough. I'll tell you at twenty after three."

"Why then? Why not now?"

He nodded at the truck's radio. "I don't want to take away from your two hours."

I reached out and hit the on-off button. Silence. "I'd like to know now."

He crumpled up the baggie from his sandwich and flipped it over his shoulder into the back seat. "Minneapolis."

"Minneapolis."

He nodded.

"Why Minneapolis?"

"Airport."

"We're going to the airport in Minneapolis?"

He nodded again.

"Why?"

"Why do people usually go to airports?"

"Okay, so we're getting on a plane at Minneapolis. Then where?"

He reached across and hit the button on the radio. Aerosmith, "I Don't Wanna Miss a Thing." "We talk at twenty after three. You don't wanna miss this thing."

Just a zany guy.

At a quarter past three, I said, "Five more minutes."

The old man looked over at me. "You don't look like I thought you would."

"What did you think I'd look like?"

"Taller, skinnier maybe … pimples."

"I'm one of the tallest kids in my class. I'm not exactly fat. And see those? Those are zits."

"I thought your hair would be brown. That's how I remembered it."

"Yours isn't brown."

"No, but your mother's is. You've got her dark eyes. I thought you'd have her hair. That's how I remembered it."

I wondered why he said that twice. "Maybe it was brown then and sort of blonded up as I got older."

"Blonded up?"

"Got lighter."

"I figured that's what 'blonded up' meant."

"So you think I look like you?" I hadn't thought about that until right then. I didn't want to look like him.

"No, you look more like your mom. I'm better looking than either of you."

I didn't laugh. I didn't plan to laugh at any of his jokes. Maybe we had a couple of rules for driving and maybe we'd had a minor conversation, but this still wasn't any damn buddy movie.

I looked at my watch. "It's twenty after three."

3

"Saigon."

That was it. One word. No explanation. Not even where exactly Saigon was. I'm not bad on geography. So I'd heard of it. Watched some war movies, so I had an idea about the place, but that was it. What I didn't have was an idea as to why people would go there. Why I was going there.

"You're kidding, right?"

"Saigon. Vietnam. Southeast Asia."

"I know where it is," I said. "Why?"

"Why what?"

"Why are we going there?"

"You might learn something."

I was getting tired of people saying that. "I learn crap all year long. That's what school's for. I don't need to learn in summer."

"School's about half of one percent of what you need to learn to get along in life."

"What's the other ninety-nine and a half percent?"

"That's what you're going to find out. Starts with Saigon."

"Does my mom know you're insane?"

He laughed hard at that. "I think she's got a pretty good idea."

"What if I just say *no*. Like drugs. Just say *no* to your old man who's a couple of beer short of a case?"

He laughed again and reached over to change the station on the radio. Back to country music.

"All this conversation is cutting into my two hours."

4

I kept waiting for him to call me "kid."

Most of his sentences sounded like they should end with "kid." You might learn something, *kid*. Starts with Saigon, *kid*. But he didn't call me *kid*. Come to think of it, he hadn't said my name either. Which fit in perfectly with the weirdness of this whole thing.

I had a couple of other questions I wanted to ask him. But I knew he wouldn't answer me during his two hours of radio time. I watched scenery go by for a while. Then a sign: Minneapolis 439 kilometres. I did a calculation. Four hours. Maybe a little more. And then what? That was the biggest question of all.

I discovered there's an upside to country music. Or maybe it was just the driving and the total boredom. Anyway, something put me to sleep. I'm betting it was Garth and Clint and Reba and all their friends. I woke up from one of those dreams you want to keep going. Jen Werz and I were at this lake. She was lying on a rubber raft, and I was in the water pushing it along. Every little while she'd lean her head over the edge and kiss me.

Except some of the time she wasn't Jen anymore. Sometimes she was a different girl, who was totally hot too, except that I couldn't remember her face after I woke up. I could only remember that she was gorgeous and hot. And weird. The non-Jen girl kept singing all the songs from *The Lion King*. Yeah, a lot of hot babes do that. But then she was Jen again and had just finished telling me she could kiss me a lot better if I'd get up on the rubber raft with her. That's when I woke up.

I looked over at the old man. He wasn't tapping or bopping or singing along. He was just driving. "Do we ever make bathroom stops on this trip?"

He smiled. "Town coming up. Last town before the border. We'd best pee, get rid of all the drugs in the car, and dig out our passports. We need fuel anyway."

I was having trouble figuring out when he was trying to be funny. His face didn't change much when he said stuff, so it was hard to tell. But I figured the drugs-in-the-car thing must have been a joke.

Or a warning. Like if I had something stashed that I shouldn't have, last opportunity to get rid of it. I'd never been in the States in my life, so I didn't know what to expect at the border. Although right then I didn't care. I was at the point where a pee stop was all I was thinking about.

That and Jen Werz. On a rubber raft.

We pulled into the pumps at a Gas Rite service station, and getting to the can I practically ran over a lady holding a totally ugly dog — one of those squished-face ones that looks like an alien with fur. I yelled "sorry" over my shoulder, but I didn't slow down. The emergency was now a stage-four crisis.

When I came out of the can, the old man was checking out the chips display. "You wash your hands?"

I looked at him. *Who asks you that?* I didn't bother to answer.

"Lots of guys don't. Think it's manly, maybe."

"Guess I'm not manly. I washed."

"Cool. Want something?"

I reached over and took a bag of Crunchits and headed for the counter.

"Just put it there with that other stuff. I'll pay for it."

"I've got money."

"I know you have. You can pay next time." He starred in the direction of the bathroom.

"Make sure you wash," I called.

He waved over his shoulder without looking back, but I could tell he was laughing.

I threw the Crunchits on the counter with some other stuff he'd put there — a couple of bananas, some little cartons of yogurt, and a Cherry Blossom chocolate bar. And some baseball magazine. Then I went outside.

The lady had put the dog on a leash, and it was sniffing around some pretty much dead flowers along the front of the service station. I watched the dog for a few seconds then looked up at the old lady. She was glaring at me. *Another drug-crazed teenage pervert purse snatcher.*

"What kind of dog is that?" I asked her.

She told me it was a cross between two words I'd never heard before.

"They all look like that?"

"What do you mean?"

"That is one very unattractive dog."

She picked up the dog and kind of held it to the side to keep it away from me. Like I was an animal killer. I thought about telling her I wasn't, but if I ever became one, I'd start with her dog. I didn't, though, and the door of the place opened, and the old man came out with a bag full of the stuff he'd bought.

He flicked the fingers of one hand and a few drops of water hit me.

"Good for you," I said.

He nodded and we climbed into the truck. As he put it in gear and we pulled away, I looked back at the lady and the dog. She was talking to it. Probably telling it, "Don't worry, Pookey, I'll protect you from that acne-covered little bastard."

"What's so funny?" The old man was looking at me and grinning.

"People," I said. "People are what's funny."

He nodded. "No argument there. You got your passport handy?"

"It's right on top of my backpack."

"Better fish it out."

I did and handed it to him. He put it beside him with his own passport and an envelope with Mom's writing on the front. All it said was *permission letter*.

"Mom said you played professional baseball."

He looked like he was going to turn up the radio but changed his mind. "Yeah, a little."

"What were you?"

"You mean what position did I play?"

I nodded.

"Mostly third base. But I wasn't good enough, so I was a utility player. That means I played all the infield positions. Only got in the game if someone was hurt or we were blowing someone out or getting blown out ourselves."

"So you were a crappy fielder."

"No, I was a pretty good fielder. I was a crappy hitter. Couldn't handle the curve ball."

"Mom said you got hurt. Had to quit."

"Tore up a knee. But I wasn't going to make it to the big leagues anyway. So it didn't matter. I just quit a little sooner than if I'd stayed healthy, that's all."

"Then what?"

"Then what ... what?"

"What did you do after you quit baseball?"

"Got a job."

"What kind of job?"

This time he did reach over and turn the sound up on the radio. I muttered "rude" under my breath, but if he heard me he didn't say anything. And then it was all about Alan Jackson telling us how great it was "way down yonder in Chattahoochee."

5

The next part of the drive was almost as boring as the part that had gone before. When I pointed that out to the old man, he said, "That's your favourite word, isn't it?"

"What?"

"Boring."

I didn't bother to answer.

The old man was nervous about crossing the border, I

could tell — he was doing this thing with his hair, kind of curling the part by his ear with his index finger. He hadn't done that until we were about a half-hour away from the border. Now he was doing it all the time.

I figured, *Sweet, the old man's a convicted drug dealer in the States, and I'm going to spend the rest of my life in some prison with bad food and black and white TV.*

But actually getting through the border wasn't that bad. The big thing was me. Like, had the old man kidnapped me at some mall and was sneaking me across the border with a fake letter from a fake mom in some fake town?

They told us to park and come inside, and they put us in separate rooms. A guy named Granfield, who was big enough to be a defensive end and soft enough to be an angel food cake, took me into a room and closed the door. He offered me a granola bar, and I shook my head. Then he told me about fifteen times that I didn't have to be afraid, I could tell him the truth, and there was nothing the man in the other room, whether he was my dad or not, could do.

Apparently, the permission letter from my mom wasn't cutting it with the border police. I knew that I could put an end to the whole summer-with-the-old-man gig right then and there. All I had to do was say something like there I was drinking a slurpee and minding my own business and that nasty man in the other room came up to me and told me my cat had been run over by a car so I got in the pickup that he hadn't even bothered to wash and the next thing I knew here we were at the border and please save me Officer Granfield. That's all it would have taken, and I'd be spending the rest of my summer reading *Catch-22* and drinking milk shakes and quite possibly doing amazing things to Jen Wertz's body.

I didn't do that. Partly because I figured even somebody as stupid as Granfield, who didn't smell real good, especially in a room that wasn't all that big and had like zero air flow, would eventually figure out I was lying. And also it wouldn't have been fair. The last thing I wanted to be doing with the next few weeks of my life was going to be freaking Saigon with the old man. But he'd been fair about it. He'd phoned Mom, and he'd obviously put out some serious money to pay for the trip, and he was even trying to make it okay for me. So I couldn't really do something as dirty as rat him out at the border for something he hadn't done.

Instead, I said to Granfield, "Why don't you just phone my mom, and she'll tell you if the letter is the real deal."

I could see Granfield was pissed. He'd been all excited about the possibility of a big international case and saving some poor kidnapped child, and I'd just burst his bubble. We were out of there about five minutes later.

Back on the endless highway. The old man didn't talk much, but I noticed he wasn't twirling the hair anymore, and he was bopping to the music again.

We stopped at a diner in a place called Thief River Falls. There was a poster on the outside of the door advertising a PBR Bull Riding at the arena that night. I'd seen a couple of bull riding events and thought they were pretty cool. But I knew we wouldn't be going to this one because we had to get our asses to Minneapolis so we could carry on to Saigon. Sweet.

"Have anything you want. I'm buyin'," the old man said

as we sat down. "They charge for airplane food except for the pretzels, and the food's crap anyway. So let's load up here."

I ordered an open-faced western sandwich and the old man ordered a double order of veal cutlets. I figured anybody who ate double orders of stuff would have to be part of the North American Obesity Problem you read about all the time, but one thing I could say for the old man — he was as far from obese as you can get.

That didn't stop him from tucking away the whole veal cutlet extravaganza. He ate fast at first, then slowed down and talked between pretty well every bite. Didn't say a lot, but he was doing more talking now than at first.

"I've crossed the border dozens of times, and I still don't like it. A lot of the border guards are pretty good guys, but every once in a while you get somebody who thinks he's Dirty Harry — and the women can be just as bad."

I didn't know who Dirty Harry was, and I didn't get a chance to ask.

"How was your guy?"

"Granfield? Fat. Stupid."

The old man nodded. "A lot of 'em carry guns now."

Granfield with a gun. Scary.

"He wanted me to say you'd kidnapped me. I think he would have liked to make a big arrest. Get some headlines."

The old man nodded. "Dirty Harry."

"Why are we going to Saigon?"

"We won't be in Saigon the whole time."

I'd noticed that I didn't get a lot of direct answers to my questions. "Where to after that?"

"The countryside."

"The countryside where?"

"Vietnam … that's where Saigon is." He cranked his head around. There was a mark on his neck, a scar or something. "Can we get a little more coffee, please?"

The waitress brought the coffee pot and topped up the old man's cup.

He looked at me over what was left of the cutlets and mashed potatoes. "How about pie, you want some pie?"

I shook my head.

"No, *thanks*," he said.

"No, thanks," I repeated. Great, now he was starting to act like a father.

He looked up at the waitress. "What kind of pie do you have?"

"Coconut cream and cherry."

"We'll have two pieces of coconut cream."

She looked at me, shrugged, and walked away.

"How is it that she gets that I didn't want pie, and you don't?"

"I'll eat it if you don't."

"Why don't you weigh four hundred pounds?"

"Metabolism."

The pie came, and I ate one bite. I'd never had coconut cream pie before and based on that bite didn't plan to ever have it again. I pushed it away. The old man dusted both pieces, but I noticed that he hadn't finished the carrots that came with the veal cutlets, so the man was probably starving.

We sat for a while. He ate and I watched him eat and looked around the diner. There were pictures on the walls, all of them of people fishing. Some were guys standing in

42

streams fly-fishing and the rest were pictures of people with the fish they'd caught. Some of the pictures were pretty old, like black and white old, so maybe they were famous people who'd caught fish nearby.

"Grab me that paper, will you?" The old man nodded at a mess of newspaper pages on a table across the diner.

I got up and went over there and tried to organize the thing so it looked like a real paper. When it was more or less sorted out, I brought it back to our table.

He read and I read. I sat, sipped on my chocolate milk and looked at the back pages of the paper as he flipped through the sections. Sometimes he'd fold the paper over, and I'd get to look at more than just the back pages.

56 DIE IN WAVE OF IRAQ SUICIDE BOMBINGS

CALIFORNIA WILDFIRES THREATEN THOUSANDS OF HOMES

YANKEES ROMP OVER RED SOX — WIN STREAK AT EIGHT

J.K. ROWLING PENS ADULT NOVEL

GLOBAL ECONOMIC RECOVERY SLOWER THAN EXPECTED

ARYAN SUPREMACY GROUP STAGES RALLY IN IDAHO TOWN

UNLIKELY SONGSTRESS THE TOAST OF BRITAIN

MAN EXPRESSES REMORSE AFTER BEATING THREE-YEAR-OLD

EDUCATION BUDGET SLASHED

I wasn't one to read the paper much. Sometimes we'd look at what was going on in the world in social studies class, but it wasn't like I paid a lot of attention to current events. I mean I wasn't stupid — I knew about Afghanistan and 9/11 and I could name the prime minister of Canada and the president of the United States, which was more than some of the kids in my school could do, but I wasn't into the news.

Out of what I was reading that morning sitting across from the old man, I was most interested in the J.K. Rowling thing. I'd read the Harry Potter books and thought they were amazing, and I'd also read somewhere that the author was now mega-rich. Maybe I'd ask her to marry me. Right after I got back from my lovely Saigon vacation.

Then it was back in the truck and Steve Earle singing "Copperhead Road." There's a line in the song, something about running whiskey in a big black Dodge. And some stuff about Vietnam too. The war. I liked Steve Earle. If all country music was like that we wouldn't have needed rule number two. I sat back and thought about what other rules might make sense.

6

I must have fallen asleep again, but this time no great dreams starring Jen Wertz and the mystery girl. When I woke up, we were parked in one of those pullouts on the side of the highway. The old man was sitting with his arms resting on the wheel. He was holding the envelope that said *permission letter* in Mom's handwriting. He didn't look over at me, but he must have known I was awake.

"Your mom used to leave little notes on a table in the living room when I was out at night. She'd write a couple of lines about her day and said she hoped my evening had gone well. I'd be out drinking or … whatever, and she'd write me a note for when I got home. Never ever missed. Always ended it with something like, 'I hope you know how much I love you.' 'Course she didn't know that I was drinking or —"

"Screwin' around."

"Because I guess I was a pretty good liar. Those notes were probably the nicest thing anybody ever did for me. Your mom's a … a … very good person."

He still hadn't looked over at me. He set the envelope back on the seat between us and started the truck. He pulled out onto the highway, and for the first time since we'd left, there was no loud music pounding out of the radio.

7

I wondered why he'd told me about the notes my mom left for him. Guilt? Didn't stop him from taking off with the teenager. Maybe she was one of the ones he was screwing when he was out at night and Mom was at home writing notes to him.

I was young when he left, so I don't really remember how she was after that, you know, how she handled the breakup. Except I remember waking up a couple of times and she was sitting beside my bed watching me sleep. It wasn't the times when I was sick or anything, so I was never sure why she was there. But thinking back on it, that might have been right around the time the old man took off.

I watched more amazing Minnesota scenery rolling by and yawned a few hundred times. But I was careful not to say the word "boring." Actually, I didn't say much of anything.

I got to thinking about the first job I'd ever had. I was eleven years old. One of the women Mom worked with lived just a few blocks from us. She was looking for a baby sitter for the summer for her five-year-old.

I got the job. I'd get up at 7:00 a.m. every weekday and ride my bike over to their house. Then I'd look after the kid — his name was Asa — from eight until four thirty when the mom got home from work.

She left lunch to be warmed up every day, usually soup or macaroni, stuff like that. The best was this soup she called red borscht. I'd never had it before. It's a cabbage and beet soup — some other vegetables and potatoes in there too. Except it was purple, not red … purple soup. It looked gross but tasted awesome. Asa and me, we really got after it on red borscht days.

The kid was okay. The best part was that even though he was five, he had a sleep every afternoon. I'd sit around and play his mom's CDs — she had pretty good taste in music — until the kid woke up.

We went for a lot of walks. Pretty much toured the whole neighbourhood. Like explorers. Sometimes we rode our bikes.

One bad day kind of wrecked the whole summer for both of us. We were out walking. Actually, Asa was riding his bike, and I was walking along beside him. It was easy because Asa didn't ride very fast. He had one of those little bikes, which made sense since he was a pretty small kid, even for five.

We were on the sidewalk by a major street called Edmonton Trail. Asa was pedalling and talking, and I

46

was off in whatever world eleven-year-olds go to when they get tired of listening to five-year-olds. We were by a playground. There were some kids playing on slides and swings and stuff. Suddenly, this little girl, maybe about Asa's age, ran out onto the road to get a ball.

I starred to yell at her not to run out there, but I didn't have time. She got hit by a car, a big boat of a car, I remember. The guy driving didn't have a chance to miss her. It was the worst sound I ever heard. I could see what was going to happen, and everything slowed down. It was like I had time to think about what it would sound like when the car hit her.

Except it didn't sound like what I thought it would. It was awful, first the thump of the car hitting the kid, then the sound of the brakes on the car, squealing but not until after it had hit the little girl, then the bump of her hitting the pavement, I bet it was twenty metres down the road.

It went on what felt like forever — that little girl rolling and rolling on the pavement. But then came the worst sound of all — it was the kid's mother who came screaming from the park out onto the road. "Carla, oh, god, oh, my god, Carla, my baby!"

She just kept yelling that. Over and over. She was bent over the little girl where she'd finally stopped rolling. I grabbed Asa, and we turned down the lane at the end of the park.

He was pretty shook up. I was too. He told his mom about it that night. She said she'd heard about a little girl being hit by a car on the news on her way home from work. She said the newscast didn't say if the girl was going to be okay or not. I always had the feeling she really did know but didn't want to say in front of Asa.

Asa didn't want to go for any walks or bike rides for a couple of weeks after that. And we never went anywhere near Edmonton Trail again that summer.

8

We hadn't had a pee stop in quite a while. I told the old man I needed to stop, and we pulled into a Conoco in Sauk Center, Minnesota. The old man told me it was pronounced like 'go soak your head.'" *The hilarity just keeps on coming.*

I saw a sign that said SINCLAIR LEWIS HOUSE, and there was an arrow pointing off to the right. I figured Sinclair Lewis must be a big deal in Go-soak-your-head Centre, Minnesota. Like in the next town to ours there was an NHL guy born there, and there's a big sign — LIBBERT, ALBERTA, HOME OF WHATEVER THE GUY'S NAME IS. In Canada, if you're a hockey star, you can get your name on the town sign.

I asked the old man if he'd ever heard of Sinclair Lewis, but he just shook his head. Then there was another sign a little further on: SINCLAIR LEWIS, 1930 NOBEL PRIZE WINNER FOR LITERATURE. I didn't figure that would get you a sign in my town. Unless you also happened to play for the Blackhawks or Penguins.

We stayed in a Motel Six just outside of Minneapolis that night. The old man said it was cheaper than getting a place in the city. *Great, we're on the economy plan.* I didn't know how I felt about not having my own room. Sharing a room with my old man. Who, let's face it, until ten or twelve hours ago, was pretty much a total stranger to me.

What if he was a pervert or something? Or walked in his sleep? Or snored real loud? Sure, Mom had said he wasn't an evil man — wasn't that how she'd put it? But hell, she hadn't seen him in forever. Maybe she didn't know him as well as she thought she did.

As soon as we checked in and dumped all our stuff in the room, we went out to an Italian restaurant. I had ravioli and meatballs, and the old man had something that had too many consonants for me to pronounce.

We didn't talk much at first. I noticed a couple of women, I'm guessing in their forties, looking over at us from another table. I doubted very much if it was me they were checking out. The old man didn't seem to notice them, or if he did, he didn't seem to care.

After I'd polished off about half of the ravioli and a couple of meatballs, I looked over at him. "You got a girlfriend?"

He was chewing, so it was a while before he could answer, but then all he did was shake his head, which he could have done *while* he was chewing. He looked at me with a look that I figured said he didn't want to have this conversation. I set my fork down.

"What happened to the teeth cleaner?"

"She was a *dental hygienist*. Name was Cindy."

"Was?"

"She went back to her husband after we'd been together for a couple of years."

"She was nineteen and had a husband?"

"They were split up when we met."

49

"She was nineteen and had split from her husband. Sounds really nice."

"She was really nice. And she was almost twenty."

"That's way better. And you and Mom?"

"What about us?"

"You weren't split up at the time."

"No, we weren't. Not until after."

"Sweet."

I have to give him credit. I was doing everything I could to really get to him, and so far he was keeping his cool. He didn't like it, but he hadn't blown up. Yet.

When the cheque came, I found out he wasn't kidding before when he said I could pay next time. Which was *this* time. I figure the chips and snacks he bought at the truck stop came to maybe eight bucks tops. The dinner at the Italian place was *thirty-eight*. The old man threw in a ten to pay for his beer, and I got the rest.

He didn't say anything on the way back to the hotel, or after we were back in our room. He took some stuff out of his suitcase and went for a shower. Ball game on TV — Seattle and Detroit, two teams I couldn't care less about. I fell asleep before the seventh inning stretch. The old man poked me awake. I brushed my teeth and climbed into one of the two beds in our $49 room.

Day one of my summer vacation was over. I wasn't sure I could stand much more of this kind of excitement. I think I fell asleep in about six seconds. Maybe that's how the motel got its name.

The next morning we were up early — 6:00 a.m., which to me is a ridiculous time of day to be doing anything but sleeping. We hurried down to the lobby for the free continental breakfast, which was coffee and a bagel for the old man, juice and a tired muffin for me. Tired as in been out in the open air way too long, Chewy.

While we were sitting there the old man handed me a pill. "Take this."

"What is it?"

"Malaria pill. You take one today and for the next few days, then for a couple of days when we get back."

"Who says I have to take it?"

"Nobody. You take it so you won't get malaria, not because somebody told you to take it."

"Think I'll pass."

"Suit yourself." He picked up the pill and dropped it in his jacket pocket.

I ate some more muffin.

"You ever know anybody that got malaria?"

He nodded. "A few. Some of 'em are still alive."

Some people say something like that, you figure it's for effect. They're being *dramatic*. With the old man, he just threw it out there like he didn't give a damn if you believed him or not.

"So what happens?"

"When you get malaria?"

"Yeah."

"Comes from mosquito bites. You get sick. Fever. Vomiting. Major muscle pain, hot then cold, big-time headache. You go to the hospital. Sometimes you get over it. Sometimes you don't. Let's go."

"Maybe I'll take the pill."

"You sure? I don't want to trample on your human rights."

I took the pill. We threw our garbage in a container in the lobby, went back to the room to brush our teeth and load up our gear. When we had packed our stuff into the truck and were sitting in the front seat waiting for the diesel to warm up, I had a thought.

"What do we do with the truck?"

"We leave it here … in Minneapolis. Not far from the airport."

"You can do that?"

"I know a guy. He's got a place."

The place was a little piece of land with a small, kind of old house on it. A couple of other buildings too. Same vintage as the house. Looked like it could have been an okay place if somebody took better care of it, and if it wasn't in the middle of an industrial area. Lots of equipment and high chain-link fences. Industrial plumbing supply outfit across the street. I thought about what industrial plumbing meant. Maybe you call these guys for the BSP — Big Shit Problems. Chase Sheet Metal on one side. Road Runner Courier Service on the other side.

The guy the old man knew, the guy who lived in this little slice of heaven, was a piece of work too. Looked like Santa Claus after a three-day drunk. I figured him to be about the same age as the old man. He was a little taller, maybe heavier but not by a lot. The thing you noticed about the guy was the white hair and beard, a lot of hair and a lot of beard. A ball cap advertising Rent-A-Wreck was perched on top of the white hair. The Rent-A-Wreck place was probably another one of his neighbours.

His face and eyes gave the impression that this was a man who hadn't been looking after himself all that well. Crack cocaine instead of fruit and vegetables — that kind of look.

The other thing about him, which I didn't notice right away, was that most of his left arm was missing. His sleeve was folded up and pinned at about the elbow. When we got out of the truck, he threw the good arm around the old man and the two of them hugged. They hugged long enough that I finally turned away and looked out at the trees that surrounded the guy's place on three sides.

The trees were a good idea. Who wanted to look at a sheet metal place all the time?

"Nathan."

I turned back, and the two of them had an arm around each other, and they were grinning, but it looked like there were tears in their eyes. I was wishing we could just ditch the truck and get out of there.

"I want you to meet one good son of a bitch." The old man was grinning and wiping his nose with his sleeve.

The good son of a bitch stuck out a hand the size of a pillow. The good hand. The only hand. I reached out and took it. No, that's not right. I didn't take his hand; he took mine. It was like my hand had disappeared. I couldn't see it anymore.

At least the GSOB didn't squeeze the crap out of it like some people do to show you how strong they are. His hand was knobby and warm. Hard too, like it had calluses. Nothing like a pillow.

"I heard about you." He was still grinning, and his eyes were still shining.

Him knowing about me, that surprised me. I didn't figure the old man told a lot of people about his kid.

"Great . . . uh . . . good to meet you," was the best I could do.

"Nathan, this is Tal Ledbetter. Tal, my son, Nathan."

Tal nodded his head like crazy. Tal. What's that short for . . . Talbert? Talisman? No, that's a book. Tallas? I didn't bother to ask.

He let go of my hand. "Let's get you boys a beer." He starred for what looked like a shop that was off to the left of the house. The old man followed him, looking back at me and jerking his head for me to follow. I followed. But first I looked at my watch. Eight thirty in the morning. Seemed early for beer but what do I know — maybe that's what good sons of bitches do.

Not a lot more was said until three lawn chairs were arranged on the cement pad out front of the shop. Tal Ledbetter handed the old man a beer and me a Dr Pepper. *Awright.* How'd he know that? Probably just luck. All he had in the fridge.

He twisted the top off another beer and sat across from me and the old man. Looked at the old man like he was memorizing him.

"By damn, you're looking good, man. Old but good."

"You think *I* look old? You passed by a mirror lately?" They both laughed like they were the two funniest guys on the planet. I sipped my Dr Pepper and looked around at the place.

It was hard to get hold of. I mean I didn't know what happened there. Sure there was a shop, but the big double doors were open and except for a John Deere tractor that

54

looked about the same age as Tal and the old man, the fridge Tal had got the drinks from, and a ride-on lawn mower, there wasn't much in there. I didn't see the tools you expect to see in a shop, you know, all arranged on the walls, hanging on metal hooks.

In fact, what was on the walls were paintings — some of people, some of countryside, a couple of horses. And there was one big one, really big, of a bald eagle sitting on the seat of a very large motorcycle — maybe a Harley. All of the paintings had this weird sort of off-kilter feel to them. The people ones were mostly women, and the people in the paintings were all at an angle so you wanted to tilt your head when you looked at them. The countryside paintings — every one of them had a big space, a white space, like there was a hole in the painting, or he'd forgotten to finish it. The space was in a different place in each of the paintings, but they all had it. The eagle on the motorcycle was the most normal painting in the place. And it wasn't all that normal, since it was an eagle on a motorcycle. No helmet. Not a safety conscious eagle.

If Tal was the artist, I didn't think he was very good. I decided not to mention that to him.

"I can't believe you're going back," Tal was saying to the old man.

"A lot of guys are. They've got tours."

"I heard about that. Don't believe I'll ever go on one."

"Okay if I walk around?" I was looking at the old man, but actually, it was Tal I was asking.

"Sure, kid, make yourself at home."

Kid. There it was.

I picked up my Dr Pepper and wandered off toward the house. One storey, maybe two, three rooms. Big enough for one person, or maybe a couple, but only if they didn't own much. Tal didn't look like he owned much. I wondered if there was a Mrs. Tal.

I circled around the house to where a lot of places have a backyard. This one had a back swamp. There was a fence around the outside but not chain-link. Wooden like you see around animal corrals. And inside the fence was a body of water too small to be a lake or even a slough but too big to be a swimming pool. It wasn't encased in concrete; it just sat there — this huge hole dug out of the ground and filled with water.

I remember reading, I think it was in a magazine or the newspaper, about water that looked "brackish." I didn't know what the word meant then and I still don't, but if I was looking for a word to describe that water, I'd go with brackish. But that wasn't all. There was a fair amount of grass around the outside of the water and also inside the fence.

And two cows. Not like a herd. And not milk cows, not the kind you see in pictures on milk containers. I figured these had to be beef cows. Who has *two* cows?

I climbed up on the fence and watched the cows eat grass for a while. I figured it was better than listening to two old guys telling each other how great they looked. Besides, I needed some time to think about a few things.

I was finding some things out about the old man, even if he wasn't very good at telling me stuff about himself. Or maybe I wasn't all that good at asking.

So what was this for? What was this about, this trip to Vietnam with a man who hadn't been part of my life for most of it, then suddenly shows up with malaria pills and two tickets to Saigon?

I finished the Dr Pepper, watched the cows for a few more minutes, and climbed down off the fence so I could throw a few rocks into the swamp. Then I walked back around to the front yard. I figured Tal and the old man had had enough time to visit. If we were going, we should get going.

When I got back to where they were sitting, they were on their second beer and laughing like two junior high girls. Looked pretty stupid on a couple of old guys, even stupider than it does on junior high girls.

Tal looked up and said, "What do you think of my moat?"

"Moat?"

"Well, that's what I call it."

"It won't be very effective keeping your enemies out. Isn't a moat supposed to go around the whole place?"

"I figure all my enemies, being the no heart sons o' bitches that they are, will try to sneak up behind me, so I only need a moat on that side."

"Makes sense." I nodded. Actually, it made no sense at all. Near as I could see, there wasn't much about Tal Ledbetter that made any sense.

"Besides, I got tired of digging." More laughing from the two of them. What the hell had been funny about that?

"You dug that whole thing?"

"Me and that John Deere. Took me three and a half days to get it the way I wanted."

"For two cows."

"I'd planned to have more. Couldn't afford 'em."

"Why have just two? If that's all you can afford, then why not just go with none?"

"Because I like cows better than cats."

Another answer that didn't make sense.

"The water looks brackish."

He nodded. "Yes, it does."

"Time to mount up, Nathan." The old man got up out of his chair.

I looked around for whatever Tal was going to drive us to the airport in. Nothing. But a taxi was pulling into his driveway. Tal and the Old Man did some more hugging while I walked over to the truck and pulled my stuff out of the back seat.

The old man did the same thing as the taxi came alongside us. The driver didn't look happy as he popped the trunk and got out to help us load our stuff. Except he didn't help. Or say anything. He just watched as we threw the old man's duffle bag and my suitcase and backpack into the trunk. He kept looking from the old man to Tal and back to the old man. He wasn't very good at hiding how much he didn't like either of them.

Maybe he'd been mugged or something and figured these were the kind of guys to do something like that. I couldn't totally blame him. They didn't look like people you'd want to meet in some dark out-of-the-way place. Like where we were right then. Except it wasn't dark.

The driver got back in the taxi as we turned back to Tal.

"See you in a couple of weeks." He punched the old man on the shoulder.

The old man nodded. Which is how I learned how long we'd be in Vietnam. Tal turned to me and grinned. "Good to meet you, kid."

I nodded. "Yeah, same. You're the first good son of a bitch I ever met."

He grinned but only for a couple of seconds, then he looked at me all serious. "You're wrong about that, kid. You're travelling with one."

I shrugged and moved away to get in the taxi. I watched Tal and the old man talking to each other, but I couldn't hear what they were saying. Handshake. Nods. The old man went around to the other side of the car and climbed in.

"Airport," he said and looked out the side window. Away from me. And away from Tal. He didn't see Tal wave to us as the taxi rolled out. I did and nodded in Tal's direction.

If our time with Tal Ledbetter was an indication of what the summer was going to be like, I was looking forward to it even less. Nothing wrong with the guy really, just strange. The kind of guy you could spend a day with and at the end of it, you'd think, *what was that all about?*

I sat in the unpleasant silence of that taxi, hoping my summer would get better but without a whole lot of confidence about it.

9

My first big international flight experience wasn't all that memorable. *I'm trying not to say boring.* First came the airport in Minneapolis, where we had to spend an extra hour and a half because the flight to Los Angeles was late. The old man was going nuts because he figured we'd miss our connection. I couldn't really have cared less. After an hour of sitting and watching planes take off and land, I just wanted to be somewhere other than in that airport.

I bought a book of Sudoku puzzles. Part of the Asian theme. Yeah, right. I didn't even think of that until the old man pointed it out. When he said it, I just shrugged. Didn't have an answer.

I'd never worked a Sudoku puzzle in my life, but by the time we got out of Minneapolis, I was pretty good. Could knock off the easy ones pretty fast. I figured I'd try some of the tougher ones in the next airport. LAX. Los Angeles.

I watched *Talladega Nights* on the plane. *Like, don't they have any recent movies on here?* Once he figured out we were still okay for our next flight, which was Los Angeles to Tokyo, the old man relaxed. In fact he slept pretty much the whole flight. If I'd known just how stupid *Talladega Nights* was, I would've done the same thing, although that would have meant missing out on the free beverage and "Cookies or Bits and Bites?" The old man was right about the food. The second time the flight attendant went through, I asked if it would like totally blow the budget if I had one of each. Apparently, the woman attendant somehow became deaf at that exact moment, because she dropped a Bits and Bites on my tray and moved on to the next row.

I'd never been to Los Angeles, and except for the inside of the airport, I still haven't. We had to hurry to get from our gate to the one for the Tokyo flight, which was in a different terminal. No time for Sudoku. *Oh, damn.* I could see tall buildings through some of the windows, and it seemed like everywhere there were these big-screen videos of amazing looking hotels. I told myself this would be a good place to bring Jen Wertz on our honeymoon. That's if she didn't fall in love with someone else while I was blowing off the whole *freaking* summer going to places I never wanted to see.

The second leg of the flight was long. That's all — long. *Ten hours long.* By the end of it, I had memorized every hair on the head of this chick who was in the aisle seat one row ahead of us. It wasn't like she was amazingly hot. It was just that after another movie, a couple of thousand games of Sudoku, and part of one of the old man's paperbacks, memorizing someone's hair made sense to me.

Actually, the movie was pretty good — *Body of Lies,* which was directed by one of my favourite Hollywood directors, Ridley Scott. I guess I know a lot about movies. You have a mom who works a fair amount, you watch more than your share of movies. Anyway, this one was decent. A couple of years old, but at least it was from this decade. Leonardo Di-Caprio, the middle east, spies, some pretty good action scenes.

The paperback wasn't that bad either. The weird part was it was about this guy taking a train across America. Long trip. Like us — travellers. Except the book all happened around Christmas. The author was this guy named Baldacci...

So okay, good movie, good book, chick with okay hair just a few seats away ... why wasn't I having a blast? If that book, that movie, and the chick with the hair had come into my life anywhere but there, and anytime but then, and if I'd been with anybody but the old man, it would all have been good.

And that's it — the highlights of my big journey. Enough said.

Except for Tokyo. I'll tell you about that part. We got in there just after noon. The weird part was we left Los Angeles on a Thursday and it was now Saturday. An entire day of my life had disappeared.

The old man seemed to think that it was really important that we make up for the lost day. At least that's what I figured he was thinking because suddenly he was in this big frenzy.

We had a four and a half hour layover, and he said if we hurried we could make it into downtown Tokyo and back in time for the next flight. All so I could "get a feel for the place."

I wasn't real nuts about getting into another mode of transportation even if it didn't ever leave the ground. I was thinking more that a couple of burgers and fries, maybe some poutine, and about a pail of Dr Pepper might actually fix me up. But no, there I was running through the airport, dodging people with luggage carts packed higher than the people pushing them.

I didn't bother to tell the old man I could probably live out the rest of my life without having a feel for Tokyo, but I wouldn't have been able to say anything even if I'd wanted to, because I had to run hard to keep up with him as he dashed for the taxi place. I'll say one thing for him — he could run pretty good for a guy his age. What pissed me off was when we'd finished a death-defying dive into the back seat of a taxi that for some reason was already moving, I was breathing hard and he wasn't. Just sitting there grinning at me. I knew what he was thinking …

Now *this* is a buddy movie.

I was thinking there's a pretty good chance I might hurl right here in this taxi. I hadn't eaten any real food in about eight hours — just chocolate bars and pop and the always tasty Bits and Bites. After the sprint through the airport, my stomach seemed to think puking was a pretty good idea. I took some deep breaths through my nose and after a minute or so, I felt more or less okay.

I don't remember a lot about Tokyo. What I do remember is that we spent most of the time driving. The old man decided we needed to see the Tokyo Tower, which is supposed to be patterned after the Eiffel Tower in Paris except the Tokyo one is a little taller. There are a couple of observation areas, and one is really high up, so you get this really awesome 360 degree view of Tokyo.

Good idea, right?

Well, it might have been if it wasn't eighty-five minutes travel time in each direction. A guy directing people to the cabs told us that in perfect English. "Eighty-five minutes," he said. "Less on Sunday, more during the week."

We'd no sooner got into the taxi than the old man started to worry about whether we'd make it back in time for the flight to Saigon.

Sweet. A nice relaxing jaunt around Tokyo. The old man looked at his watch about every four minutes and kept telling the driver to hurry up, step on it, go faster and several other expressions that meant about the same thing. The driver kept saying stuff back to the old man but, of course, it was in Japanese. I figured he was probably saying *shut up, stupid*. I was getting one of my headaches. All very nice.

"Maybe we should just turn around and go back," I said. The old man looked at me like I was nuts. "No way," he said. "No problem."

I have to admit, the tower was actually pretty cool. The driver got us there in seventy-nine minutes, six minutes quicker than what we'd been told at the airport, so the old man finally started to chill. Twelve thousand yen for the cab fare — one way. That's almost a hundred and fifty bucks American. He never said how much we had to pay to go up to the observatory, but I bet it was a bunch.

I was beginning to think the old man had some serious coin. Either that or he saved up big-time for this trip.

Once we got up in the observatory, my head started feeling better, and I kind of enjoyed the view. We walked around the whole platform so we saw the city in every direction. There was another tower, newer and taller — called the Tokyo Sky Tree — off in the distance. Impressive.

But the best part was Mount Fuji. I've seen mountains, some of them close up, but I'd have to say that was the most amazing, and biggest, mountain I'd ever seen.

"If it's cloudy or there's too much smog, you don't see the mountain," the old man told me three or four times, like the fact that it was a clear day was all his doing. Part of the "old man tour of Tokyo."

The ride back to Narita Airport was a replay of the ride to the tower. Eighty-two minutes this time. We ran our asses off getting back through the airport, then through the security line and back to our departure gate about five minutes before they started boarding the plane.

Now the old man was grinning. "Not bad, eh? You see some of Tokyo, and we're back here in time, just like I planned it. Nothing to it."

Yeah, nothing to it.

1

Okay, what I said before about being pretty good with geography? Forget that. I expected Saigon to be all huts and mud — little orphaned kids everywhere holding out their hands and begging in these little pathetic voices, *American man you rice … give little money.* I expected to be standing in line at weird little shops (more huts), so I could buy a bowl of wet rice that I'd have to go through with my chopsticks to filter out the bugs crawling around in the bowl. I expected a city that was not like any city I'd ever see. I expected … a dump.

And I was wrong. First of all, it's not even called Saigon any more. It's Ho Chi Minh City. Okay, that was partly the old man's fault; how would I know that? He called it Saigon, so I called it Saigon. And in fairness to him, a lot of the locals still call it Saigon too. I found that out later. But officially, at the end of the war, when South Vietnam and the Americans lost and the North Vietnamese took over, the leader of North Vietnam was Ho Chi Minh, and he decided to re-name Saigon after himself. Nothing like a healthy dose of self-esteem.

No huts, at least not in any of the parts of the city I saw. Skyscrapers, neon lights, clubs, restaurants, palaces, and parks — some people begging, quite a few of them actually, but not many of them were kids. If it wasn't for the totally different trees and flowers, the gazillion people on little motorbikes and another gazillion people on bicycles and the fact that most of those gazillions of people were Vietnamese, I could have been in Toronto.

And I was wrong about that too — the everybody-being-Vietnamese thing. The old man told me that a pretty big part of the population of Saigon is Chinese. Especially in the centre of town.

Since we'd arrived at eleven thirty at night, I was pretty tired by the time we got our stuff off the luggage carousel, and the old man had flagged down a taxi outside. We were staying at a place called the Rex Hotel — the old man told me that while we were watching luggage drift past us on the carousel. Watching and getting pushed out of the way by rude people, who seemed to think that if they didn't get their suitcase *right now*, the world was going to come to an end.

I got pushed out of the way three different times. By the third time, I was getting seriously annoyed, and I was about to educate the little Asian guy who did the pushing on some of the more creative ways to use English swear words when I noticed that he was a she. A tough little she, but a she just the same. I stepped back beside the old man, who was grinning and shaking his head. I might have thought it was a little funnier if I hadn't been so damn tired.

Before we left the airport, the old man rented two cellphones at a little kiosk, one for each of us. "Our phones don't work over here. so we'll need these. Don't lose it, or it'll cost us, well actually cost *you*, a bunch."

One of the top five prettiest women I'd ever seen in my life explained how the phone worked and what our numbers were. I wanted to ask a bunch of questions just so we could keep talking to her, but exhaustion from the plane ride had ground my male hormones into powder, so I settled for nodding a lot.

She spoke excellent English, but a couple of times she couldn't find the word she wanted and fell back into Vietnamese. The old man seemed to understand, and even spoke a few words himself. I don't know why, but I thought that was pretty impressive. I didn't bother to tell him that though.

The taxi ride was another adventure. I expected the first words out of the old man's mouth to be Rex Hotel, but instead he said some stuff in Vietnamese. Then we discovered the driver spoke English, so the old man said, "Just drive around for a while."

I looked at him in the dark of the back seat. "You're kidding, right?"

"Just for a few minutes. Go to sleep if you want." Then he turned to the window on his side and stared out like a kid watching for Santa Claus. It was like I wasn't there.

It was close to midnight, yet there was an awful lot of light. Neon lights and street lights and the lights from cars and motorbikes. It felt like four o'clock in the afternoon.

And there were a lot of people on the streets of Ho Chi Minh City. That surprised me, since it was pretty late. Most were still in shirt sleeves because it felt like a summer afternoon feels back home. Lots of movement. There didn't seem to be anybody just standing around. Quite a few eating places and most of them seemed pretty busy for that time of night. Except for the people eating in those places, everyone seemed to be in a hurry. A blur of moving bodies and vehicles of all types.

Noise too, lots of it. The driver had his window down, and there was this din — car horns honking, music coming from several different places, the rattle-hum of motorbike engines … and voices, loud voices that seemed to be speaking in syllables instead of sentences.

The other thing I noticed was the smells. A big mix of smells. From the streets we drove down, there was the smell of food, kind of like when you go into a Chinese restaurant in a Canadian or American city. It was jumbled together with gasoline fumes and the occasional whiff of garbage. There was the smell of the inside of the taxi, too, a mix of body odour and beer, I think that's what it was. And from somewhere, there was the hint of a flower smell. Like you were in a garden or a flower shop. But that smell wasn't there all the time. It seemed like the other stuff overpowered it.

"Stop here!" The old man had yelled it, and I jumped. Then he yelled again, something in what I guessed was Vietnamese. The driver looked in the rear-view mirror and shook his head, but he stopped the car.

I looked over, and the old man was leaning forward and staring at a building. It didn't look like much to me, just a store that sold vegetables and fruit. The produce was in bins and baskets both inside the store and outside on the sidewalk. Like one of those fruit stands you see in British Columbia. Then there were apartments or maybe offices above that for five floors.

The old man opened the door of the taxi and stepped out. He said, "Wait," without looking back, so I couldn't tell if he was talking to me or the driver. Both of us waited, and both of us watched the old man.

He walked slowly to the building, looking up and down at it as he walked. Taking it all in. It had to have been a place that he knew for some reason when he'd been here before. Was it a grocer's shop back then? I'd ask him later, but there was no guarantee he'd tell me. It didn't seem like he was going to be telling me much.

There was a skinny little guy selling the vegetables, but he looked like he was putting stuff away. Closing up. About time, it had to be after midnight. The old man talked to the vegetable guy for a couple of minutes. The guy pointed up the street. The old man looked where he was pointing, then he nodded, and the skinny guy went back to packing up his groceries, covering baskets full of stuff and setting them inside the door of the shop.

The old man looked at the building some more, then reached out and touched the brick wall, left his hand just resting against the wall for a couple of minutes. Then he backed up toward the taxi, but he kept his eyes on the building.

He turned, climbed in the car and said, "Let's go." Then turned to look out the window again. He didn't look at me or say anything to me.

We drove for a while longer. I noticed something else. Another sound. Loudspeakers. Not everywhere and not all the time, but every once in a while you'd hear these loudspeakers. Sometimes it was music; other times it was people talking, in Vietnamese, of course, so I couldn't tell what they were saying. Mostly it was men talking, but sometimes it was a woman. When it was a woman's voice, I got the feeling maybe it was like a commercial for something. The men's voices, I couldn't tell. It seemed harsher though, like the preachers on those TV shows where they tell you to smarten up your life and send money.

One thing was for sure. Ho Chi Minh City had like a major night life — clubs, lots of them. I could hear some of the music as we went by. Some oriental, some American. Even some oldies rock and roll. As we went past one place I could hear and see the band, all Asian guys pounding out a version of "At the Hop." My mom loves that oldies stuff, so I know a lot of the songs from hearing them at home. These guys weren't bad. People were dancing, and they were pretty good too.

Next was a karaoke place. I could see through the windows, some people dancing, some just watching. Two girls trying to sing "Roxanne," the Police song. They sucked.

We drove a little farther, going pretty slow because of the traffic. That's when it occurred to me — it was Saturday night here. See, I told you I'd lost a day of my life. I was thinking Friday.

Something else I didn't expect — that Vietnam would be all about partying on a Saturday night. Then the old man said, "This is good right here."

I looked around. Terrific. No hotel in sight. So we were going to haul our stuff around the streets of Ho Chi Minh City in the middle of the night for a while. This was getting to be more fun all the time.

The old man paid the driver, and a minute later we were standing in the middle of a brightly lit street. Big-time crowded.

"Now what?" I started to organize my stuff into walking mode. "You forget that we had a hotel, or did you lie to me about that? We just going to wander the streets until morning."

"The Rex isn't far from here. We need to eat first."

"A lot of guys might have dropped their bags off first then walked back to this charming little spot for dinner." I waved my arm around to indicate the charm.

"Yeah, we could've done it that way, but we didn't, so now we eat, then we'll head for the Rex. And, by the way, you complain way too much."

He pointed to what looked like an outdoor lunch counter. People were sitting at seats that faced into the part where the cooks were making stuff. There were some benches a few feet back from where the people were eating. Every time somebody finished eating and stood up to leave, someone from the benches would race in there like this was the most exclusive restaurant in Asia and you were lucky to get in. It looked pretty dumpy to me. Especially compared to a lot of the places I'd seen as we were driving around. No band in this place and no karaoke.

I kept my mouth shut. I'd hate to be labelled a complainer. Especially when we were having all this fun.

We took over one of the benches, got our stuff gathered close around us, and watched the backs of the people who were eating. I tried to get a read on who'd finish next from the way they were sitting and making little eating movements. Couldn't really tell.

It started to rain. Perfect. Not hard, but even soft rain's still wet. The people at the counter who were eating were under a sort of canvas canopy. Out of the rain. The people at the benches — as in *us* — weren't.

I looked over at the old man. He seemed to be, I guess you'd say, intense. Alive. Interested. Not at all bothered by the rain. He turned to me and said, "It rains a fair bit in Vietnam, so get used to it." Heading me off before I could complain.

Sure, nothing to it. I'd get used to the rain just like I'd get used to hauling luggage around the streets of the city on foot in the middle of the night and sitting on a bench getting wet and cold waiting for a turn to eat at a place that looked like the ol' health inspectors just might have missed it. Hell, anybody would get used to that, right?

We sat there for about fifteen minutes. Some people left. Others took their places at the counter. Finally, it looked like it was getting to be our turn. A couple of people finished eating in front of us, and I got ready to make my move. The old man put his hand on my arm. He nodded at a really old lady and a kid maybe my age. They were at the next bench to us, and I was pretty sure they'd got there after us.

They stepped forward and took the two spots at the counter. Didn't even look at the old man to thank him or anything.

"That was stupid," I said. "That old lady already has like a million wrinkles. The rain isn't going to do anything to her."

The old man smiled. "We're next."

Our turn finally came, and we took a couple of seats at the counter. I wasn't all that comfortable, mostly because I had jammed everything I owned in where my feet

72

were meant to go. I was sure we were surrounded by bandits or Asian gang members just waiting for some pathetic North American kid to come along so they could steal his stuff. We were sitting with our backs to the street, which I didn't like either because I figured that made things even easier for bandits or Asian gang members just waiting for some pathetic North American kid to come along so they could steal his stuff.

The old man didn't seem all that worried about it. He was concentrating on ordering. There was no menu, just signs on the wall and hanging from the ceiling above where the cooking was going on. The signs were in Vietnamese, which meant I couldn't figure out squat that was on them. The Vietnamese alphabet is like ours, as opposed to the symbols that are the Chinese and Japanese alphabets, but that only helps to a point. French uses the same alphabet as us too, but if you're not French, you still can't read it.

There were a couple of pictures of food, but I didn't recognize any of it. The old man studied the signs.

"What do you suggest?" I asked him

He didn't answer, and it was pretty loud in there, so I tried again, louder this time. "What's any good?"

"Noodles."

"What if I don't like noodles?"

"Then you shouldn't have got off the plane."

"There's a lot of stuff written up there. It can't all be noodles."

"I'll order for you."

"Are you going to tell me what it is, or will it be a surprise?"

The guy who seemed to be taking orders came along just then, so I didn't get an answer. The old man did some pointing, held up four fingers and threw out a few words in Vietnamese. The order guy said some stuff back. It sounded like he was giving the old man hell for something. Then he looked at me, not real friendly, and walked away, shouting in the direction of the people who were cooking.

"So what am I having?"

"Noodles and fish."

"Is the fish cooked?"

The old man shrugged.

"Will it be dead at least?"

"Pretty much."

"You speak very much Vietnamese?"

"Some. I used to be pretty good. But I've forgotten a lot."

That was it for conversation. The old man didn't seem to feel like talking, and I was too tired to try.

I'll say one thing — the place got the food out really fast. It was maybe a minute or so before I was staring down at a plate full of noodles and some things sitting on top of the noodles that I assumed — and hoped — were chunks of fish. It was all steaming and, actually, didn't look or smell, that bad. I took the chopsticks and moved some of the noodles around, checking for anything that crawled. I didn't see anything.

For a few minutes the old man and I just ate, no talking. The thing is I'm okay with chopsticks, but I kind of have to work at it. So I was concentrating pretty hard.

"Not bad," I shouted after I'd worked my way through some of the noodles and one piece of the fish. "What kind of fish is it?"

The old man didn't answer. He pointed at one of the pictures, which was exactly zero help. I got the feeling that whenever he thought I might not like the answer to one of my questions, he just didn't bother to respond.

He chewed for a while, then looked at me. "You play any baseball?"

"Whar?" It wasn't the conversation I expected to be having in that place at that exact time.

"Baseball. You play any?"

"Little League."

"You any good?"

"Not bad, I guess. I played shortstop and once in a while catcher. Our team made it to the city finals one year. But we lost. I made an error in the last inning. Probably cost us the game."

"Shit happens."

"I thought we had a rule about saying shit."

"We have a rule about *you* saying shit."

"That's not fair."

The old man swallowed some more noodles and nodded. "You're right. No more shit. Eat."

We ate. But before I could finish, I was falling asleep. Sitting there surrounded by noise and chaos, I was afraid I'd slump forward head first into the noodles. The old man said something about Vietnam being a big-time baseball country. I was too tired to answer. Or care. He stood up, paid the guy who'd taken our order, and stepped back from the counter. I barely got my gear pulled out from under the counter before two business-men-looking guys (what kind of business happens at

75

midnight on a Saturday night?) piled into the seats we had just vacated.

We stepped out into the street. "Want me to carry something?"

I shook my head. "I'm good."

He headed off in what I hoped was the direction of the Rex Hotel. We were maybe ten minutes getting there, and there was constant noise and movement and light going on around us the whole time. But I don't remember much more than that because I was in a total zombie state for most of the walk.

2

Which is probably why I don't remember much of that first look at the Rex Hotel either.

I woke up the next morning a little confused. The light was streaming in on top of me from a large window next to my bed. I didn't have a shirt on, but I was still wearing the jeans and socks I'd had on the day before. I couldn't remember getting undressed for bed. I guess that's because I didn't, not really.

I sat up and looked around. I was alone in the room. No sign of the old man. There was a clock on a shelf that jutted from the wall near the window. Ten sixteen. I was like *whoa, I never sleep that long.*

I got up and went into the bathroom to wash my face and brush my teeth. When I came out, the old man still hadn't come back from wherever he'd gone. I got dressed, unpacked my clothes, and turned on the TV. I was still trying to find a channel that was in English when the old man came through the door.

"Hey, Sleeping Beauty's finally up and moving."

"Sorry," I said, "I don't usually sleep in like that."

"Don't sweat it. Jet lag. Let's go get some breakfast."

"Is it going to be sort of … normal food?" The idea of noodles first thing in the morning was enough to make me give up eating for as long as we were in Vietnam.

"Bacon and eggs normal enough for you?"

I did the fist pump. "Oh, yeah."

We ate in the rooftop restaurant. It was outdoors with a pretty cool view of the centre part of the city. That surprised me too, the city itself. Seeing them in daylight, the buildings weren't what I expected. I mean, inside me, I knew it wasn't *really* going to be all huts and grass shacks. But still I hadn't expected *this*.

For starters, everything was bigger than I thought it would be. And the architecture was a lot different from what I expected. Some Asian looking buildings, pagodas and stuff, some fancy what looked like European architecture and some really modern looking places like you'd see in Los Angeles. That is if you ever got out of the airport and actually *saw* Los Angeles.

It was hot already, but there were some clouds around that looked like there might be some rain.

The waiter spoke English, and the old man ordered three orders of bacon and eggs, "one for you, one for me, and one for backup" was how he put it. This time I totally agreed with his food order.

I ate and the old man ate, but his eating wasn't like mine. It was like he was sitting on something itchy. He kept moving around, looking around, and sometimes he'd just stare at something like he was trying to memorize it. Or remember it. A couple of times he shook his head. So maybe he wasn't trying to remember. Maybe he was wanting to forget.

"So I figured it out," I said as I dabbed toast in runny egg yolk.

"What did you figure out?"

"Why we're here."

"And why's that?"

"You fought here in that war, the Vietnam War. The one the U.S. lost. You and Tal probably fought together. And now you've come back here to see what's happened to the country since you left. Am I right? Is that it?"

"Something like that." He was still looking around while we were talking, but then he looked at me. "This hotel and especially this restaurant were a big deal with American soldiers, especially officers. I came here a few times. It was a good place to forget … forget what was happening when you weren't in places like this."

"Were you an officer?"

"No," he sipped coffee. "But sometimes the grunts … the regular soldiers, came here. Not often. A few times."

"Nice place."

"Yeah."

He didn't say any more. We concentrated on eating again, and he seemed less jumpy, less intense for a while. We shared the backup order of bacon and eggs. Ate everything. Sat back afterwards like stuffed hogs.

3

I have to admit it was a pretty good day. It was like the old man suddenly realized he had a kid with him, and it might be nice to do some stuff that a kid might like.

First, we went to the City Zoo, but we didn't stay long. It pretty much sucked. I'd been to zoos back home, and they were all better than this one, even the smaller ones. The City Zoo in Saigon didn't have many animals, and the ones that were there didn't look like they got fed all that regularly.

I could see the old man was feeling bad that the zoo wasn't great, so I said something about the gardens and the flowers being real impressive, but I don't think he bought it.

Next we hit the Reunification Palace. When I hear *palace*, I think old. Like Buckingham Palace. This palace wasn't actually all that old, 1960s. As we wandered through the halls and the grounds outside, I read some of the plaques that explained stuff. It was designed by a Vietnamese architect who got his training in France. Before the war and during the war, the place was known as the Presidential Palace, but when the North Vietnamese overran the country in 1975, their tanks smashed through the gates of the Presidential Palace. And pretty soon the place got renamed — the Palace of Reunification.

I noticed that references to the war didn't exactly heap a lot of praise on the Americans. Lots of stuff about how they used cluster bombs to slaughter women and children and committed every atrocity you can imagine. The old man didn't spend a lot of time looking at that stuff.

More of the same when we crossed the street and went into the War Remnants Museum. Not a happy place. And if you'd fought on the side the old man had, it had to be tough going through there. It wasn't *all* bad. There was a cannon that had a range of twenty miles, a tank, and a helicopter — all in the grounds around the museum. It was American equipment that got left behind when they pulled out. I think the old man wanted me to learn something about the war, but this wasn't what he wanted me to learn. Inside the museum there were endless pictures of all the bad stuff the Americans did to people and to the countryside during those years. That was another short visit.

Next stop was Dam Sen Park, sort of Disneyland-Vietnam. The best thing was the elephant ride. Real elephants. The old man and me, we both went for a ride. It was cool, I have to admit. I asked the guy running the elephant place if mine had a name. He just shrugged like he didn't understand me. I named mine Elly. I told the old man, and he named his Fant. Buddy movie stuff.

I was getting hungry, so we went to the downtown area called Cholon, Saigon's Chinatown. The old man told me Cholon means "big market." To me it was big chaos. Plenty of shouting, people in a major hurry, lots of Asian architecture, pagodas, and statues of dragons, and these lion-dogs that sent jets of water into goldfish ponds.

"This is where we came for excitement when we had time off. Opium dens, sex, gambling — it was all here. Looks like they've cleaned it up some since then." The old man had to shout that whole speech so I could hear him over the human noise.

"So which ones did you do?" I yelled back.

"All of 'em. The opium less often than the other stuff."

We found a place that looked like it had pretty good food. We were right ... the most amazing won ton soup ever. Not that I've had it a lot — Mom and I don't dine out a bunch — but I've had won ton soup a few times and this stuff was awesome.

We didn't talk — or yell — much during lunch, and it wasn't until we were out of the busiest part of Cholon that we tried conversation again.

"There's something I want you to see," the old man said. "I'll take us a little while to get there."

We walked for a while, then got on this bus and sat about halfway back. I wanted to ask the old man where we were going, but by then I knew better. He'd tell me if he felt like it. We drove through the city, and this time it was my turn to stare out the window. I can't say I was liking Saigon, but it was definitely interesting. Okay, maybe I was liking it a little.

It seemed to me that a lot of the people on the bus were tourists, not a lot of Vietnamese. Several different languages were being spoken around us. Not much English. Quite a few backpackers.

There were three people sitting across from us. They were Caucasian and speaking English, with an accent. Husband, wife, daughter, about my age. The daughter smiled at me. I gave her a little smile back. Reminded myself I was saving my love for Jen Wertz. The two adults — they looked about Mom's age — nodded at us and we nodded back.

"Where you from?" the old man asked.

"Australia. You? Yank?"

"Canadian."

"You going to Cu Chi? The tunnels?" the lady asked.

"Yeah."

I looked at the old man, wondering why it was so tough for him to tell me the stuff he could tell somebody we'd only just met.

The Australian guy leaned forward, looked at the old man. "You look the right age to have been here during the war. You a veteran?"

The old man didn't answer, just turned and looked out the window. Not real friendly, I thought. The Australian guy sat back and looked at his wife. I couldn't tell what the look meant. The daughter smiled at me again. I figured I knew what *that* look meant.

"What's your name?" I said.

"Jennifer."

Jennifer. Jen. *Whoa, what are the chances?*

As we were getting off the bus, the Australian man stepped up close to the old man. "Listen, I'm in the middle of writing a book about Vietnam, the Australian experience, you know? But I want it to be on the mark, get it right. Talk about the war America and its allies lost, how Kennedy and Johnson and Nixon, how all of them screwed up … how it was the most unpopular war the west ever fought, even more than Iraq. What I need is the perspective of the American soldier——"

"No."

"Look, mate, I wouldn't take up a lot of your time, I really only need you to——"

"I really only need you to shut the hell up ... mate." When the old man said that, the Australian guy took a couple of quick steps backward. He was nervous — maybe even scared. Scared of someone in his sixties.

The weird thing is, if I'd been him, I'd have been scared of the old man too. There was something about the way he was looking at the Aussie writer that was kind of crazy — off base, like he wasn't totally with the program. Guys like that are scary and right at that moment the old man was a scary guy.

The writer dude from Australia shut the hell up. And got out of there, dragging the family with him. They were moving quite rapidly

I thought about trying to say something funny. Like *well, I guess I won't be taking her to the prom*. But I changed my mind. Maybe not the time for Huffman humour.

We moved away from the bus and followed the crowd that all seemed to be heading the same way. Cu Chi was a town. But we weren't there to see the town. Nobody was. It turned out everyone on the bus, and all the people from all the other buses, were there to see the tunnels. The Cu Chi Tunnels.

I figured this would be more boring than the Saigon zoo with its *No Animals* policy. Now we'd be poking around a couple of little tunnels with those things hanging down — stalactites. Total yawner.

I was way wrong.

The old man led me over to where you pay for the tour. He went up to this sort of cage and paid. He came back and handed me a piece of paper.

"Where's yours?"

"I'm not going."

"Why not? I don't want to go by myself."

"I've been in tunnels. Not these tunnels but others like them. Charlie was very good at digging."

"Who's Charlie?"

"It's what we called them … the enemy. We called them other names too. But a lot of the time it was Charlie."

"So why are we here if you're not even going in there?"

"I don't need to go down there."

I shook my head. "Well, I don't *need* to go down there either. I thought this was about you. You're the one who was in the war."

"This is about us. I've been in tunnels, you haven't. You better get going. Your tour guide is leaving."

I wanted to tell him this was crap, but there were a lot of people around, and I didn't want to look like the pain-in-the-ass teenager. I shook my head again and turned to follow the tour guide and about ten people who were in our group.

The guide didn't say much at first, just walked off and signalled for us to follow her. She looked like she was having a bad day.

There were maybe twelve of us. We hadn't gone far when suddenly this guy popped out of the ground right in front of us. He was wearing a black army shirt that looked like it came from Value Village and a floppy green bush hat. He was holding the hatch over his head like one of those sewer covers and grinning like crazy at us. He made his fingers in the shape of a gun.

"Bang, bang, you all dead now," he said, still grinning. I could see what he was saying. A bunch of soldiers walking along and suddenly, this guy is there with a machine gun or a grenade or something and yeah, everybody's dead.

Everyone snapped pictures like crazy for a couple of minutes. Everyone but me. I wasn't going to waste film on a guy doing an impersonation of a jack-in-the-box and wearing cheap black pajamas. We walked on and eventually came to an exhibit. I've been to a few museums on field trips and stuff, but I'd never seen an exhibit like this one.

The whole exhibit was booby traps that the Viet Cong used to kill guys. The worst one for me was this pit that was covered over just like the hole the guy had come out of. When the thatch cover was pulled away from over top of the pit, there were all these sharp bamboo stakes at the bottom, pointing up.

I tried to imagine what it would be like to be walking along and falling into one of those pits. I had this picture in my mind of these soldiers looking down into the pit where one of their buddies was spread out with those stakes all through him. Trying to think of a way to help him. To get him out.

Something I'd noticed: whenever you saw anything about American war crimes, it was all *those rotten bastards*. But anybody who ran into one of the booby traps I saw displayed there was going to die a pretty horrible death. Cruel. But this exhibit was like a celebration. Like somebody had won the Stanley Cup. *We showed 'em.* I guess they did.

I was glad we didn't spend a lot of time at that exhibit. Next we got to go down into one section of the tunnels ourselves. The guide told us there were 125 miles of these tunnels. Three tiers of them that had kitchens, first aid stations, weapons caches — it was unreal. And the Viet Cong, who were the communists in South Vietnam — Charlie — they did a lot of their war preparations from down there. And launched attacks from inside the tunnels.

The guide said there were guys on the American side called tunnel rats. Their job was to go down into these tunnels and try to find and destroy the enemy. I tried to imagine what that job would have been like. The guide said guys volunteered for that job. He sounded like he actually admired people who would do that. I knew one thing — there was no freaking way I'd have volunteered to go down there and look for the enemy.

I got tired of listening to the guide, so after we'd been down there awhile, I wandered off by myself. This part of the tunnel had been a command post. I moved slowly through it and came out into what had been a dormitory — probably big enough for about twenty people to sleep in. Some of the bunks were still there.

"Hi."

I turned and there was the Australian chick, Jennifer, standing there. "Hi."

I looked around. There were other people in the room, another tour group, but I didn't see Jennifer's parents.

"Where're your mom and dad?"

She shrugged. "*We're* not interested in the same things."

I nodded. Tried to think of something to say. "Uh . . . what did you think of that bamboo pit deal?"

She made a face. "Gross. Scary."

"Yeah, no kidding."

"So your dad — did he fight in the war here?"

"Yeah. I guess so. He doesn't say much."

"But when he does …" She had a little smile on her face.

"Yeah, sorry about that … he wasn't exactly polite to your dad."

"It's okay. Dad can be like so annoying. There've been a few times when I wouldn't have minded telling him that myself."

"I know what you mean."

We just stood there for a couple of minutes, looking like kids the first day in a new school — totally lost. "You want to walk around?" I wasn't sure why I asked her that, and I figured she'd do the *I better get back to my parents* thing but she didn't.

"Okay."

"Okay." We stood there for another little while. Then I decided, if we were going to walk around together, we should probably do some actual walking.

I started off around the outside of the room. Looked at the beds, the walls. The dirt ceiling with wooden beams holding things up.

"You never told me your name."

"Oh sorry, you're right. It's Nathan … Nate."

"Which one?"

"I like Nate better."

"Me too. I'm Jen … Jen … Jen Dodsworth."

Jen Wertz … Jen Dodsworth … sweet.

We walked around, not saying a lot. Making little comments about stuff we were looking at.

"How long have you been here?" I asked her.

"Eight days." Sounded like she was keeping track. Wanting to get the hell home. "And we don't go back for another whole week. You?"

"I'm not sure. This whole thing was my old man's idea. He doesn't tell me much. Another few days maybe."

"I miss my dog."

"Oh, yeah ... uh ... what's its name?"

"Farnsworth."

Farnsworth Dodsworth. Nice.

"What kind of dog is he?" She hadn't said it was a he, but I figured nobody names a female dog Farnsworth. If the dog was a golden retriever, I decided I'd run out of the tunnels and throw myself into the bamboo pit.

"Dalmatian."

Not a golden retriever. I didn't like Dalmatians either, but then I didn't like any kind of dog. I decided not to share that information with her.

There were quite a few places where the tunnels got narrow and small and we had to scootch down and duck walk to get through. Scootching down and getting close to Jen wasn't all that bad, even in a tunnel.

We worked our way through a few more rooms — a kitchen, a weapons storage area, a printing shop, and then we came to another dormitory. Either that or a hospital. More beds. This time we were by ourselves in there.

"I wonder if they had sex down here."

I looked over at her. I wondered if that was her way of being flirty or if she was showing me how adult she was or what. I shrugged. "The guide said there were women down here as well as men so I guess ... maybe."

I wasn't sure where the conversation was going to go from there, but it didn't go anywhere because that's when her mom and dad showed up.

"Jennifer, where did you get ..." her mom stopped in mid-sentence when she saw me. "Oh, hello."

"Hi again," I said.

"Where's your father?" Mr. Dodsworth (or was it Farnsworth?) asked me.

"He stayed up top."

"He didn't come with you? Sent you down here by yourself?"

"He said he's seen enough tunnels."

"He was bloody rude to me, I'd have to say. All I did was ask a question. He didn't have to swear ... quite rude."

"Yeah, well, my old man's a rude son of a bitch."

That seemed to be a conversation stopper. Mr. Dodsworth turned toward the exit and spoke over his shoulder. "We better be getting along, we seem to have lost our group, Jennifer."

The three of them started off toward the doorway. Jennifer stopped and looked back at me. "Jendoll at westcom dot au. Will you remember?"

I nodded. "Jendoll at westcom dot au. I'll remember. Oh, and I've thought about what you asked me ... you know, about having sex down here in the tunnels. The answer's a definite yes."

Her face turned bright red, but she was laughing as her parents hurried her out the door. They weren't laughing.

I'd seen enough of the tunnels, so I worked my way back to where we'd come in and went back outside. For a minute I stood there blinking, trying to get my eyes to work in the bright sunlight. I spotted the old man sitting on a bench drinking a coffee and reading a newspaper. I walked over to where he was sitting. The newspaper was in Vietnamese … definitely not English.

"Can you read that?"

He didn't look up. "Not a word."

I sat down on the bench. He put the paper down.

"How was it?"

"The tour? Interesting."

"That's it … interesting?"

"You know how parents ask their kids how they liked something and the kids say *interesting* but what they really mean is *that bored the crap out of me?*"

"I've heard that happens," he smiled.

"It happens. I said interesting, and I meant interesting."

"Good. You hungry?"

"I'm hungry for a Big Mac."

"How about a Big Spring Roll?"

"Terrific." I looked around, praying for a set of golden arches to pop out of the ground like the guy in the Value Village army uniform.

"We'll eat, then we best be heading back. Need our sleep tonight. Tomorrow it's feet on the floor at oh six hundred hours."

That's what he actually said … *oh six hundred hours.*

Military talk.

Sir. Yes, sir.

4

0600 hours was about oh three hours less sleep than I would have liked.

I knew about thirty seconds after I had my "feet on the floor" that today was a big deal. The old man was different. He wasn't twirling his hair like he had at the border, but I knew something was going on inside him.

He was quiet, pointed to the bathroom and said, "I'm done, it's yours." When I came out, there was fruit and cereal and milk on the table. Since we didn't have any of that stuff with us, I knew he must have ordered room service. I hadn't thought of the old man as a room service kind of guy.

While I ate, he rolled clothes and other stuff we'd need into two sleeping bags, then threw them into two dull green duffel bags. He also threw in some sandwiches, matches, bug spray, and a knife the size of a small sword. Maybe it was a machete. I wasn't sure since I'd never seen a machete up close. If we needed to chop our way through the forest, I figured that thing would do the job.

When I'd finished eating, the old man told me to brush my teeth and put my toothbrush and some clothes in my backpack. He said I wouldn't need my duffel bag. Okay, so that meant we were sleeping somewhere else tonight. Of course, the sleeping bags were pretty much a giveaway, but the toothbrush thing sealed the deal.

There was a knock at the door. I answered it and found myself looking at a guy about a hundred years old who came up to my chin. He looked serious, not grumpy exactly, but *real* serious. He looked like the kind of person who was serious all the time. Chinese or Vietnamese, I couldn't tell. He also weighed maybe 125 pounds total. Not a big guy, but even with the age and how little he was, he didn't look like a guy you'd want to mess with. Kind of like the old man that way.

He was wearing a black shirt over a black T-shirt and green real baggy pants like the kind you see American soldiers wearing in war movies. Except they looked a few sizes too big. He was also wearing a Pittsburgh Penguins ball cap. That made no sense to me. *Watch a lot of hockey do ya, little fella?*

The old man stepped around me and shook hands with the guy, invited him in.

"This is Mr. Vinh. Mr. Vinh — my son Nathan."

"Nate," I said.

Mr. Vinh nodded but didn't offer to shake my hand.

"Mr. Vinh and me, we got some stuff to talk about."

The old man pulled some money out of his pocket and handed it to me. "Why don't you go shopping or something for a half hour?"

I handed it back to him. "First of all, I've got money. Second of all, since it's oh six hundred hours plus about twenty minutes, I figure the shopping is going to be a bit scarce. Third of all, I get that you want me out of here. So this is me leaving."

I started to leave, then stopped and turned back. "We're coming back here right? To this hotel?"

The old man nodded.

As I walked through the door into the hall, I heard him say, "Thanks, Nate," behind me, but I kept going toward the elevator.

I'd seen a computer in the lobby and there were a couple of things I wanted to do. I bought a coffee at the little restaurant on the main floor, got a password from a drop-dead gorgeous Vietnamese woman at the desk and set myself up at the computer.

First thing. Jendoll at westcom dot au. I worked my way to the email function, typed in Jen's address and started tapping out an email.

Hey, I'm the guy you met at the tunnels. How you doing? My old man and I are going somewhere for what looks like a couple of days, then I should be back here. Feel like taking in a movie or just getting a burger or something? Notice I didn't invite you for noodles, which should tell you that I'm a really nice guy. You can email me if you want to at Nathanh@telcomworld.net

LOL
Nate

I hit send. I figured she'd still be sleeping like most of the normal people in the world at that moment, so I didn't expect an answer back. Maybe later. Maybe.

Then I googled something called *My Lai*. It was something I'd seen pictures of in the War Remnants Museum. I wanted to know more about it.

I spent twenty minutes reading and looking at pictures. It's a good thing I'd already eaten because I wouldn't have wanted to after I finished finding out about My Lai.

I could have just cut and pasted something from Wikipedia or some other site, but I wanted to write it out in my own words. This is My Lai …

March 16, 1968.

American soldiers went into two small villages — one was called My Lai, pronounced Me Lie. The soldiers killed over four hundred people — unarmed men, and women, and children. They herded them together and machine gunned them, bayoneted them, even killed the animals that lived in the villages. There were pictures of groups of women holding their little children and babies just a few minutes before they were all shot. One old man was thrown into a well and then shot after he was down there. Some soldiers refused to kill innocent civilians, but most didn't. When the world found out what had happened that day, twenty-six American soldiers were tried for murder and other war crimes. One was convicted.

I was still sitting at the computer looking at one of the pictures — it was these people, all women and little kids dead in this ditch — when the old man came down to get me. I minimized before he saw what I was looking at.

"We're ready to go. Come on up and help us with the stuff."

I shut off the computer, stood up, and followed him to the stairs. I was having trouble getting the pictures I'd seen from My Lai out of my head.

When we were back in the room, I saw that Mr. Vinh had one of the duffel bags over his shoulder and was just reaching for the other one.

The old man and I both said "I'll take that" at about the same time. The old man got there first and took the duffel bag. I offered to take the one Mr. Vinh had slung over what there was of his shoulder, but he shook his head and made for the door.

The old man pointed to a briefcase-looking thing on the bed. "You can bring that. Don't set it down, and don't lose it." It was one of those old-style ones, rectangle shape, and there was masking tape wrapped around it a few times to keep it together.

Great. I get to look like a total nerd out there.

"And leave your cellphone here. Where we're going you won't need it, and you could lose it."

I tucked the phone into my duffel bag, which wasn't making the trip, and shoved the duffel bag in a corner, not hidden but not totally out in the open. My style of security.

I pulled my backpack on, picked up the briefcase, and followed Mr. Vinh down the hotel stairs. The old man came down behind me.

Don't set it down, and don't lose it. So it's either a bomb, or drugs, or money. And I'm carrying it. Lovely.

5

I know now why the iPod was invented. It's for driving through Vietnam in a Land Rover that looks like it could quit at any moment and never ever go again with two guys, one who doesn't speak English and the other who doesn't feel like talking. In any language.

For a couple of hours I looked out the window, especially when we passed through some village. The brief case was at my feet, which didn't leave a lot of room for actual feet, but god forbid I should lose our drug stash.

Ever play that game where you count horses while you're driving? I played that same game except with pagodas. Since I was the only one playing, I won twenty-six to nothing.

Then I fell asleep. When I woke up, I discovered something else about the Land Rover. It didn't have air conditioning. It was the hottest day since we'd arrived — as in *freaking* hot — and after I sat there soaking in my own sweat for a while, I pulled off my T-shirt and stashed it in my backpack. Went with the bare chest look. That helped a little.

We seemed to be driving along or near a coast. I could see water … sometimes in the distance, sometimes right alongside us. I had decided I wouldn't ask the old man where we were going or how long it would take to get there. I figured he wouldn't answer anyway and if he did, it would be one of those answers that didn't make any sense.

He was like he'd been that first night in Saigon. Looking at everything as we drove, his ass on barbecue coals — big-time intense.

More iPod music. We passed rice paddies, and little villages, (the huts at last), and fields of crops that I didn't recognize. And, of course, we went through jungle — although most of that was just on the edges, so it didn't look like much more than a big forest. Which, come to think of it, is what jungle is, right?

We were on something called the AH 1 — the old man did tell me that much. A main highway in Vietnam. We were on that road for about five hours — two stops — one for a pee break, the other for coffee that had the colour of a urine sample and a taste that didn't convince me it wasn't.

I was bored, and I was getting stiff from the back seat of the Land Rover. We were in a sort of mountain range, so the view was pretty good for a while. The ocean, if that's what it was, was below us now and still on our right. Endless dense, bushy looking forest to our left. As I shifted my body for the fiftieth time, I could see we were approaching a big place. Civilization. The old man turned around and looked at me for the first time since we'd left Ho Chi Minh City.

"Da Nang. Big air base during the war."

That was it. He turned back and faced the front again.

Yeah, thanks for the in-depth guided tour. I pretty well know everything there is to know now.

We came down out of the mountain range and onto flatter ground. Just before we got to the edge of the city, we left the AH 1 and headed west toward some hills, more mountains and jungle terrain off in the distance. This was a shorter leg of the trip, less than an hour until we turned right into what looked like a gravel driveway except that it went for quite a ways. When we stopped, I wasn't sure why. Then I noticed what looked like a camp tucked into some trees.

A couple of tents, pretty big ones. A Vietnamese woman standing by a big campfire between the tents. There was a big pot over the fire, and she was looking into it. Didn't look up at us at all.

You ever see the play *Macbeth*, you know, Shakespeare? They did it at our school last year — I ran the lights for it. The woman by the fire looked like one of the witches from *Macbeth*. Just needed two more witches and you could have had that . . .

Double, double, toil and trouble;
Fire burn and cauldron bubble.

It's not like she was ugly or nasty looking; it's just that standing there all bent over and stirring whatever was in the big pot that was sitting over the fire, well, that's what she reminded me of. Mr. Vinh turned off the Land Rover. He and the old man climbed out.

I pulled my earphones, put the iPod into my back-pack, and followed them out into the outdoors . . . and what felt like a sauna. I got my T-shirt and pulled it on over my head. Modesty — there was a lady present.

Mr. Vinh walked over and looked into the pot. Grunted. I didn't know if the grunt meant, *mmm, delicious* or *what is that slop?* I could smell whatever it was she was cooking, and I would have said somewhere in between.

The old man said something to Mr. Vinh, who shook his head and said something back. The old man spoke again, I think he said the same thing that he'd said before, but this time he threw in a bunch of gestures and pointing, somewhere into the brush behind the camp. Mr Vinh responded with some arm waving and pointing of his own. His pointing was at the pot. My guess was that the old man wanted to get going, and Mr. Vinh wanted to sample whatever was on the menu first.

The lady stirred some more, but still hadn't looked up at any of us. She said something, and that set Mr. Vinh off again with yelling and more waving.

The old man shook his head and walked over to me. Pissed off. "Might as well sit down. He wants to eat before we go on."

I was with Mr. Vinh on this one — especially if what we were going to eat was edible — meaning *not* noodles.

"Sit down where?" I looked around. There was a shortage of lawn chairs, picnic tables and blankets.

"On the goddamn ground."

Okay, that clinched it, the old man was not a happy dude.

I found a spot where there were maybe three blades of grass and a couple of weeds and sat. Mr. Vinh brought me a wooden bowl and chopsticks.

Noodles. *Just kill me now.*

"What a nice surprise," I told him.

The old man helped himself to a bowl of the noodles, threw me a canteen of water from his duffel bag and one of our sandwiches. He sat next to me.

"Don't take all day eating that."

"You know something, you're starting to be a pain in the ass to be around."

He set his bowl down, and I figured I was about to find out just how tough this sixty-some-year-old guy was. I waited to get hit.

He shrugged. "You know something — you're right. I'm sorry. I'm way over the top here. Sorry. Enjoy the noodles, I know they're your favourite." He grinned at me.

"That Mr. Vinh's wife?"

He nodded, slurped noodles. "That's what I'm thinking."

We ate. The noodles weren't bad. There was other stuff mixed in with them, vegetables of some kind — no bugs. The sandwiches were tomato. Kind of plain.

"You fight around here? Some battle?"

He nodded. "Among other places. This was the last one."

"Last one for you? Or of the whole war?"

"Last one for me. Tal was in more shit after this."

I'd almost forgotten about Tal.

The old man was working the contents of his bowl pretty hard and not looking at me. I was starting to figure out his signals. He didn't want to talk anymore. I finished the noodles, got up, and took my bowl and chopsticks to the lady, who was still busy with the pot on the fire.

"Thanks, Mrs. Vinh. Excellent noodles."

She didn't say anything, but she did look up. First time she'd done that. Grunted. That seemed to be an important part of the Vinhs' vocabulary. I grunted back at her, hoping I was being polite.

She went back to work. Mr. Vinh was sitting close to the fire, eating. I wondered when Mrs. Vinh ate.

The old man came over to where I was. He looked at Mr. Vinh. "Ready to go?"

Mr. Vinh stood up. Threw the last of his noodles on the ground. Didn't look happy — although I wasn't sure I'd be able to tell when either of the Vinhs *were* happy.

"You might want to use the facilities before we go." The old man pointed at the edge of the jungle out behind the tents. "And use this — generously." He passed me a can of mosquito spray.

"I'm fine on the bathroom thing, but I will have a shot of that."

I sprayed my arms, the backs of my hands, and a little around my neck, basically exposed skin. The old man grabbed the can out of my hands and started spraying me like it was bathroom spray and I was a bad smell.

"Okay, take it easy." I backed away. "That stuff's toxic."

"So are the mosquitoes."

"What now?" I asked as he sprayed himself.

"A little hike." The old man heaved one of the duffel bags up over his shoulder. Mr. Vinh did the same thing with the other one. I noticed he had the machete-looking thing in one hand. I hoped it was for knocking down a vine or two and not for fighting off boa constrictors and stuff.

My job was the backpack and canteens. There were three canteens. And the dorky looking briefcase. I had a little trouble getting it all sorted and hanging from various places on my body, but after a few tries I was more or less organized.

"Let's make a move," the old man said, but he stepped back to let Mr. Vinh lead. Apparently, Mr. Vinh knew better than the old man where we were going.

I fell in behind the old man, but on the way out of the camp, I looked back at Mrs. Vinh. She had stepped away from the fire and was smoking a cigarette. She looked up at me. Nodded. I waved a little wave at her and turned to follow Mr. Vinh and the old man.

I wondered if we'd be coming back here other than to get the Land Rover. I knew there was at least one tent in one of the duffel bags so maybe not. We hadn't gone more than a few hundred metres when I learned my next big lesson about Vietnam. There's forest and there's woods and there's brush and thickets and growth and timberland. All of them together don't make jungle. *Jungle* makes jungle. And five minutes out of that camp, we were up to our asses in jungle.

Mr. Vinh was very good with the machete. No wasted motion. In fact, it didn't look like he was working all that hard. He whacked away and carved a path where there hadn't been one before. The machete had to have been ultra sharp. I decided not to do anything to upset Mr. Vinh.

6

If I'd thought Mr. Vinh's camp felt like a sauna, I revised my opinion real quick. I figured out that back there was air-conditioned comfort. *This* was a sauna.

I had to walk fast because when he wasn't carving a hole in the jungle, Mr. Vinh had this little trotting thing he did which covered a lot of ground in a short time. The old man had a long stride so he was right behind Mr. Vinh.

I had to haul ass to keep them in sight. And I noticed that neither of them looked back. That meant I either kept up or got lost in the jungle to be eaten by whatever creatures were making the noises I heard all around us.

I thought that was just in the movies. But there were noises, animal and bird noises, and not one of them sounded like any animals or birds I knew. The noises died away as we got closer to whatever creatures were out there and started up again behind us as soon as we passed them. No, not behind *us* ... behind *me*. I was at the back. I hoped none of the noisemakers was hungry.

Then things got worse. We, stopped at this swamp-looking body of water that stretched out in front of us for what looked like half a football field. I finally caught up to the old man and Mr. Vinh. They were at the edge of the swamp and the old man was digging into the duffel bag he'd been carrying. Pulled out two sets of rubber boots. Rubber boots with attitude. About a metre long.

"Hip waders," he said. "Put them on."

"We're not going in there?" I looked at him like he was nuts. Which he was if he thought I was setting foot in that ... water. With or without hip waders. "It's the colour of sewage and it doesn't smell good and who knows what's in there."

"So, what's your point?"

"My point is I'm not going in there."

"Okay, first of all, nothing bad will happen to you in there. You won't drown, and you won't get eaten by a great white shark."

"That's because no shark in his right mind would be caught dead in that crap."

"Second of all, we're crossing this, and if you decide you're not going to, then I'll see you back at the truck. You can leave now."

I looked back at the jungle we'd just come through.

I thought about the noises I'd heard in there. Plus, even though there was sort of a path, I wasn't totally positive I could find my way back to Mrs. Vinh and the campfire.

"Are you sure there isn't a better way? Like maybe we could go around this?"

"There's no better way. If Mr. Vinh says we have to cross this, then we have to cross it. Put on the damn hip waders."

Mr. Vinh launched into some Vietnamese lecture. Sounded like an English teacher when you don't hand something in.

The old man nodded. "He wants us to hurry up."

"Give me the damn hip waders."

They were too big, and I had trouble walking in them. The old man took bungee cords and wrapped them around my legs a couple of times to keep them on. He made the cords so tight they hurt.

"You've cut off my circulation."

"Then we better get going. It'd be a bitch if your legs fell off out there in the middle." He waved his arm in the direction of the swamp.

I noticed Mr. Vinh didn't have hip waders. "Is he going to cross like that?"

The old man shrugged. "He's tougher than us."

"He's stupider than us."

The old man actually cracked a smile. "Let's go." He nodded at Mr. Vinh, who did his little trot-shuffle step up to the swamp, then stepped out into it.

I was relieved that he didn't disappear straight down and out of sight. He held his arms out to the side like he was balancing, but he moved pretty fast. I was wishing the guy had more than one speed.

The old man gathered up the duffel bag and stepped into the water, then moved off a few metres into the swamp. But this time he at least stopped and looked back to see how I was getting along. I had my canteens and backpack all arranged, but holding the briefcase up chest high meant I couldn't use my arms to balance myself.

"This place takes brackish to a whole other level," I don't think anybody heard me.

There are earthworms that move faster than I was moving right then, and I figured it wouldn't be long before I heard about it. But this time the old man was patient. Even said all that encouraging stuff. "Doin' just fine, Nate…. Looking good, buddy." That kind of stuff.

And I *was* looking good until a little past the midway point of our crossing. The water was up to about the middle of my thighs. I think my foot must have slipped off a rock on the bottom, and I lost my balance. I tried like crazy to get my feet back under me, but as I was scrambling around, I tripped over something — a submerged log or something and fell backwards into the swamp.

I was only totally in the water for like a second and a half, but I swallowed what I was sure was a lethal dose of swamp water. I scrambled and splashed my way back to my feet sputtering, choking and trying to say "Shit," all at the same time.

The amazing thing is I kept the briefcase from going in the water. Kept my arms up as I was falling. Could've drowned, probably poisoned myself, but I saved a briefcase I'd never even seen the inside of. Genius.

"You okay?"

I had a feeling the old man was trying to keep from laughing.

"Just ducky," I said.

The rest of the way to the other side went okay considering I was feeling like I'd been slimed. The water was cool so that part had been okay. At least it got some of the sweat off me.

By the time the old man and I got the hip waders off and back in the duffel bag, Mr. Vinh had disappeared into the jungle ahead. I hoped the old man knew where he'd gone.

I wanted to take time to wring out my T-shirt, but the old man shook his head.

"Saddle up. We're moving out … now."

Was it just me or was he starting to sound like somebody out of a war movie? I didn't have time to think about it because he headed off down what looked like a bit of a jungle path, moving even faster than he had before.

I saddled up and hustled after him, the canteens jouncing around as I sort of jog/sloshed off into the jungle. I was able to catch up even though neither Mr. Vinh, who I could just make out up ahead, nor the old man slowed down even a little bit.

I wasn't sure how long we'd been hiking, but I was sure of one thing. I was tired to the point I could have fallen over. I was walking with my head down, and I almost ran into the old man. He'd stopped suddenly, and Mr. Vinh was just a couple of metres ahead.

I looked up. We were at the edge of a huge clearing that looked like someone had gone through and cut down all the trees and left a lawn. The grass was a little long for a lawn, but I was so happy to be out of the jungle I wasn't about to criticize the groundskeeper. It was a space about the size of our school gymnasium, maybe a little bigger.

The old man dropped his duffel bag. Mr. Vinh did the same thing. The old man said some stuff, some English, some Vietnamese, and threw in a few hand signals. I was getting used to their way of communication, and I figured out that the old man and I were going to set up the tents while Mr. Vinh's job was to get the food out.

"Where are we?" I dropped the canteens and backpack on the ground. Then I set the briefcase down very carefully. I still didn't know what was in it, but after the effort I'd made to keep the thing dry back there in the swamp, I wasn't about to let anything happen to it now.

"A clearing. It was an LZ — Landing Zone. Places like this choppers used to set down to drop guys for search-and-destroy missions. Evacuate wounded too."

That was a big explanation for the old man, so I decided not to push it. I looked around, tried to imagine helicopters coming in, getting shot at from the jungle all around, landing, taking off again. I shivered. Part of it was because my clothes were still soaked, and it was getting cooler. But I don't think that was all of it.

"We'll stay right here tonight, push on again in the morning. There're dry clothes in the duffel bag Mr. Vinh was carrying. Better get changed."

"Change like right out here?"

"The master bedroom's occupied. And I don't recommend you go back into the jungle and start peeling off clothes. No telling what might happen." This time he didn't try to keep the grin off his face. Didn't matter. I wasn't setting foot into anything that looked like jungle without the old man and Mr. Vinh real close by.

The old man started setting up one of the tents and Mr. Vinh was doing something to do with food. I got some dry gonch and socks and another T-shirt and jeans out of the duffel bag. Then I turned away from them and tried to change. Going for privacy. It wasn't easy. The clothes I had on were sticky, and the ground was uneven, so I was hopping around trying to get the wet jeans off and the other pair on. It took a lot longer than I wanted it to.

I had one leg in the dry jeans and was trying to get the other leg in without losing my balance when I heard laughing behind me.

"You try it, you think it's so easy," I yelled over my shoulder.

I got the other leg into the jeans and whipped around to look at them while I did up the button and the fly. The old man was looking at me, still grinning but not actually laughing. I looked over at Mr. Vinh. He was bent over, and he was killing himself laughing. Making little Vietnamese comments to the old man, who was nodding.

"And just when I thought ol' Mr. Vinh had no sense of humour at all." I gave them both my best pissed-off face, but that got Mr. Vinh laughing even harder. "You son of a bitch," I said.

But the thing is, it *was* funny. And for the first time since I'd started on this whole stupid summer from hell, my old man and I laughed at the same time. But neither of us was coming close to Mr. Vinh in the laughter department. I thought the old guy would have a heart attack or something.

"Actually, you're both sons of bitches." I threw my soggy T-shirt at Mr. Vinh.

It wasn't long before we had two tents set up, my wet clothes hanging from a tree on the edge of the clearing, and we were eating. Something. Some of it I recognized. There was bread and a can of some kind of meatballs that we passed around, each of us spearing a meatball when it was our turn.

The rest of it I wasn't sure about and didn't ask. There was some kind of fish; at least I thought it was fish, raw fish. There were cold noodles (what's a meal without noodles), and this salad looking stuff that didn't taste like salad. I drank quite a bit of water with that meal.

7

Dark came in fast and I was real tired, but I didn't want to go to bed. Not yet. We'd cleaned up from our meal, and the old man was sitting down against one of the folded up sleeping bags and looking up at the darkening sky. Mr. Vinh was sitting cross-legged and smoking a pipe.

I spread out my sleeping bag on the ground and lay down on it, my head propped on one elbow. I watched them. I was trying to figure out what was going on.

"You feel like sleeping, that's our tent." The old man pointed.

"I feel like sleeping, but I feel more like talking … that is if anybody wants to talk to me."

"I can't speak for Mr. Vinh." The old man went back to looking at the sky.

"I was thinking more that I'd like it if *you* talked to me." I'd noticed that now we were actually out here, the old man seemed a lot calmer, more settled than when we'd been travelling to get here.

"What would you like to talk about, Nathan?"

"Nate."

"What would you like to talk about, Nate?"

"How about where are we for starters?"

He pointed back over his shoulder. "In that direction is the A Shau Valley. That's where we're headed. During the war, this valley was part of something called the Ho Chi Minh Trail. North Vietnamese soldiers used this as their main infiltration route into the south. A lot of battles were fought around here. A hell of a lot of people died in that valley."

"And this is where the battle you told me about, the one you and Tal were in, this is where that battle happened?"

"Yeah."

"Why did you want to come back here?"

"Jesus, Nate, you could be one of those interviewers on *60 Minutes* or something. These are tough questions."

"Sorry."

"A lot of guys come back. Visit the places where shit happened. I don't know exactly why. I never wanted to experience anything like that ever again. And I didn't think I'd want to be reminded of what happened here. So I can't explain exactly why we're here, except that I guess I changed my mind."

"It just seems weird to me after all this time."

"Forty years."

"Seriously? Forty years?"

"Yeah."

"Can you remember stuff that happened that long ago?"

"Like it happened this morning."

"I still don't get why . . . after forty years."

"It's the right time."

I shook my head. That didn't make sense. But I was too tired to try to figure it out.

"What happens tomorrow?"

"We walk. Five miles to a place I want to see. A place I want you to see. After that I don't know."

I stopped listening after the *five miles* part. I hoped there weren't any more swamps. I picked up the sleeping bag and pushed it into the tent. I fell asleep like somebody had hit me over the head with a brick.

The A Shau Valley

1

I woke up and freaked.

In the pre-dawn semi-light, I was sure of one thing — I'd been carried off to a giant jungle spider's web. The spider's webbing was all around me. I tried to move my eyes without moving my head so that whatever it was that had taken me prisoner wouldn't know I was still alive. Or awake.

I didn't see a spider. But I did hear the old man's voice outside the tent, talking softly, and Mr. Vinh's high-pitched singsong answering.

"Uh ... morning," I called out. I didn't want to let on that I might need to be rescued from a bloodthirsty insect, but I wouldn't have minded if the old man happened to look into the tent right about then.

He didn't. "Hey, Nathan, gather up that mosquito netting as you're getting up. We'll need it again tonight."

I pulled my hand out from under the covers and gently reached up, touched the spider's web. *Mosquito netting.*

"Uh, yeah, mosquito netting. I'll gather up the mosquito netting. I'll just gather it up. No problem."

"Good." I heard the old man saying something to Mr. Vinh. I was pretty sure the phrase "strange kid" was part of what he said.

I gave up on the netting long enough to pull on the rest of my clothes. It didn't take long since I hadn't totally undressed the night before. I'd pulled off my shirt and running shoes and that was it. I had this feeling that sleeping in your gonch in the jungle was an open invitation for some creature to sneak into your sleeping bag and start gnawing on some private area best left un-gnawed.

I'd just finished getting the shirt and shoes back on and picked up the jumble of netting when the old man and Mr. Vinh stomped into the tent, wearing slickers but looking wet anyway. Raining outside. The old man was carrying the briefcase. He opened it and pulled out what looked like some maps … and a couple of old photographs.

They both sat on the floor of the tent. The old man was sitting cross-legged with the briefcase in his lap, lid down, and one of the maps lying on its surface. Mr. Vinh sat next to him. Both were staring hard at the map.

The old man pointed at a couple of points on the map. Mr. Vinh nodded and spoke in a mix of Vietnamese and English that was pretty well gibberish to me. The old man answered him also with a mix of words, most of them one syllable. As usual, I understood pretty well nothing.

But it was quite an animated conversation. A couple of times Mr. Vinh didn't seem to know the answer to whatever the old man wanted to know. When that happened, he shrugged and shook his head. The old man's voice got pretty loud right about then. After maybe the third time it happened, the old man looked up at me. It was like he suddenly realized I was there, still sorting mosquito netting and watching the two of them.

"Get that sleeping bag rolled up and into that duffel bag outside, the bigger one. The mosquito netting too." That was it. He went back to the map, except that now he had some of the photographs spread out on the briefcase, and he was pointing at them too.

I gathered up the netting and sleeping bag and stepped out of the tent. The rain wasn't hard, but there was enough of it that I knew I'd be soaked pretty fast. There was a gathering of branches next to the tent, sort of a lean-to and the two duffel bags were under it. I didn't remember the lean-to from the night before. Maybe they'd put it up after I'd gone to bed or maybe it was there from before. I didn't know and it didn't matter. What mattered was that it was dry under there. I took my time packing up the rest of the gear.

The old man and Mr. Vinh came out of the tent, and the old man tossed a slicker to me. I pulled it over my head, lifted the hood into position and stepped out from under the lean-to. It was raining harder now, a lot harder. Even with the slicker I got pretty wet … pretty fast. Not as bad as after the swamp episode but fairly damp just the same.

I went around to the other side of the lean-to to take a leak. It was the most privacy I could hope for unless I wanted to go out into the jungle a ways. And I didn't want to do that.

We ate bananas, two each, under the lean-to before heading out. Nobody was going to get fat on this trip. That was obvious. I pulled my hood back just long enough to check the sky. It looked like the clouds were about fifty metres above our heads and the rain was coming down even harder. Nice day for a walk in the jungle.

I gathered the canteens and the backpack. The old man had stashed the briefcase in the bigger duffel bag, so I didn't have to carry it anymore. Mr. Vinh grunted a couple of times and started off across the clearing, machete in hand, toward the jungle that was on the other side. This time the old man nodded that he wanted me to go next and that he'd be at the back. I didn't mind that actually. At least this way I wouldn't get lost in the jungle or picked off by some python without anyone even knowing.

2

I don't know how long we walked. I do know that the rain stopped. Trouble was, it was actually worse after that. Hot with a humidity of maybe four hundred percent. Steam was actually rising off the jungle floor. I pulled off the slicker, but it didn't matter. I think I was wetter when it wasn't raining than when it was. I laid on my second layer of mosquito repellant. I noticed something unpleasant. The mix of sweat and mosquito juice and the lack of shower facilities (I didn't count my dip in the swamp) didn't make for a really great-smelling boy. I was pretty sure neither of the Jens would have found me all that attractive right about then.

We finally came out of the jungle, and there was this field stretched across in front of us. Neat rows of plants stood maybe a foot high in a layer of water across the whole field. The water looked to be about fifteen centimetres deep. Maybe more. The old man came up alongside me.

"Rice paddy," he said. "There was one in about this area the last time I made this walk. May be the same one."

I was thinking *who cares.*

Then he pointed. There was another stretch of jungle on the other side of the rice paddy, not very big this time, and a hill that kind of rose up out of it. Behind that hill there were a couple of good-sized looking mountains.

"That's where we're going. Hill 453. Not a very exotic name is it? Not like Hamburger Hill, the one they made the movie about — that's over there." He waved an arm in an arc to his right, but there were lots of hills and mountains in that direction, so I didn't know which one he meant. I'd seen the movie but I couldn't remember very much about it, other than the name.

I looked at the hill we were heading for. Not a real big deal. Hill 453 definitely didn't look like it was worth fighting for. Or dying for. I wondered if people had died on that hill during whatever happened when the old man was there. And I wondered if I'd find out.

"Stay as close to him as you can," the old man told me, nodding toward Mr. Vinh. "And don't decide to stroll off the path any."

"What path?" I wasn't trying to be funny. If there was a path, I was having a tough time seeing it. Yet there had to be one since Mr. Vinh's machete was hanging from his belt as he walked through the growth.

"Just stay in his line. Step in his footsteps if you can."

I looked at him. I was going to ask why, but he beat me to it. "Unexploded ordnance. Shells and stuff that didn't explode. An average of five people a day die in this country from coming in contact with unexploded ordnance. And this is a bad area. Walk where he walks."

No kidding. Unexploded ordnance. Doesn't sound all that nasty. Oh, look a shell. Make a great souvenir. Think I'll just ... BOOM!

I hustled after Mr. Vinh at pretty close to a sprint. I didn't want him out of my sight. This was one time I wasn't going to argue with the old man. If he said walk in Mr. Vinh's footsteps, that's what I planned to do. I wondered whether the old man had mentioned unexploded ordnance when he'd talked Mom into letting me go on a little summer road trip.

We set out across the rice paddy. No hip waders this time. Just sloshing water up to your ankles and in your shoes and soaking your socks. Just as we got to the other side, a woman came running up to us. She was yelling and waving her arms. My guess was that she was pissed off about us walking through the rice paddy. *Her* rice paddy. I didn't know if we had wrecked any of the plants or not — I'd tried not to — but I could see her point.

The old man kept walking, and I figured I'd better follow along. *Don't forget the unexploded ordnance.* We left Mr. Vinh to deal with the rice paddy lady. Almost immediately we were once again surrounded by dense jungle growth and animal noises. This part of the jungle seemed noisier than any we'd been in so far. I wondered why that would be. The water maybe. Greater number of animals because of the water right close by. Although water didn't seem to be something that was in real short supply in the jungle. We'd walked through lots of little puddles and pools.

The old man hadn't been BS-ing. There actually was a path in this part of the jungle. It wasn't very wide, and sometimes you had to duck your head, but it *was* a path.

Mr. Vinh caught up to us and went right by without saying anything. Took the lead again. I never found out what happened with him and the rice paddy lady after the old man and I got our butts out of there.

3

I'd had this piece of jungle figured right. It didn't go for long, and pretty soon we were at the base of a hill. I'd lost track during our trek, but I figured this was the hill the old man had pointed to. Hill 453.

There were some trees and brush on the lower part of the hill, but it wasn't nearly as dense as in the jungle. The old man spread one of the slickers on the ground and motioned for me to sit down. He pulled out the sandwiches — I'd almost forgotten about them — and passed them around. Mine was jam.

"Sorry, there's no meat. I figured it would go bad in this heat, and we'd all get sick if we ate them."

"Jam's fine," I said.

Mr. Vinh didn't say anything, but he pretty much attacked his sandwich. And for the next twenty minutes we had this weird picnic, sitting on a slicker at the bottom of Hill 453. We polished off one entire canteen. All of us were thirsty.

After we finished eating, the old man dug out the briefcase again. This time he didn't bother with the map. He mostly seemed interested in the photographs. He'd look at a photo, then at the hill, craning his head around like he was trying to get some sort of bearings. Mr. Vinh was mostly ignoring him. Kind of nodding off.

I watched, but I didn't say anything.

"Okay, let's go." The old man stood up. He didn't pick up the duffel bag this time. Just moved it over beside Mr. Vinh, who hadn't moved a muscle except to unfasten the machete from his belt and hand it to the old man. It was obvious the old man and I were on our own from here on.

I wasn't sure I liked that. Mr. Vinh knew his way around, that was clear. The old man hadn't been here for forty years, couldn't possibly remember. I was hoping he wouldn't get us lost or up to our chins in quicksand or something. *Is there quicksand in the jungle? Probably — right next to the unexploded ordinance.*

He took the briefcase, and I grabbed the backpack and one canteen.

"Let's go," he said again.

We started across the lower face of the hill going up a bit of an incline as we walked. Okay, first of all, Hill 453 wasn't really a hill. More like a mountain that hadn't totally grown up.

I discovered this as the old man and I were working our way up the slope. It wasn't too bad at first, not real steep and not tons of jungle growth. Neither of those lasted long. It got steep pretty fast, and at about the same time, it seemed like we were having to fight our way through major growth.

The old man stopped to catch his breath. Or maybe it was to let me catch my breath. "Triple canopy. That's what you call jungle that's got growth along the ground, at about head height and overhead as well. We're in triple canopy here. Makes for hard going."

Ya think?

119

A couple of times I lost sight of him but could still hear the swish-whack of the machete as he carved a path up the side of the hill.

It wasn't long until I couldn't see the sky at all. And a weird thing was happening. I was scared. Okay, maybe not scared but nervous. I still didn't know what had happened here, but I had this strange feeling, like when you have the flu, and you're hot, and then you're cold. It just felt like this was a bad place.

I tried to stay behind the old man, but the truth is he could go up some places I couldn't. Though the rain had stopped, the ground was muddy and slippery, and a couple of times I went down to my knees. There were some big palms to my right, and I figured I could use the leaves to pull myself up the slope.

I yelled. Loud. And jerked my hand off the first leaf. I was bleeding. The old man slid back down the hill to where I was and looked at my hand.

"You're okay. It'll bleed a bit, but it's not poisonous or anything. I should have told you about those. Nipa palms. The leaves have sharp edges. But I guess you already figured that out."

He pulled a not-very-clean piece of cloth out of a pocket and wrapped it around my hand. "This won't stop the bleeding, but it should keep some of the mud out of the cut. The bleeding will stop on its own."

He pointed to an area to our left. "It's not quite as steep over there. We'll go that way."

"Yeah," I said.

"You okay?"

"Yeah."

"You're doin' good, Nate."

For some reason I liked hearing him say that I wasn't at all sure I was doing good, but I wasn't doing all that bad either. And I realized something, I hadn't complained about anything, not really, for at least a couple of days. Ruining my image.

4

In the next half hour my guess was that we covered a hundred and fifty yards, maybe less. The only good part was that the old man was having as much trouble as I was. At least I didn't look like a total jerk trying to get up that hill.

I'd pretty well forgotten about my hand, but the handkerchief had been a good idea. I lost count of the times I had my hands in the mud up to my wrists trying to get a little further up that slope.

I lost track of the old man again, this time for longer than the time before. Sometimes I could hear him, and I could see where he'd worked his way up the hill. I tried to follow as closely as I could his exact route. That whole unexploded shells thing had spooked me. I tried to look down too as I scrambled through the mud. But I wasn't sure that I'd see anything even if it was there. It could be covered in mud. Or buried just far enough to be out of sight.

For most of this trip I'd been either bored or pissed off that I was there at all. That it was killing my well-planned summer. Now there was something else. There was danger here. An average of five people a day, the old man had said. And they probably weren't scrambling through a battlefield on their hands and knees.

I called out a couple of times, but he didn't answer. I wanted to stop. Every muscle was tired, and I was totally out of breath. Sweat was pouring out of me. And the old man wasn't answering me.

Terrific.

I finally caught up, but only because he'd stopped. As I came up behind him, he was looking around. I couldn't see that where we were looked any different from where we'd been twenty minutes earlier. And looking ahead, it didn't look like the next twenty minutes would change much either.

But something *was* different. The old man was different. I flopped down on my side, propped myself on one elbow trying to catch my breath. I looked at him. He turned toward me, and what I saw scared me more than the idea of hidden exploding stuff.

His eyes were open wide, and he was making some kind of moaning noises. I was pretty sure he wasn't seeing me even though I was five feet away at the most. I thought maybe he was having a heart attack or something. I wasn't sure what I was supposed to do. What I *could* do.

"Are you okay?"

He didn't answer me. I tried to get up to where he was, but I kept slipping back. Finally I was able to get my feet against some rocks and push my way up beside him. Both of us were covered in mud.

He was on his belly now, his head barely off the ground, looking up the slope. I reached out and took his arm. He jumped and grabbed me by the shoulder. Hard. Scared the crap out of me. He was looking at me like he was seeing something else. Maybe *someone* else. Someone he wanted to hurt.

"It's me. It's me, Nate, Nathan," I told him. I said some other stuff too, but I can't remember what exactly it was. I still couldn't tell what was wrong with him. But even through all the mud and stuff, I saw that his face was all changed. There was a look, no, not a look, not an expression, something more than that — it was like his face was all out of shape. Like he was in pain.

He wasn't the only one. He still hadn't let go of my shoulder. And it was starting to hurt like hell.

"It's okay. It's just me, Nate. Your son."

It felt weird to hear those last words coming out of my mouth. I managed to get hold of one of the canteens, got the top of off, held it toward him. "Here," I said.

I wasn't sure he understood at first. But finally he let go of my shoulder and took the canteen. He twisted over on his side. Drank like he was someone in the desert. Like people you see in movies, the water rolling down the sides of their mouths.

5

After that he started to look more normal, breathe more normal. He passed the canteen back to me, and I took a drink, then twisted the top back on.

"You okay?" I asked again.

He didn't answer, but I thought maybe he nodded his head, just a small nod, but something, I was pretty sure.

He took some deep breaths, trying to get himself back. He pulled himself off his belly and sat up, still looking around, but his eyes looked more like they usually did. Intense but not crazy. Not like they'd been a couple of minutes before.

"Over there," he pointed. "Work our way over there."

I looked where he was pointing. Up a little ways and to the right. The jungle growth did seem a little less there. There was nowhere for him to get by me, so I led the way this time. We slid our way up and over to where he'd indicated, to a bit of a clearing. Not as much mud there. It was steep, but there were a couple of trees, not nipa palms. I sat down in a small depression right next to one of the trees. I could kind of brace myself against the up-slope side to keep from sliding. It was grassy and fairly dry. Better. Almost comfortable.

We sat there close together, both still breathing heavy, sweating. Looking up the slope.

I was too tired to talk. I just wanted to breathe, but each breath hurt my chest. It was quite awhile before the old man said anything. When he spoke, it wasn't much more than a whisper.

And he wasn't talking to me. Not really. He was just talking.

"I was so scared here. So scared. I never knew a person could be as scared as I was that day. I'd been in firefights before, been shelled before, even wounded once, not much more than a scratch, but still I'd been in the heat of battle. I knew what it was like to have people shooting at me, trying to kill me. And I'd been afraid before, being afraid in a battle isn't being a coward ... but nothing like this. Nothing like here."

He shifted his weight, leaned back against a tree trunk.

"It was an alpha-bravo, that's the term we used for ambush. *Bo Doi,* Uniformed North Vietnamese Army regulars. Tough, well-trained fighters. Used to fighting in the jungle, and damn good at it.

"We were Delta Company, two platoons. Ninety men. Our platoon, we called ourselves *The Fighting Ninth*. Hadn't really done all that much fighting. A few firefights, not big ones. But this was different, this was something not even the cowboys in our group, the guys who craved action — not even those guys wanted this. I figured Kiner, he was our sergeant, and maybe our lieutenant, maybe those guys had seen this kind of combat before. For the rest of us, this was a whole new ball game. We were scared, and we were fighting for our lives."

He spoke slowly, his voice still barely more than a whisper. And it was flat, no emotion. Not like his eyes. His words were telling the story, but it seemed like his eyes were living it.

"I don't know how many died in the first minutes. Fifteen, twenty, maybe more. We tried to fight back. Do what we were trained to do. Couldn't see shit for the dust, the smoke, sure as hell couldn't see Charlie. But he was out there, above us, on both sides of us. Maybe below us. We didn't know."

The old man stopped talking. Reached for the canteen, took another drink. Poured some over his face. He set the canteen down on the ground between us.

"The noise is the worst … what I hated most. One minute it's so quiet you can hear the sweat running down your chest and the next minute you can't think for the noise. That's not some bullshit statement. You *can not* think. Guns, mortars. Guys on both sides yelling. Some screaming. The worst was 'help me.' Wounded guys yelled, 'Medic,' or 'I'm hit.' Dying guys yelled, or they whispered, 'Help me.'

"I remember the lieutenant and a radio guy next to me, both of them yelling as loud as they could. Trying to be heard over the noise. Trying to get help. I remember some of it. *Blue Water One … This is Blue Water Five … Blue Water One, this is Blue Water Five … Delta Company, Delta Company … Hill 453 south slope, alpha bravo, alpha bravo. Boo koo Bo Doi. Deep serious. Need close air support. Immediate. Repeat. Deep serious … deep shit. Need close air support and dustoff. Can't give zulu. Need dustoff.*

"But it didn't matter how much shit we were in. The weather had closed in over us. Low cloud. Nothing that flew could even see the hill, let alone see us, or get our wounded men out. That's called dustoff. Couldn't even give a zulu … casualty report. Nobody knew who was dead and who was alive. All we knew was there was a lot fewer of us now than when we started.

"We got spread out … too far apart. Couldn't communicate with each other. I saw a guy. Charlie. There were maybe a few hundred of them, and I finally saw one. Bet I fired forty rounds at the son of a bitch. No idea if I hit him.

"I was sure I was going to die that day. Right here where we are. This is where we dug in, tried to hold on. Still calling for help.

"I'd been in country for nine months. Lots of search and destroy patrols. That's what they called it when you went looking for Charlie, so you could shoot his ass. Got wounded on one of those. I was point — the guy at the front."

"Is that the scar on your neck?"

126

He nodded. "Trouble was the only time you found Charlie was when he wanted you to find him. When he was hidden and ready. Like he was that day. Here. I remember looking back down the hill, and the lieutenant and the radio guy, Cletis, they were both dead."

He stopped talking again, took a couple of breaths, had a fit of coughing, then recovered.

I looked around again. All I could see was jungle. I tried to imagine what it must have been like that day. But I couldn't, not really. All the movies I'd seen, it had to be like that, right?

But I knew that what the old man was talking about wasn't like any movie I'd ever seen. I closed my eyes, but I still couldn't see it. Scrunched my eyes tighter. And there was ... something. So weird. I couldn't see anything ... but it was like I could hear it. Shooting, stuff exploding, people screaming. It scared me and I opened my eyes quick.

Silence.

"We'll rest here." The old man's voice. "Let me see the rucksack."

I pulled the backpack off my shoulders and passed it to him. He pulled a couple of oranges out of it and handed me one.

For a few minutes we didn't say anything, just ate the oranges. When we'd finished, he pulled out a camera and took some pictures of the area around where we were sitting. He didn't take any pictures of me and didn't ask me to take any of him. This wasn't a family holiday at the Grand Canyon.

He put the camera back in the backpack, pulled out a little folding shovel, and handed it to me.

"You're sitting in a foxhole."

"Foxhole, that's what you dug and got down into, right?"

I looked down at the depression I was sitting in. I guessed it had filled in quite a bit since it was a foxhole for some soldier.

"Yeah. These ones weren't very deep. We didn't have much time. They were still shelling the shit out of us and giving it to us pretty good with AK-47's at the same time. From over there was the worst." He pointed to the right. The jungle was thickest there. Maybe it was back then too.

"That's where I saw that first guy I shot at."

My butt was sore, and my back was getting stiff, so I shifted my weight. Tried to get more comfortable.

"Go ahead, dig right there, at the bottom of your foxhole."

"What for?"

"Guys sometimes buried stuff there. Or just left it in the foxhole when they moved out. Or got killed."

"I don't know if I want to."

"It's okay," he nodded. "Go ahead."

I stood up and unfolded the shovel. "Where should I dig?"

"Anywhere. In the bottom of the hole."

I dug. It wasn't easy. There was grass and roots from the trees and other stuff growing around there. I didn't really think I'd find anything. And at first I didn't. But then there was something. I didn't know what it was; it looked like part of a little tin can or something. There were words on the side, but I couldn't make them out. I reached down, lifted it out of the hole … handed it to the old man.

He looked at it, then looked up at me, sort of smiling. "C rations. What we ate when we were in the field came in these little tins. This one was ham and lima beans, the worst shit they ever put in C rations. Every guy hated it. We called it ham and chokers. There were worse names too, but ham and chokers says it real well."

He tossed the tin back to me. "Got yourself a souvenir."

A souvenir. Something to make me remember a summer I wanted to forget. I handed the tin and the shovel back to him. He put them both in the backpack.

I sat back down in the foxhole. "Listen, I'm not pissed off or anything, but I'm still wondering why you brought me here."

He did up the backpack, pulled it behind his head, lay back on it. "Sometimes the most important thing that happens in your life isn't a good thing. This is the most important thing that ever happened to me. I wish I could say it was your mom. Or you. But it was this. I want you to know me. To know me you have to know this."

"I don't get why you were in that war. You … we're … Canadian."

"There were other Canadians who fought in Vietnam."

"That doesn't answer my question."

The corners of the old man's mouth turned up just a little.

"The truth? I didn't have anything else to do. My baseball career was over. I'd had a couple of jobs, hated them … I wanted to do something, have an adventure, care about something."

"Yeah, I guess."

"Don't try to understand it, Nate. I don't totally my-self. I remember reading all this stuff about how if this place became communist, then all these other countries would too. They called it the domino effect. Back then communism, that was a bad word. I guess it still is, but then it seemed like a big deal to stop them from taking over this part of the world. And I thought, 'yeah, that's something I can do. That's the thing I can care about.'"

He waited for a while before he said, "I had it completely wrong."

"Can I ask you something?"

He smiled a bit bigger this time. "You already asked me some things. Quite a few things."

"I know. One more."

He nodded.

"In the war museum there were all these photos. A place called My Lai."

His eyes narrowed when I said the name. He nodded. I wasn't sure how to say what I wanted to say. Without making him mad. "You ever … you know … "

"Was I ever involved in something like My Lai? Is that what you want to know?"

I looked down at the ground.

"The answer is no. Nothing like that. My Lai happened after my tour was over, but it made all of us sick. All of us who had tried to do our jobs and knew the whole time that so many people back home hated what we were doing and then those guys go nuts and massacre all those people, those kids … babies … "

"Sorry. I guess I shouldn't have asked that."

"Nate, I can't sit here and say I didn't do some things I wish I hadn't done. War brings out the worst … and maybe sometimes the best in people. It wasn't like I thought it would be — them and us, good guys and bad guys, white hats and black hats. There was a lot of bad shit happened on both sides."

He paused, reached for the canteen but didn't take a drink. "That doesn't make My Lai right. I hate that those guys were on our side. I'm just saying there was stuff that happened that made me wish I'd never come here."

I didn't answer at first. He drank, then handed me the canteen, and I took a long drink. I wiped my mouth with the back of my hand. "Even though I'm here I'm not sure I understand very much about what happened in that war. I mean you want me to know this so I can know you, know who you are. But I can't say, if that's happening."

"I get that, Nate. I really do. I don't know that I've figured out a lot of it myself."

"How did it end?"

"The war? We lost, plain and simple. America lost the stomach to keep fighting when most Americans didn't know what it was they were fighting for."

"I meant here." I looked around us. "Hill 453. How did it end?"

It was a long time before he answered, so long that I thought we'd gone back to me asking about stuff and him not telling me. But that wasn't it. I watched, and his face twitched a couple of times. He was looking away, into the trees. I figured he was seeing it again. But this time he seemed in control.

Finally, he took a deep breath, let it out slow, looked back at me. "We hung on until help got to us," he said.

"That's the short answer. They could have overrun us anytime they wanted to. But they didn't. I don't know why. I'll never know why.

"There was a thunderstorm that night. Real light show. They didn't let up shelling, and it was the damndest thing, not being able to tell the difference between the thunder and lightning and incoming shells. Then, when the thunderstorm stopped, the shelling stopped. It was like it was all part of their battle plan.

"In the morning, the sky cleared, and they probably figured help would be coming. So they really let us have it. An hour or more ... it was the ... the worst yet. A lot of people died right around here that morning. We were sure we'd be overrun, and that it would happen any minute. It's funny but I wasn't as scared anymore. I guess once you've figured out that these people are going to kill you, you just want to make them pay for the privilege.

"We called again for close air support and this time a couple of Huns, F-100s, came in, blew the shit of the place.

"The Hueys were able get in for dustoffs, and we got the wounded out. A company of marines was part of the same mission we were on — Operation Blue Water. They started out as soon the word got out that we'd been ambushed. They arrived about mid-morning. Army hates being rescued by marines, but I was just fine with it."

"So that was it."

The old man shook his head. "No, that wasn't it. To show you how screwed up that war was, after all that we'd taken in that twenty-four hours, we got orders to move out. Take the summit; that was our orders, with the marines in reserve. We had sixty, maybe sixty-five guys left, and we were told to take the summit of 453."

"What did you do?"

"We took the summit. The Huns made a few more passes, and we began an assault on the top. It took three hours, more guys died, maybe a dozen or so ... a few others wounded. When we made it to the top, there were forty-seven people left in Delta Company.

"Half what you started with."

"Yeah. When we finally got up there, there wasn't a leaf left on a tree. It looked like something from a science fiction movie. A few blackened sticks poking out of the ground. That's all that was left of jungle that was as thick as this until that day. And Charlie was gone too. We got up there, and we were by ourselves. There were eleven bodies from their side up there. I'm sure there was a lot more dead than that, and they'd taken the bodies with them when they left."

"You and Tal ... you were okay, you weren't wounded?"

"We were ... okay. I took shrapnel in the hand. I didn't think it was bad, but it was bad enough that I spent the rest of my tour in Saigon. And Tal ..."

He was staring off into space again, and his face was contorted. Like it had been before. I knew this was something I couldn't ask him about. But he told me anyway.

"Tal was in a foxhole up the hill a ways from me. There were two other guys, his buddies, one on either side of him. They were in foxholes too. The next morning when the NVA really sent a lot of shit at us ... there were some incoming shells, and we all ducked down ... tried to somehow get into that dirt just a little further. When the shelling let up a little,

133

Tal looked out and both of those guys were gone. Not just dead. Gone. Tal fought like hell the rest of that day ... was the first one to the top, but he was never ... the same after that."

The old man stood up, looked around, pointed up the slope. "I have to go for a walk, Nate. I have to go up there a ways. By myself. You stay here. You'll be fine. I won't be long."

I nodded, but I wasn't real sure I liked being left behind. But I also knew I might not be able to go much further up that hill. I was just too tired.

"You'll be fine," he said again.

"Sure, yeah ... I'll be right here."

He turned and started scrambling up the hill, slipping in the mud but making some progress. He got to a bunch of thick undergrowth, started whacking with the machete. Eventually, he disappeared into the jungle. I couldn't see him or hear him. I leaned my head back against the tree behind me.

6

I slept. I don't know how long. Dreaming. It was one of those strange dreams, way too real. There was war noise in my dream, no not war, different noise. And not in the dream.

I opened my eyes. Blinked for a few seconds, heard the noise again. A man, Vietnamese, stood over me. Just up the hill from me. He was holding a dog on a chain. The dog was huge; it was snarling and growling, its jaws not more than a metre from my face.

The man was grinning and talking. I didn't understand what he was saying, but I heard the word "dog" and the word "kill" and a lot of what sounded like Vietnamese. I slid down so I was lying flat on the ground, trying to get lower somehow, to get away from the dog. But there was nowhere to go. The tree behind me kept me where I was. I tried to make myself smaller, to get further down into the foxhole I'd been sitting in.

The man was screaming now. I wanted to say something ... tell him I hadn't been doing anything. I was just waiting for someone.

But I couldn't. I couldn't say anything. I was too scared to get words out. Too scared to do anything. I pushed my face further into the ground ... still trying to get away. I was sure the dog would take a hold of me any second, rip into me with those teeth, those jaws. The man moved down the hill a little ... the dog was even closer. I could feel his breath ... smell it....

I was scared, so scared.

I never knew a person could be as scared as I was....

The noise was the worst.

Then it got quiet. I heard a voice, a different voice this time.

"It's okay, Nate ... you're okay. You can get up."

I waited a few seconds more, then turned and lifted my head a few inches and turned it far enough to see.

The old man was standing a few feet away from the dog, the machete raised over his head. He was looking at the man with the dog. The man was still grinning. The dog had at least stopped growling, snarling.

The old man spoke in a voice that was soft and terrible. "*Caca dau. Caca dau.* I'll kill you, right here ... right now. First I kill your dog, then I kill you. *Caca dau,* you piece of shit."

I was pretty sure as I looked at the old man that he meant exactly what he said. He'd kill them both. The guy with the dog didn't seem even a little bit worried.

"You friends die here, fucker American. You friends die here. You shit pants here while they die. We kill lots fucker Americans here. We kill lots you friends."

"The war's over, asshole. But there's gonna be two more dead on this hill if you and your dog don't back off *now*."

The Vietnamese stepped back maybe two steps and pulled the dog back far enough that I felt I could get to my knees. I tried to shake some of the dirt out of my mouth. The dog growled again. I gagged and threw up. I wiped my face to get the tears and the puke off me, but mostly I just added dirt to what was already on my face.

The Vietnamese was still grinning. He looked at me.

"You scared, little boy, little American. You cry, you puke like baby. Brave like fucker Americans we kill here. You shit pants, little scared American?"

"Last time I'm saying it." The old man took a step toward the dog. "You move out now or you die."

The Vietnamese laughed. "Like old times, eh, American? You scared that day, scared like you little boy."

"You're dead right, asshole. I was scared that day. But I'm not scared right now. And I'd love to shiv that goddamn dog from one end to the other. And you right after him. So what do you say, how about this American make you dead? *Caca dau.*"

The Vietnamese laughed a high-pitched cackle kind of laugh and pulled his dog back. They starred past us down the hill, but we could hear him talking — then yelling as he went.

"We scare Americans. Like before when we kill them. They shit pants, then die. Here."

I didn't move until they were far down the hill. Then I turned my body so I was sitting up, leaning back against the tree again.

The old man bent down beside me. Pulled a cloth out of the backpack, poured canteen water out onto my face and washed me off. I spat out some dirt and finally drank some water.

"You okay? That dog, he ...?"

I shook my head. "No, he didn't bite me. Just scared me awful ... awful bad."

"I know," the old man said softly. "I know."

"I didn't know what to do. I ... couldn't do anything."

"You did fine here, Nate." He put a hand on my shoulder. "You've been through a load of stuff. And you got through it all."

"No, I didn't. I was so scared I cried ... and threw up. How's that doing fine?"

"What that gook ... " he hesitated. "What that ... piece of crap said ... about us shitting our pants here that day. He was right. Some guys might have done that. I didn't, but only because I was loaded up on what we called cork. It was a drug they gave us to keep us from having to crap in battle. If men shit their pants, it's because they were scared just like you were. But they were brave men."

"I wasn't brave. I didn't fight back. I didn't do anything."

"We can't always fight back. There was nothing you could do. That dog would have torn you apart. You did the right thing. You stayed alive, in one piece ... for

137

another day. You survived."

I thought about what he'd said. Shook my head.

"I just don't — "

"Every guy who was on this hill that day was thinking one thing. Please, God, let me survive this day. Some did, some didn't, but we prayed for that … just that. I prayed harder than I ever have in my life. Please let me live through this day.

"And I did. I lived through it. So did you."

"What … what do you think would have happened if you hadn't come back? Would he have …?"

The old man shrugged. "I don't know, Nate. Hard to know what someone will do if they hate enough."

I stood up. My knees weren't right. I wasn't sure they'd hold me up. But I didn't want to be in that foxhole anymore.

"Let's go. It's time we were leaving."

I brushed some of the dirt off my shirtfront. Tried putting weight on one leg, then the other. Seemed okay.

"Yeah, I guess so."

7

We never looked back at the hill. We slipped and slogged our way to the bottom, but we didn't look back. Not once. I was kind of surprised by that. I didn't want to look back. I didn't want to ever see that place again. But I figured the old man might stop and glance back that way, at least one last time.

He didn't. By the time we got back to where Mr. Vinh was waiting for us, it was raining again. The cloud had settled down low over us, maybe like it had been that day of the … what had the old man called it … the alpha-bravo?

The ambush on Hill 453.

Mr. Vinh had everything packed up and was wearing his slicker, ready to go. He and the old man didn't say anything. The old man nodded once, and Mr. Vinh took the lead just like he had most of the way here.

And we walked out of the A Shau Valley. Not much to say about the hike out. Except it was pretty funny when we got back to the rice paddy. I mean, I'm not kidding — that lady was really old, even older than Mr. Vinh, and weighed maybe ninety pounds with her shoes full of paddy mud. And here were three guys, yes, I was one of them, sneaking through that waterlogged field of rice like we were all scared of her.

That's because we *were* all scared of her. When we got back into the jungle on the other side, we all tried to act totally normal, like nothing had happened. But all of us, even Mr. Vinh, had been holding our breath hoping she wouldn't show up. I bet if she had we all would have run like hell.

It was funny, but nobody laughed. Not then anyway. After what had happened on Hill 453, I'd had all the laughter knocked out of me. And I think it was the same with the old man. And Mr. Vinh, well, he just didn't laugh much ... ever. Unless somebody fell in a swamp.

A lot of it gets hazy after that. As we slogged through the rain in the jungle, I was wishing I was four years old so someone would carry me. I didn't even think about the unexploded ordnance. I guess by then I was pretty much programmed to walk in the line of whoever was ahead of me.

We stayed overnight in the same place we had the night before. Mr. Vinh's wife had something cooked up when we got back, but I didn't eat any of it. Not because it looked or smelled bad or anything. I was just too tired to eat.

I probably would have fallen asleep just sitting there except the old man and Mr. Vinh got in a big shouting match. It was the same as all of their conversations, only louder. Some Vietnamese, a little English and a bunch of hand gestures.

The old man was real pissed off. Eventually, he threw his hands in the air and came over to where I was sitting on a stump. He sat down on the ground next to me.

Then Mr. Vinh got into it with Mrs. Vinh. Big-time argument. No English this time. Just foreign language yelling. Lots of it and loud.

"What's all the hollering about? Just in case I decide to sleep at some point tonight."

The old man shook his head. "The guy on the hill, the guy with the dog, turns out he does that shit a lot. Likes to hassle vets who come back here. Two of his brothers were killed there."

"You mean in the ambush that you —"

"Yeah. It's his way of getting even. Mr. Vinh says he doesn't think he's ever let the dog attack anyone. I gave him hell for not warning me. Says he wasn't sure the guy would be there. Dumb son of a bitch."

I wasn't sure who he was calling a son of a bitch — the guy on the hill or Mr. Vinh. Maybe both of them. Right at that moment, I didn't really care.

As soon as the tent was set up, I stumbled inside and fell asleep in maybe fifteen seconds tops. Too tired to take my boots off.

Saigon, the Second Time

1

The next morning we started the drive back to Ho Chi Minh City. I slept most of the way back. I don't know how long. I woke up with the old man shaking my shoulder. I sat up and looked around, expecting to see the Rex. I was actually looking forward to seeing something that looked familiar. At least, a little normal.

What I was looking at definitely wasn't the Rex. Or normal. Not really.

Instead we were facing these narrow apartments, I guess that's what they were — the one right in front of us was four storeys high. When I say narrow, what I mean is *narrow*. One room wide, so I figured the rooms must run one behind the other with some little hallway connecting them. Or maybe just little doors between the rooms.

Up to now I'd only seen the tourist stuff and the countryside. This was my first look at how the average Vietnamese person lived.

"Tube houses. They've been around a long time," the old man said.

"What?"

"That's what they're called … tube houses."

"Why?"

The old man shrugged. "Maybe because they're as narrow as a tube. Or maybe there's some kind of tube hallway that connects it all together."

Which is just what I'd thought. Maybe I was getting smarter about this country. "I take it we're back in Saigon."

"Uh-huh."

"And we're here why?"

"This is where our hotel is."

"No, I mean *here* here."

"Because this is where Mr. Vinh lives. We're dropping him off and keeping the Land Rover for a few more days."

On cue, Mr. Vinh climbed out of the driver's seat. He went around to the back of the Land Rover and opened the door to take out a pack that I hadn't really noticed before. I guessed it had his stuff in it. Light packer, Mr. Vinh was.

The old man climbed out too, and I followed him. I wanted to at least say goodbye to Mr. Vinh. He came back around to where we were standing and stopped in front of the old man. It didn't look like they were back to being buddies yet.

We had to be careful, because I swear to god we were engulfed in people on motorbikes. Hundreds of them. Most of them were on the street behind us, but some veered off and went around the Land Rover and up on the sidewalk to get around us. Save time. These were kamikaze bikers, and there were a hell of a lot of them. Lots of hollering and motorbike horns sounding too. Like non-stop.

The old man reached into his pocket and pulled out a wad of money.

142

The currency in Vietnam is called the dong. Pronounced dom. Trouble is, there's about fifteen or sixteen thousand dong to one American dollar. So you carry tons of paper money around with you all the time. Now the old man was peeling off reams of the stuff and giving it to Mr. Vinh.

I tried to keep track but gave up after a while. "Will we see him again?"

"Not likely. He's taking out a group of vets tomorrow. They're going to Hue." From the tone of his voice I could tell I was right. They were still pissed off at each other from before.

"Why didn't Mrs. Vinh come back with us?"

"She stayed at the camp. Probably that next bunch of guys will stay there overnight. Like we did."

I couldn't tell if Mr. Vinh knew that we were talking about him. When he had been paid, he nodded and started for the apartment. The tube house. I ran up alongside him. He stopped and looked at me.

I didn't know if I should try to shake his hand or bow or what. "I just wanted to say goodbye."

He didn't smile, but I didn't think he looked mad either. "You try not fall in water."

Ha, ha, ha. He turned and dodged a couple more motorbikes on the way to his apartment. I didn't stop watching until he disappeared inside. I liked the guy, and I didn't really care what the old man thought.

When I turned around, the old man was getting into the Land Rover. I walked around and climbed in the passenger side. I cranked my head around and looked at the gazillion or so motorbikes. I had no idea how we'd actually get back out on the street.

"This should be fun," I said.

The old man decided this wasn't the time for Canadian road courtesy. He was probably right. He leaned on the horn and started backing up. Somehow he wedged us back out onto the street without killing anyone. I was pretty sure there was more horn honking and yelling than there had been before, but what the hell, we were out there.

I could have rolled down my window and had a face-to-face conversation with all kinds of people as they inched by us and we inched back in front of them. I didn't.

"So what's next?"

"I got some shit to do."

"I thought we weren't supposed to say 'shit.'"

"Based on what was said on 453, I think we can put a moratorium on the shit moratorium."

I nodded. "Probably. What time is it?"

"Coming up on four o'clock. Rush hour in Saigon."

"Sweet."

It took a real long time to get back to the Rex. I now knew how ants felt. Or bees in a hive. Or all those millions of buffalo that roamed North America 150 years ago. Anyway, you get what I mean.

By the time we were parked and out of the Land Rover, I had made a career decision. I'd open a motorbike dealership in downtown Saigon. Should be able to retire at about twenty-three. We grabbed our gear and headed for the room.

When we got there, I had the longest bath of my life. Every time the water cooled off a little, I ran more hot into the tub. I don't know how long I was in there, but I still wasn't convinced I was clean. Or ever would be again.

144

The old man had gone back to not talking much during the drive back to the Rex. That had been okay with me. I'd been mentally putting together my motorbike business plan.

When I got out of the bathtub, there was a note on a table in the room: *Nathan. I'll be back in a couple of hours. Here's money. Get something to eat.*

And there *was* money sitting next to the note. Even though I had some of my own, I didn't mind taking some from the old man — especially after the last couple of days. I figured he owed me, so I got dressed, pocketed the dong, and wrote my own note. I left it on top of his.

I'll be back in a couple of hours. Thanks for the money. I'm going to use it to buy heroin. P.S. It's Nate, not Nathan.

I headed downstairs. Two hours to myself in Saigon. The thing I wanted most was a grilled cheese sandwich. I doubted I'd find one of those anywhere in Saigon, but I was hungry enough that even noodles sounded okay.

But first I stopped at the lobby computer to check my email. Jackpot. Jen (the Australian version) had answered the email I'd sent her before our trip to the A Shau Valley. What was really weird was that it seemed like the old man and I had been gone for a couple of weeks, not a couple of days. There'd be time to think about that later. Right now, there was Jen.

Hi Nate

I'm really glad you remembered my email address. And yes I'd love to do a movie or a burger or both with you when you get back. My cell is 04-7010-9211. And we're

staying at the Grand Hotel, Room 519.
Call me. I'll tell my dad you're a pizza
delivery guy. For some reason he doesn't like
you. Or your dad. Can't imagine why.

LOL

Jen

There's some stuff I don't get. How is it that a guy who couldn't buy a date in Canada can get hooked up a few thousand miles from home with a totally hot chick who is also a few thousand miles from home?

I called her cell, and got her message, so I called the room. That took some doing, but the woman at the desk helped me, and I eventually got through. Jen's dad answered. I did the worst impersonation of a Vietnamese guy that's ever been done.

"I spreak to Jen-rady, prease. Pizza she order is leady."

"What?"

I said all the same stuff again.

"You must have the wrong number."

"No. No long numbah. I speak to Jen-rady … pizza leady."

I could hear them talking in the background. Then Jen came on the line.

"Yes?"

"Yeah, I don't think he bought the whole pizza delivery thing. Mostly because I sound like crap as a Vietnamese person."

Her voice got a little louder. "I'm sorry I didn't order a pizza. I just asked for some … uh … information about your pizza."

146

I figured her dad must be standing close by.

"Information about pizza? What the hell does that mean? You aren't any better at this than I am. Tell you what, I'll be in the lobby of your hotel in fifteen minutes. I'm hoping you'll be down there. I'll be the guy without a pizza."

"Yes, thank you, that'll be fine." She hung up.

I was hoping her dad was either very trusting or incredibly stupid. Either way, I planned to be in the lobby of the Grand Hotel in fifteen minutes. Which reminded me that I had no idea where the place was.

2

The same woman at the desk made my night. The Grand was a ten-minute walk from the Rex. There *is* a god.

I strolled out onto the streets of Saigon. It was evening, I figured about seven o'clock, still warm but nothing like the jungle. Okay, so rush hour was over, and there was still the same number of motorbikes on the road. I abandoned my career as a motorbike sales guy. I was already sick of the things.

There was an unreal feel to everything that was happening to me. Thirty hours before, I'd been puking on a mud-covered hill with a killer dog about to tear my face off.

And now here I was walking down the street like Robert Downey Jr. in all those *Iron Man* movies, like nothing had happened. But something *had* happened to me. Something I'd never forget. Something that made me different from what I'd been before. More stuff to think about later.

The Grand is another nice hotel. I wandered through the front doors and looked around. No sign of Jen. What if she didn't come down? What if her dad *wasn't* stupid and wouldn't let her come down?

I sat down in a big soft chair that faced the elevators and waited. I didn't have to wait long. The elevator doors opened, and she stepped out, wearing a white sleeveless top and tight jeans. I reminded myself that Jen was a very good-looking chick. And hot.

I stood up and smiled, trying to think of something funny or brilliant to say. Funny *and* brilliant would be even better. Unfortunately, I had nothin'.

She crossed the lobby, laughing — a good sign — and when she got to me, put her arms around my neck and hugged me. Brushed her lips across my cheek. These were even better signs. She stepped back, still laughing, kept her hands on my shoulders.

"You're crazy, you know that, right?"

"A few people have mentioned that." I looked behind her at the elevator. "Should I be watching for your dad to be following you … maybe carrying a rifle?"

"I think he knows I was coming down here to meet a guy. He just doesn't know *what* guy. That's probably for the best."

"Are you saying my amazing Vietnamese pizza guy impersonation didn't work? It's never failed me before."

"Let's just say selling pizza in Ho Chi Minh City — not a good career move for you. So what are we doing?"

"Uh … " Until that moment I hadn't thought about that. I mean it was a date, sort of. I was supposed to have a plan.

148

"Do you happen to know where a guy can get a grilled cheese sandwich?" When in doubt, buy time with some really lame humour.

"No, but I do know where we can get an amazing burger."

"Serious?"

"And it's not even far from here. Come on." She grabbed my hand, and we started for the door. But when we got outside, I pulled her to a stop. "I just have to make a quick stop at my hotel. It's not very far. I have to tell the old man that we're going out. I kind of didn't."

Jen shrugged. "Sure. Where to?"

"This way." Now it was my time to guide her. Which meant crossing the street through the usual motorbike mayhem and navigating our way through the crowd that seemed to be growing by the minute. Didn't anybody in this town stay home?

We tried to talk. *So what've you been doing?* That kind of stuff but mostly one of us hollered something, and the other one yelled "What?" Really loud. Not a great way to have a conversation. We gave up until we got inside the lobby of the Rex.

Then it got tricky. Do I invite her to come up to the room while I update the note to the old man? How does that look? But is that worse than abandoning her down here in the lobby?

I was still working that over in my mind when I heard, "Nathan."

I turned around and the old man was standing there. Problem solved.

"Hi, I was just going up to the room to leave you a note. I ... uh we ... we're going out for a burger."

The old man looked at me with a little smile playing around the corners of his mouth.

"Good, I hope you have fun." The smile got bigger ... like he meant it.

"Oh ... uh, this is Jen. She's from —"

"Australia. I know." The old man held out his hand to shake hers, which meant she had to let go of *my* hand. I'd forgotten we were still holding hands. *Awkward moment.*

They shook. "We've met. Your dad too. We had a nice heart to heart."

"Yeah, I know." Jen looked like she didn't know whether she was supposed to smile or not.

"I'd really like you to tell him I'm sorry. We met at a bad moment, and I was a bit hard on him."

"If I tell him that, he'll want to know when he can interview you for his book."

"No interview. Just mention I apologized. Nathan, can I speak to you a minute?"

He started to walk off. I looked at Jen, shrugged and followed the old man as he walked over to where there were some couches. He didn't sit down. I couldn't tell if he was mad or what.

He kind of moved his head like he wanted me to come closer. *Secret talk.* I moved closer.

He reached into his back pocket, pulled out his wallet.

"I already have money. I took the stuff you left me on the table."

He nodded. "Listen, I'll make this quick. I don't want

to keep you from your girl for long. I … don't know how much you know. You got any of these?"

I had to look down because he was keeping his hand tight to his body. He opened his hand to let me see. He was holding a condom. All the years he never sent me a Christmas present, and now here he was sneaking his kid a condom.

"Hey, we're going for a burger."

"Yeah, I know that. You got any of these?"

"No, but I —"

"Shut up. I'm not telling you you're supposed to try to make it with that girl. I'm just telling you that if something happens, it would be a hell of a lot better if you had one of these."

I looked down again. This was uncomfortable. Like we were wrapping up a drug deal. I looked around. It felt like people were watching us even though I didn't actually see anyone looking our way. Jen was turned away from us, staring out the front window.

"Okay." I reached out, palmed the condom and slid it into my jeans pocket. "Uh … thanks."

"You sure you got enough money?"

"Yeah, I'm fine, honest. Thanks."

He nodded and started walking away. Then he stopped and turned back to me. "Have fun. And if it turns out you didn't need that, it doesn't mean the night was a failure."

What does that mean? "I know how to go on a date."

"I wouldn't have onions on the burger." He grinned at me.

"You are really weird."

"Yeah." He nodded then waved past me at Jen. As I turned away from him, Jen was waving back.

When I got to her, she took my hand again. "Your dad is actually nice."

"I guess."

"What did he want?"

"He … just wanted to make sure I had enough money. Wanted us to have a good time."

"He's really nice," she said again.

"Yeah."

3

The Black Cat (*Meo Den* in Vietnamese) was as good as Jen said it would be. The burger was one of the best I'd ever had, and the place looked like it could have been in Calgary or Minneapolis.

Most of the people in the place weren't Vietnamese, which meant that there was a lot of English being spoken. It's surprising how much you miss your own language when everyone around you is speaking something else.

Jen and I had found a table against a wall and a guy had brought us two menus. I looked at it but mostly I was trying to think of stuff to talk about. For some reason there seemed to be a short circuit between the part of my brain that thinks of stuff to say and the part of my face that says it.

This kid I know at school told me he was crazy about this chick, but she wasn't a big talker, which meant that when the guy phoned her it was pretty much up to him to keep the conversation moving along. He told me he'd write out stuff before he phoned her, little notes about things he could say or ask her about.

Thing is that might work on the phone, but I'm pretty sure the first time a guy pulls out the ol' notepad when he's sitting across from a girl and it's like *So … Sally, it's Sally, right? Yeah I was wondering … uh … uh …* (flipping open notebook) *… oh, uh yeah … so, how old are you?* Game, set, match. She's outta there, and you've got nothing but your notepad for company.

"I guess most people order the hamburgers when they come here."

"Yeah, but not everybody. They've got really good Mexican too. At least, that's what my dad said. He had it."

I looked around again. "Mexican *and* burgers. I guess I wasn't expecting that."

"Me neither. It's like I had the whole place wrong. I thought we were coming to this totally like third-world country with peasants and people with baskets on their heads."

I nodded. "Same. Guess I should have googled."

She laughed. "Anyway, they have a burger here, it's 1.4 kilograms. It's supposed to be like the biggest burger in the world. The place is famous for that burger."

I looked at her. "Are you kidding me? There's a place in Canada that serves this big burger, I think it's a third of a pound. The one you're talking about would be like nine of those."

Jen laughed again. She had a great laugh. One that made you want to laugh with her. "I don't know if anybody's ever finished one. When I was here before, this guy ordered one, big guy too, but he didn't get through half of it."

The whole conversation thing was getting easier. "Think I'll go with a normal-sized burger."

"Me too. You can order them. I'll go get us a beer."

She got up and left before I could say anything.

I looked around. Some people were drinking, but none of them were kids. I watched Jen stroll up to the bar, positive she'd be turned away and come back to our table with an embarrassed smile on her face.

I was right about the smile, except she wasn't embarrassed, and in her hands were two cans of Coors Light. She set them down and sat back down in her seat, looking at me. I think maybe I was staring.

"What?"

"Nothing," I answered, "it's just that getting arrested on our first date, I don't know if that's a good idea."

"You worried about the beer?"

"Well … I guess … yeah."

"You know what the drinking age is in Vietnam?"

I shook my head.

"There isn't one."

"You're kidding, right?"

"Actually, I've heard two stories about that. One is that there is no drinking age, and the second is that there is one, but nobody has ever asked anybody for ID in the history of the country."

"Cool."

"And you know something else? They have very few problems with drunk kids getting into trouble."

"How do you know this stuff?" I asked her.

"Research. When I found out we were coming here, I decided to find out a few things about the place."

"Research. If you know all that stuff, how come you

still thought it was a third-world country and all primitive?"

"I guess I didn't research that part."

I looked around. "No baskets on heads." I grinned at her so she'd know I was kidding.

"You wanna know something else. In 1990, there were 600,000 motorbikes in Vietnam. By 1993, there were 2.5 million. And there's 400,000 more come into the country every year. Do the math. By now there must be a couple of gazillion."

I nodded. "Maybe three gazillion. I didn't get to do any research. I didn't know we were coming here until we were on our way."

"Well, I'm glad you're here now." She hoisted her beer, held it toward me. "Here's to us."

I picked up my beer, tapped cans with hers. "To us." We drank. It tasted real good, especially after the heat and bugs and sweat of the jungle.

"So tell me about it," she looked at me.

"About what?"

"What you've been doing since you sent me that first email? You said you and your dad were going somewhere."

"Yeah."

"So where did you go?"

"Uh … we … out into the countryside … the jungle."

"What for?"

"Some stuff I … uh … guess the old man wanted to see."

"Some battle he'd been in? That's what my dad thought."

"I … I'm not … sure. We just went out into the jungle. Saw some stuff."

I don't know why I didn't want to tell her, why I didn't

want to talk about it. Or maybe I did know. How do you explain something like the old man telling me about the fight on Hill 453 … or how scared I was when I thought that crazy creep and his dog were going to rip me apart? And how I'd been puking and trying so hard to get down into the hard ground I even had dirt in my mouth? How do you tell somebody that stuff and know that they'll get it? That they'll understand something you're not sure you understand yourself even though you were there?

And there was something else. The stuff that happened on Hill 453, that was about me and the old man. Just us. I didn't want to share that with Jen. Or anybody else.

The server came then and took our order. I thought Jen would be mad that I didn't really answer her question. Because she had to know I was bullshitting. When the server left, I made a big deal about looking at the stuff on the walls.

"It's okay, Nate. You don't have to tell me."

"There's not much to talk about really. Just some stuff we saw. Some stuff that happened. You're really okay with it if we don't talk about it?"

She took a drink of the beer and nodded. "I'm okay with it. I was just asking so I'd have something to say." "Thanks."

And then it was okay. *We* were okay. We ate our burgers and French fries, we drank beer, two cans each, and we talked. I told her about Canada, Mom, and school; she told me about Australia, and her girlfriends, and her private girls' school.

I even told her about my list, my five points for summer self-improvement. She kind of laughed, but she said she liked that I wanted to do something, not just waste the summer. I decided not to mention my previous summers as the 7-Eleven king.

I left out Jan Wertz too. I figured too much information. She'd been right, the place made a real good burger. When the burgers were gone we talked some more.

"What do you think of Vietnam so far?" She waved her arm around like the Black Cat pretty much represented the whole country.

"It's okay, I guess. I mean I sort of like it. What about you?"

"You know, it's weird. At first, I hated it — too noisy, too crowded, too busy, too ... Asian. Does that make me sound racist?"

I shook my head. "I know what you mean. It's just not what we're used to. It's not like I have anything against Vietnamese people. It's just that sometimes I just want to hear English, eat North American food. ... maybe go to a football game."

"Football. Oh my god, that game you people play — I don't get any of it. Now Aussie Rules Football, that's a game." I'd seen Aussie Rules Football a few times on TV. "It's okay, I guess. I like the referees' arm signals."

"Anyway, after I'd been here awhile, I really started to like it. All of it. Weird, right?"

I shook my head. "No, not weird. I'm starting to like the place better too. Especially now that I found out you don't have to eat noodles all the time. And that thing with the drinking age ... not bad."

We both laughed and sipped our beers, before she spoke again.

"I've decided what I want to do when I'm finished school."

"Yeah? What?" I didn't have a clue what I'd be doing when I finished school. I'm not sure I'd thought that far ahead. Ever.

"My dad told me that once you have your degree, you can come here, and other countries too, and teach English. I checked it out, and there are tons of schools that hire people from English-speaking countries to come here and teach English to the Vietnamese."

She seemed pretty excited about the idea. I wondered how you got excited about something that was maybe five years or more away. But I didn't want to burst her bubble, so I listened while she told me more about it ... how you didn't make a lot of money ... that you'd probably teach in a private school, and there were plenty of them right in Saigon ... that you'd live in temporary housing for teachers. She'd obviously done a lot of thinking, a lot of checking the whole thing out.

Her eyes were sort of shining while she was telling me all this, and I have to admit I didn't concentrate on everything she said. Jen was a great looking girl — and hot (I think I mentioned that), and when she got all excited about something, like she was about teaching English in Vietnam, and you factor in the cool Aussie accent, she went even higher on the hot-o-metre.

After we ate, she asked me if I wanted to go to a movie. I hesitated at first because I hadn't really cleared that part with the old man, but then I figured if the guy was giving me condoms, he'd probably be okay with me going to a movie with a girl.

We went to the Cinebox 212. A bunch of theatres. Mostly Asian films. One English language movie. *Batman Begins*. I'd seen it before, but I'd never seen it with a girl next to me holding my hand and every little bit bringing her face over close to mine. We didn't make out exactly, but there were a few light kisses, the kind that make you think there might be more and better coming later.

You might remember that earlier on I mentioned that I spent a lot of the last year or two in a state of never-ending horniness. Yeah, that was nothing compared to what was going on inside me sitting next to Jen. I was horn-dog in the extreme, and none of what I was feeling had anything to do with what was happening on the screen in the Cinebox 212.

A couple of times I ran my hand down to where my jeans pocket was — just checking that the condom was in position, ready to be put to work when needed.

The problem was, where do teenagers go for privacy in Saigon? It's not like we could check into something called the Sunset Motel for a couple of hours. And I didn't think under a tree in a park somewhere was the answer.

I shouldn't have worried. Jen had things figured out.

We weren't going to any Sunset Motel. We were going back to the Grand Hotel to her family's room. Her mom and dad wouldn't be back for "ages" because they had gone to some formal dinner with a bunch of news media people. I was okay with her plan; at least I thought I was.

When we got back to the room, I was pretty spooked, expecting her parents to come marching through the door along about the time Jen and I were getting to the good part.

Of course, I had no idea what the good part would be. Jen and I had been together five maybe six hours total. It was a little out there to think we might actually get it on after the first, and maybe last, date.

I mean there was that little thing about how we lived on separate continents. Jen must have been thinking the same thing because we just got settled on the couch in her parents' suite when she said, "I don't want you to think I usually go this fast with guys."

"I don't."

"It's just that I like you, and once we leave here, I know we might not see each other for like a really long time."

"I know. And I like you too."

She moved closer to me, which didn't take much since she wasn't all that far away to start with. And we kissed, all gentle at first like we were both shy. Which we were — at least I was.

Then the kissing got a little more … uh … energetic. Then a *lot* more. Jen was a spectacular kisser. I waited what I thought was a respectable amount of time — it probably wasn't more than five minutes. Then I got my hand up under her top and up to her bra.

Another thing you might remember me mentioning awhile back was that I wasn't exactly Mr. Stud back home … meaning I was already in uncharted territory. Which might explain why I was as clumsy as I was. I got my hand around behind her back and tried to undo her bra.

After I fumbled around for a while, Jen pulled back and said, "Here, this will make it easier." And she put her hands over her head so I could pull her top off. After that, things got a little hazy. I remember her moaning as I touched her and I remember not having my T-shirt on any more and our chests coming together, and I remember reaching behind her and trying again to get that damn bra undone.

And I remember the freaking phone ringing.

"Don't answer it."

"I have to." She started to move away from me.

"No, you don't. It's probably a telemarketer."

"It's midnight. Telemarketers don't call hotel rooms, and they don't call at midnight."

"I think they do."

But it didn't matter. The phone kept ringing, and this was a very loud phone, and it was killing the mood anyway.

"Okay." I moved so she could get up. I watched her walk to the phone. I stopped listening after "Oh … hi, Dad. You and Mom are on your way up? Cool."

I got my T-shirt back on and tucked in a time that was definitely a personal best. If I thought Jen had some amazing moves up to that point, they were nothing compared to the magic she displayed getting her top back on and hair more or less organized.

When her mom and dad came through the door, Jen and I were drinking Cokes and watching TV. I think my breathing had pretty well returned to normal and I was confident I could stand up without having parts of my body give away what we'd been doing moments before.

Her dad came over and stood in front of the couch, looking down at me. *Oh shit, here it comes.* But he seemed to be okay with me being the guy his daughter had spent the evening with.

"Hello, again."

"Hello, sir."

"Please tell your dad that if he changes his mind I'd still like to do that interview with him."

"I will, sir." *Yeah, right.*

The parents kind of hung around, and it didn't look like they were going off to bed to give us a little more alone time so I took a couple more drinks of Coke and got up to leave.

Jen kissed me good night at the door, which I thought was cool. I said good night to her parents and left in a pretty good mood, considering I'd been that close to … needing the condom.

I never did figure out why her dad phoned on the way up to the room. Jen texted me later that she figured he and her mom had an idea we might be making out and were decent enough to warn us.

That's what I call good parenting.

The evening almost ended badly. I guess I wasn't paying attention, and I came close to being run over by a swarm of motorbikes. Got yelled at. Yelled back.

It was worth it.

When I got back to the hotel, the old man was in bed reading a magazine.

"How was the burger?"

"Good. We went to a movie too. *Batman Begins.*" I figured I should name the movie just in case he didn't believe me.

"Any good?"

"Yeah, I've seen it before."

He reached over and switched off the little light by his bed. "I'll see you in the morning, Nathan."

"It's Nate. Not oh six hundred hours or anything like that?"

"Not tomorrow."

I went into the bathroom and brushed my teeth, came back, and climbed into bed. I lay there staring up into the dark for a while.

I figured the old man was asleep. I was wrong.

"You skip the onions?"

"Good night," I said. I hoped my tone let him know I thought he was insane.

"How about your date? She have the onions?"

I couldn't help it. I laughed. I could hear him laughing too.

4

Good day, bad day.

The good? I got to sleep in until almost noon, had the second best scrambled eggs I've ever had (my Aunt Rita makes the best — I think it's the pound of butter she cooks them in), and on maybe the hottest day since we'd arrived in Vietnam, the old man and I went swimming for a good part of the afternoon.

The bad? After the swim, the old man left for a while, said he had a meeting with someone. I called Jen, hoping I might be able to see her, even for a little while. She told me her dad had arranged a late flight to Hanoi to interview some former North Vietnamese Army Officers. They would be gone two, maybe three days.

I didn't even know if we'd still be here when she got back. She sounded sad, but there was nothing she could do about it. They were leaving for the airport in just a few minutes. She told me she'd texted me earlier. I hadn't looked at my phone since before the swim. *Stupid.*

Talk about sappy. I actually ran all the way to the Grand Hotel hoping to — I don't know — yell goodbye to her. I got there as the taxi was pulling out into the sea of motorbikes.

I could make out the back of her head in the back seat, but she didn't see me. So much for young love. I mean I liked her, and it seemed like she liked me back, but I might not ever see her again unless I wanted to make a quick trip over to Australia sometime.

Bad day.

5

Actually, it was an evening of mostly boring stuff. The old man told me I should buy a present for Mom, which I had to admit wasn't a bad idea. Except I hate shopping. And besides, how was I supposed to know what to get her? I was at it most of the afternoon.

I found a street called Le Thanh Ton. Big-time shopping. Pretty expensive. I paid a lot of dong for a handbag that I didn't even know if Mom would like.

Shopping for her reminded me I hadn't phoned her yet, so we found a fairly quiet little park, and I called home. I don't know what time it was there, but Mom sounded fine. It was great to hear her voice. I didn't realize how much I missed her. I told her that and she asked a few things — just general stuff. Then before we hung up she told me to take care of myself.

"And take care of your dad too."

I thought that was a weird thing to say.

After the call home, I sent Jen a pretty mushy text and then checked my phone about every fifteen minutes. No response that day.

Watched some TV, CNN, yeah, that was fun. Went to bed early because the next day would start at — you guessed it — oh six hundred hours.

Sweet.

Dalat

1

We got up, showered, packed up some clothes — no brief case, no duffel bags — and headed out on the highway. It was the same one we'd been on when we'd gone to the A Shau Valley, but the old man wasn't all tense and weird like he'd been on that other trip.

I knew better than to ask where we were going, so I listened to FM 105.5, actual English radio, and stared out the window counting pagodas again.

And fell asleep.

When I woke up, we were stopped. I sat up and looked through the windshield. For the second time, I had woken up looking at something kind of unique. First, Mr. Vinh's tube house … now this. Except this baby was *real* unique. Thing is, I wasn't sure what it was I was looking at. It was like a place you'd see in a weird dream. Or maybe if you were on a banned substance. A house maybe. Or maybe not.

"Where are we?"

"This is where we get out," the old man answered.

"Yeah, but where are we?"

"Dalat." That's all he said. He climbed out of the Land Rover and started pulling our stuff out and onto the ground. A kid about my age came running out of the weird looking place. He started grabbing our gear.

I pointed at the kid. "Is that okay?"

The old man nodded. "The kid works here. Why don't you help him?"

"Help him do what?"

"Carry our stuff inside … to our room."

"Our room? We're staying here? Whoever built this place had psychological problems. It looks like Disneyland on crack."

The old man nodded and smiled. "Can't argue with that. I guess that's why it's called the Crazy House."

The Crazy House was actually very cool. The bottom of it was a tree trunk, and the house grew out and above it with branches sticking out all over so it was sort of like a tree house. Nothing, I mean *nothing* was straight. Rooms, walls, ceilings, beds, tables, mirrors — the whole place was … crazy.

I read the sign that stood crookedly by the gate. The architect was a woman named Hang Nga, which I guess is why it's called Hang Nga's Guest House. But everybody knows it as the Crazy House. I stared at the place for quite a while before I helped the kid carry our stuff inside and down a twisting hall to a bedroom that would have been perfect for Alice in Wonderland.

I couldn't figure out what we were doing there, but I knew I'd find out eventually. In the meantime, it was kind of fun. I was looking in a mirror that had seven or eight sides to it when the old man came in.

"What do you think? I built it myself. I bet you didn't know I was a carpenter." He flopped down on the bed.

I shook my head. "How'd you find this place? What's it called — Dalat?"

"It's pretty famous. Dalat was a favourite getaway haunt for officers and higher ups from both sides to come for a little R and R during the war. There was a gentleman's agreement that nobody would attack the place. And nobody did. Until the Tet Offensive in '68. Tet is the name of the lunar new year, big Vietnamese holiday. That's when the Viet Cong attacked a lot of the towns and cities in South Vietnam. Saigon got hit real hard. Dalat got it too.

"Grunts never got to come here. We all heard about it though. I told myself that if I lived through the war, I'd get here someday. Today's the day."

"What's the big deal? What's it famous for?"

"Scenery. The climate. It's cooler here. That kind of stuff. This house too, it's sort of a museum. Of course, it wasn't here during the war. And Dalat is also a big-time honeymoon place."

"One lousy date and you're trying to marry me off."

I heard him chuckle. "How's that going anyway? You talk to the lucky girl today?"

I nodded. "They've all gone to Hanoi. Her dad's got meetings or something. She said she'll be back in two or three days."

I had a thought. "How long are we going to be in Vietnam?"

He sat up, shrugged. "A few more days anyway. Why, you worried you might not see her again?"

"I guess the thought crossed my mind."

"How about I promise you we won't leave before she gets back?"

"Really?"

"Sure."

"Okay, thanks. So what are we here for, the scenery or the climate."

"Neither. We're here to be cowboys."

2

He wasn't kidding. An hour later we were sitting on two horses the old man had rented from a stable next to a place called Victory Lake.

The old man was arguing with our guide. The guy was dressed like a cowboy, except totally fake, cheap green cowboy hat, clothes you'd only wear on Halloween, and plastic guns. I'm not kidding—plastic guns in these crappy cardboard-looking holsters. I figured they had to be paying the guy a lot of dong to look that stupid every day.

He spoke some English, so I kind of knew what the argument was about. The old man was trying to get rid of the guy, and the guide was wanting to do his cowboy job and ride ahead of us. I guess if some dangerous outlaw jumped out of the woods, he'd shoot the crap out of the guy with the plastic pistols.

When there was a pause in their argument, I said, "I don't know. I'd feel a lot safer if Tex went along with us. He looks tough, and there's no telling what could be out there."

"Shut up, Nathan."

They argued for a while longer, and finally, as near as I could figure, the old man paid the guy twice as much not to guide us as he would have got to guide us. And we rode off along this path that skirted the outside of the lake. The old man was in front.

"I think you'd look a lot better with the hat and those guns."

"Shut up, Nathan."

"It's Nate."

I've been on a few horses, but I wouldn't say I was a good rider. The old man looked pretty comfortable on his horse, like he'd done a fair amount of riding. I decided to take his advice and just enjoy the ride, take in the scenery.

The old man had been right about that part. The scenery, especially *this* scenery, was pretty spectacular. The path went up and down, and after an hour or so of riding, we came to a waterfall. The old man stopped his horse, and I pulled up alongside. This was the first place the path had been wide enough for two horses to be side by side.

I looked at the waterfall. Of course, with a waterfall, you don't just look. You also listen. For a few minutes I listened to the roar of the water crashing against rocks on the way down and into a pool at the bottom of the falls. The old man hadn't looked away from the waterfall since we'd got there. I looked over at him. He looked serious, like he was thinking about stuff.

"You bring your camera?"

I'd almost forgotten. I'd bought a disposable camera when I'd been shopping for a gift for Mom. "Yeah."

I'd been keeping it in a nylon jacket I was wearing. Anything more was too hot, and the long sleeves at least kept some of the mosquitoes off me. I took a few pictures of the waterfall. Thought I maybe got a couple of good ones.

"You ready?"

I tucked the camera back in my jacket pocket. "For what?"

He didn't answer. He just turned his horse and kicked it in the sides a couple of times. He took off down the path at a pretty good speed. I wasn't sure if I wanted to go quite that fast, but I didn't have a choice. My horse apparently didn't like the idea of being left behind and took off after them.

I'm not sure how long we raced up and down through the hills around there, but I know I wasn't checking out much scenery for a while. The old man finally pulled his horse up alongside another lake, a different one from before. I don't know what it was called.

I pulled up alongside, and we looked at each other, laughing and breathing hard. I didn't know riding a horse at full speed could be work, but it was also a blast. We let the horses rest and stood there for quite a while looking at that lake. Different sound from what we'd heard at the waterfall. This time it was mostly bird calls and whistles. Most of them were sounds I hadn't heard before.

I looked over at the old man. "I don't think I thanked you, not really, for getting that dog away from me on that hill."

He shrugged. "No big deal."

"Yes, it was. It was to me. I was ... I was really ..."

He nodded. "I know. And you're welcome."

"Would you really have killed that guy? *Caca dau.* That's what that means, right? 'I'll kill you?'"

"Pretty close. I don't know what I would have done, Nate. Probably killed the dog, then seen where it went from there."

"Yeah."

I waited a minute or so. There was something I'd been wanting to ask. "How do you do that? I mean kill somebody?"

"When I was here before, I killed people because I wanted to stay alive. Because if I didn't kill them, they were going to kill me. At least that's what I thought at the time."

"You don't think that anymore?"

"I don't know."

I thought that answer was a little strange, but I didn't say anything more.

"Let me ask you, Nate. If you'd had a gun and that dog had attacked you, and the man let him do it, *made* him do it, what would you have done?"

I tried to make myself remember what it was like on Hill 453, how scared I was. "I guess I'd have shot the dog."

"Then what?"

I shivered. Twenty-five degrees Celsius, and I shivered. "Then seen where it went from there."

The horses were pretty well breathing normally by then, but the old man made no move to leave.

"You like horses?"

I petted my horse on the neck. "Yeah, I like 'em, I guess."

"You probably don't know that I have a ranch … in Arizona."

For some reason that pissed me off. I wanted to say, *No, I don't know that, I don't know squat about you because that's the way you've wanted it all these years.* But I didn't say anything.

"Not a big place. Three and a half sections over by Tucson. Pretty good water. Decent house, not fancy. Thirty head of longhorn cows and twenty-five horses, quarter horses, actually thirty counting the foals from this spring."

I was watching him as he spieled off the details of the place. I wasn't sure what the look on his face meant. Pride? He wasn't bragging, I didn't think. Just telling me. Like it was something I should care about.

I didn't.

"I'm not there as much as I'd like. I seem to be on the move a lot with some of the other stuff I do. It's a pretty spot. Saguaro cactus, some pretty good grass. And the water, I guess I mentioned that, but water is important in that part of the world."

I nodded. Trying to be polite. I still didn't care. Even with the water. "What other stuff?"

"What?"

"You said you're not at the ranch because you do other stuff. What other stuff?"

He took a breath. "I've got a brother in upstate New York. He's a floral broker. Brings flowers into the country. Exotic ones, from different countries. Anyway, I'm a partner in the company. So I go up there and help him sometimes."

"You help him with flowers."

"Yeah."

That seemed funny to me for some reason, but I tried hard not to laugh. I didn't think he'd want me to laugh.

"It's called Cactus West Land and Cattle Company. My ranch." It seemed he wanted to get off the flowers and back to the ranch. "The name came with the place. I thought it was catchy when I bought it."

I nodded again. "Yeah, it sounds okay. The name I mean."

His turn to nod. He was still looking out over the lake. "Anyway, it's yours."

It takes a little time to make sense of something like that. "What?"

"The ranch. It'll be yours."

"I don't ... get that."

"I'm giving it to you. It'll be yours."

"Why?"

"You can change the name if you don't like Cactus West Land and Cattle Company."

"What are you talking about? I don't know anything about ranching or horses or long neck cattle."

"Long *horn*. Texas Longhorns. Mine have real good horn."

"I don't know anything about ranching," I said again. "Nothing."

"You don't have to know anything. I got a guy, Gilbert Ruiz, that runs the place. All you do is fly down there once in a while, count the cows, maybe look at the horses, make sure they're not starving, get back on the plane and fly home. Get a cheque in the mail every now and then. And hell, if you don't like it, just sell the place...."

"Whoa. Listen, I'm going into eleventh grade. After high school, I've been thinking about university. Why don't we talk about this then? I'm not trying to be a jerk here. I really appreciate —"

"Doesn't work."

"What?"

"It won't work."

"What won't work?"

"Waiting until you're done college. This needs to happen sooner than that."

"Why? What's the big deal?"

He hadn't looked at me once during that whole conversation. He turned and looked at me now.

"Because I don't have that long."

It takes a few minutes for a statement like that to sink in. Even more than when somebody tells you they're giving you a ranch. And when it does sink in, what exactly are you supposed to say?

"What? Is this like your farewell tour or something?" I wished afterwards I'd said something different. That sounded like I thought what he was telling me wasn't serious.

"Something like that."

"You mean ... you're ..."

"Dying. Yeah, that's what I mean."

"But how ... why ... I mean ..."

The old man sort of half grinned and shook his head. "You sound like me when I found out. Okay, so here it is. You know who Patrick Swayze is ... was?"

"Yeah, the actor, the *Dirty Dancing* guy who died awhile back."

"Right. Pancreatic cancer. That's me ... same thing. Same as Patrick Swayze, except I'm better looking."

Bad joke. But any joke would have sucked right then.

"So anyway, they said six months, maybe a year if I take a bunch of shit treatments. I didn't take any of it."

"So … you don't look sick. I mean you're kind of skinny … uh … thin, I guess, but I other than that … do you feel okay, does it hurt?"

"Some days I feel great. Other days, not so hot. But overall, it's not that bad. I guess it'll get worse."

I looked out at the lake. Peaceful. Sun shining across it like a painting.

"What are you going to do?"

He shrugged. "I'm doing it. Way too late but I'm doing it."

I was having to swallow more than usual.

"I know I'm sorry doesn't mean a hell of a lot, Nate, but I am. I'm so sorry I wasn't there when you were growing up. I wish I'd taken you fishing, built snowmen with you, taught you about longhorn cows. I wish I'd been your dad, I mean *really* been your dad. I wasn't, and I'm real sorry about that."

"I don't like fishing." My joke wasn't any better than his. What was I supposed to say? *It's okay. Growing up without a dad isn't a big deal. I don't mind that you thought a teenage girl was worth blowing off me and Mom for.*

"I'm sorry that … I mean I … wish you weren't dying."

"Me too, Nate. I wish that too."

Some birds that looked like swans, I don't know if that's what they were, came gliding in over the lake and landed with a flutter of wings and a swish of water.

"You're finally calling me Nate. Thanks."

"About time we started back." The old man turned his horse back the way we'd come. "I'd hate for Wyatt Earp to come looking for us."

I turned my horse.

"Why don't you lead this time?" he said. "Just follow the path. And even if you get lost, I'm betting these horses would get us back there without any help from us."

I nodded, touched my horse's sides with my heels, and starred back up the trail. The sun was lower now, and shadows crisscrossed through the trees and onto the path ahead.

3

I'd be lying if I said Dalat was much fun after the horseback ride. The old man tried to keep it light, but it wasn't working, and he knew it wasn't working.

We toured the Crazy House, the part that was a museum, and it was okay. We had a nice lady trying to make it interesting, but I wasn't interested.

I checked my phone about every fifteen minutes but no texts from Jen. No answers to the two texts I'd sent her earlier in the day.

The old man took me to a restaurant called the Long Hoa (we decided that must be Vietnamese for Longhorn), which was totally Vietnamese except for one dish — spaghetti. I had the spaghetti. I wasn't bad at using my spoon to curl noodles around my fork. The meatballs were pretty good and I ate most of it, which kind of surprised me since I didn't really feel like eating.

They served homemade yogurt for dessert, and it was pretty good too, but I left most of it in the bowl. By then, I'd kind of lost interest.

The old man was finished eating too and was sipping some kind of coffee with booze in it. Didn't smell great, but he seemed to like it.

"What are you going to do?" I asked him.

He looked at me and back at his coffee cup, but he didn't say anything. I started to say it again. "I mean now, what are ——?"

"I know what you mean."

"You know, you could probably come to our house and ——"

He shook his head. "No, I couldn't do that. That wouldn't really be fair to your mom, would it? I run off on her, don't see her for almost a dozen years and then move back in so she can nurse me while I die. Even I'm not that big a jerk."

"She's a pretty amazing nurse. It's what I think she'd really like to be if she could."

He didn't seem to hear that. "And you've already had enough bad thoughts about me in your life without having to watch me do this."

Watch me do this. Dying is something you do.

"So what then? You can't just drive around the country in that dirty black Dodge. And you said the guy at the ranch pretty much runs it."

He nodded. "I talked about it with Tal. I figure I'll go stay with him. Help him around the place as long as I can. Tal's seen lots of soldiers die. He can handle one more."

"Are you going to see Mom when we get back to Canada?"

"I don't think so. I ... can take your mom hating me, but I really can't take her feeling sorry for me."

"She doesn't hate you."

"She should."

178

And that was Dalat. The next morning we slept in, had breakfast and went for a walk. Didn't talk any more about dying. The old man had been right. It was cooler in Dalat. For almost twenty-four hours I hadn't really sweated.

About noon we drove out of there and back to Saigon. Weird ... I was looking forward to getting back. The noise, the lights, the fumes. Even the motorbikes.

Saigon, the Last Time

1

What was it Jen had said? Four hundred thousand more motorbikes every year in Vietnam. That's more than a thousand a day, and even though not all of them end up in Saigon, it was weird to think that there were probably five hundred more motorbikes in the place than there had been when we left for Dalat. I wondered where they'd squeeze them all in.

We were almost to the hotel when Jen texted me:

So sorry. Busy me. But so BRD. BBT. LOL

J

That wasn't all that helpful. Yeah, you're bored and you'll be back tomorrow, but do you want to see me? Should I call you? Have you been grounded for the next several months ... what? And which LOL is that? Lots of Love, Loads of Laughs, Later on Loser? Hell, there was only one thing I was sure of. Having a girlfriend, if that's what this was, is way harder than just wishing you had one.

We dropped our stuff in the room, and the old man said he'd be out for an hour, maybe a little longer, and was I okay with that?

I said sure and wandered down to the lobby. Dialled up pancreatic cancer on the guest computer. Lots of pretty dismal information. I looked up Patrick Swayze and that wasn't real cheery either. I gave that up pretty fast.

BRD. No freaking kidding. There was one thing I kind of wanted to do before we left Saigon, and I figured I might as well make use of the free time the old man had just dropped on me.

It was something I'd seen while we were driving back into Saigon from Dalat. Something I wanted to take a closer look at, find out a little more about. I'd tried to memorize where the place was from the Rex and how I'd get back there. I didn't think it was all that far away. I decided to find out. I'd start out walking and if I couldn't find it or if it was too far away, I'd jump on a cyclo, which was what they called these bicycle-taxi things. They don't go all that fast, but it didn't matter; *nothing* went fast on the streets of Saigon.

The North American English Language School. I'd been thinking about what Jen had told me about teaching English here someday. The more I thought about it the more I thought it might be a cool thing to do for a while after I got through school.

I know what I said before about thinking about stuff that was a few years away, but it really couldn't hurt, could it?

I wasn't sure what time it was, I was guessing maybe six o'clock, so maybe there wouldn't be anyone at the North

American English Language School. But that didn't make sense either — a lot of people taking the classes must work during the day, so evenings should be like action central around the place.

I found the place, no problem, in maybe forty-five minutes, and lights were on all through the building. It was two storeys high, and looked like a combination office building/Canadian Tire store. It didn't really resemble a school except that there were a lot of people going in and out of the place. Most of them were carrying books. Students.

Over the front door of the building — where you'd expect to see the name of the school — was a massive Coca-Cola sign. There was a high chain-link fence around the outside of the schoolyard, but you could walk right through the schoolyard and up to the front door. I did.

I hesitated when I got there but finally decided to go inside. I walked in and up a few steps just inside the door to what was the main floor. There were classrooms on both sides and ahead was what looked like an administration office. I stopped outside one of the classrooms and leaned against the wall next to the open door. I could hear perfectly everything that was going on.

I took a quick peek, then stepped back and just listened. The teacher was maybe my mom's age and was speaking English with a German accent. At least I think it was a German accent. Sometimes he'd say something in Vietnamese, but most of what was going on in there was in English.

It seemed that the class was discussing the weather. Specifically, winter weather. I heard one of the students say,

"That is a very bad blizzard outside." Then the teacher said, "Yes, we will need to wear our parkas and scarves today."

Yeah, I bet that blizzard topic comes up all the time around here. I had heard that in the northern part of the country there were more mountains, and they did get some cold and snowy weather. But right here in Saigon, the parka business was doing right poorly.

Still, I liked what I was hearing in the class. I took another peek. The students in this class were all adults, maybe twenty to a lot older — people the old man's age, maybe even older than that.

The atmosphere in the classroom seemed happy. There was some laughter, but I couldn't tell if they were laughing at something the teacher had said or if it was at each other and the way they were pronouncing the words. Some were better than others. Some were pretty hard to understand. The teacher put up a slide of a snowman and that brought big-time laughs.

A couple of people walked by me in the hall and looked at me a little funny. Suspicious. I figured I'd better move on. I went to the office and thought about going in to talk to someone, but there were brochures in racks on both sides of the door, so I took a couple and drifted off.

I went out a different set of doors than I had come in through. Just outside, sitting on a concrete retaining wall was a little Vietnamese girl maybe seven or eight. She was reading an English picture book, something about a farm. There was a horse and a pig and a chicken on the cover of the book. There was something wrong with the little girl's face. One side kind of drooped and one eye seemed to sit lower than the other. I couldn't tell if it was from an injury or if it was a birth thing, but it didn't matter. Somehow, even with the defect, she was really pretty, especially when she smiled, which she did right then.

"Hi," she said, practising her English.

"Hi," I said back to her.

A dog on a leash was lying at her feet looking up at me.

"It is a very nice tonight."

"Yes, it is," I agreed. *No blizzards, don't even need a parka.*

She held out her book. "This is a book."

I took it and looked at it. "Yes, it is. It's called *Fun Day at the Farm.*" I pointed to the words on the cover.

"*Fun Day at the Farm,*" she repeated.

I handed the book back to her. "Are you a student here?"

She nodded. "Student, yes."

"Do you like English?"

She said "yes" but looked a little puzzled.

"You like to speak English?" I pointed to my mouth as I said "speak English" and that seemed to help.

She smiled the big smile again. "Yes, I like to speak English."

I wasn't sure how long I should talk to her. In Canada you have to be really careful around little kids. People get suspicious in a hurry. In a foreign country, I didn't figure I wanted to push it. I turned to leave.

"What is your name?" She was still smiling. Enjoying the conversation in English.

"My name is Nate." I turned back to her. "What is your name?"

"My name is An Lien." The dog stood up, stretched.

"That's a very nice name, An Lien."

I took a half-step back. The dog was small, looked like a bichon or something. The tail was wagging. But it was still a dog.

"You like my dog?"

"Uh … sure, I like your … dog. Is he friendly?"

She tipped her head to one side and looked at me. Didn't understand … probably the word "friendly."

"Your dog … uh, what is its name?"

"Name … is Tu."

I remembered that Madame Benoit, our French teacher, always made us answer in complete sentences. And because Madame Benoit was *très* gorgeous and had a *très* nice body, I remembered this part of my French education.

"My dog's name is Tu," I said.

An Lien looked at me like I was nuts. *I also had a dog named Tu.*

I pointed at her. "You say, 'my dog's name is Tu.'"

She smiled and looked down, petted the dog and looked back up at me. "My dog's name is Tu."

"Awright." That confused her too, but I didn't explain that. I didn't know how.

"I have to go now," I said.

She nodded. "You like … touch my dog Tu?"

"We say 'pet' the dog. Yes, I would like to pet your dog, Tu."

Which, of course, was bullshit. For all I knew, Tu might mean "Kill that white bastard" in Vietnamese. But I'd kind of got myself in it. No choice unless I wanted a little Vietnamese girl to know I was afraid of a dog that stood maybe twenty centimetres high from bottom to top.

I bent down slowly. Reached my hand gently towards Tu. Back of the hand first. I'd read that in an article somewhere. I hoped that Tu had read the same article. I left my hand a few centimetres from Tu's nose. He looked at it, took a couple of tentative steps forward and sniffed my hand.

I felt hot. Maybe I was sweating, I wasn't sure. I mean this wasn't anything like Hill 453, but I still wasn't having a nice time. I left my hand there, hoping the dog wasn't thinking of my fingers as tasty looking hors d'oeuvre. He looked up at me, then back at my hand. Gave a couple of fingers a little lick, then another one.

I slowly extended my hand a little farther, gently petted his back, my eyes totally focused on his tail. Still wagging, good.

I scratched behind his ears, and Tu flopped down on his belly. He was liking it.

An Tien laughed. "He likes you. He likes you pet him."

Pet. She had learned a new word. I had taught her a new word. How cool was that?

I stood up, took a deep breath. "I like him too," I said.

"You live here — Ho Chi Minh City?"

"No, I live in Canada. I am going home, back to Canada — in a few days." Then for the second time, "I have to go now, An Lien."

She nodded and jumped down off the retaining wall.

"I go in class now. Goodbye, Nate."

"Goodbye, An Lien." Her hands were kind of full with the book and the dog leash so I reached over and opened the door for her. She went inside, climbed the stairs and looked back at me.

"Will you come back to Vietnam …Nate?"

I laughed. "An Lien, I might. I just might come back to Vietnam one day."

She nodded, smiled, and hurried off down the hall.

I turned and headed for the Rex. I stopped along the way at one of those food stands and got myself a bowl of noodles. I ate them as I walked.

Noodles, for god's sake.

2

It was the second time I had run into the old man in the lobby before I got to the elevator.

He was sitting on the arm of one of the couches in the lobby. Looking serious. I thought I must be in shit.

"You got any plans for tonight?"

No *hello, hey, how ya doin'*. Nothing.

"Not really."

"There's someone I'm going to meet. I'd like you to come along."

I shrugged. "Sure, but I wouldn't mind a bathroom stop."

"Go ahead. I'll wait here for you."

It didn't look like he was pissed at me, but he wasn't joking around either. I went up to the bathroom, had a quick look at my phone — nothing — then back down to the lobby. The old man was standing up, ready to go.

I tried to get a read on his mood. He was bouncing lightly on the balls of his feet. Looking around. Having trouble standing still. Nervous. Not like when we went to Hill 453 but nervous.

"So what's up?"

"Let's go."

He wasn't telling me. Now there's a surprise. We went out to the parking lot and climbed in the Land Rover. Eased out into traffic, traffic that was barely moving. It was worse even than usual. More yelling, more honking, more arm waving from the people on motorbikes. The old man wasn't trying to weave his way through traffic, so I figured we must be okay for time — whatever it was we were doing.

We got as far as a stoplight, then stopped dead. Now we could see the problem. An accident just ahead. A car turned totally sideways. A motorbike on its side. A couple of guys standing in the street screaming Vietnamese insults at each other.

It didn't look like we'd go anywhere for a few minutes at least. I reached forward to turn the radio on.

"Don't," the old man said.

I pulled back and looked at him. He was looking ahead, but it was like on the hill. He wasn't seeing what he was looking at.

He didn't say anything at first. When he did, his voice was soft, flat.

"About four months after I was in country, we relieved a company of marines over near Hue. They'd been in some hell-shit fighting for weeks, lost a lot of people. They finally took control of the area, and we were sent in to mop up.

"We'd just got there, been there a couple of hours maybe and a Chinook, that's a helicopter, came in to re-supply and pick up some of those guys, take them back to Hue. While the Chinook was coming in, the door gunner was shot, fell out of the chopper, maybe two hundred feet to the ground. When the guy hit, some of those marines cheered."

He stopped. I waited for more. Nothing.

"You mean, they cheered when their own guy got killed?"

He nodded. "War makes people crazy, Nate."

I still thought there might be more to the story. There wasn't. The road was opening up ahead of us, and we started moving again.

We made a few turns, and after a while I wasn't sure where exactly we were. But it looked familiar. I'd seen some of this before. Then I remembered. We'd come this way from the airport that first night in Saigon.

Cholon, the Chinese sector of the city. Lots of shopping, a big market. We'd walked through here the day before we went to the A Shau Valley. The old man pulled over and parked the Land Rover, motioned at me to get out.

A woman was waiting near a building. She was watching us. When we got out of the car, she started forward.

So that's it. The old man's got himself a Vietnamese girl-friend. Probably met her online from back in North America. Finally figured the kid should meet her. That explained the condoms.

Actually, it explained exactly zero. Didn't even make sense. I couldn't see a guy planning a trip to Vietnam to relive some of the shit of a former life and then thinking what the hell, I might as well go online and see if I can get hooked up while I'm over there.

I guess my mind goes off in weird directions sometimes. The old man stopped in front of the woman. "Thank you for coming. For doing this," he said.

He started to take money from his pocket, but the woman shook her head. "You pay later."

Pay for what?

The old man looked at me. "This is my son, Nathan ... Nate. He'll be coming with us. Nate, this is Madame Nguyen Thi Soon, Mrs. Soon. She's an interpreter. We're going to speak to someone, and I know a little Vietnamese but not enough. Not enough for tonight. Mrs. Soon will interpret."

I nodded at Mrs Soon, who nodded back at me.

The old man said to her, "You're sure she's the person I'm looking for."

"I have spoken to her. She is the one."

"What did you say to her about me?"

"I told her a man from North America requests the honour of speaking to her about her brother. That is all I told her."

Mrs. Soon didn't look like someone who smiled a lot. Not unfriendly exactly, just not a lot of fun. She was taller than a lot of the Vietnamese people I'd met so far. She was well-dressed, expensive-looking clothes. She was pretty too, and I guessed she was about Mom's age.

She was looking at me. "Are you sure you want him there, Mr. Huffman?"

Mr. Huffman. First time I'd heard him called that. It felt weird to be reminded that we had the same last name.

"I'm sure. Let's go."

Mrs. Soon led off down the street. The old man walked beside her some of the time, behind her when the sidewalk got too crowded. Both sides of the street were lined with shops. Commerce. It looked like you could buy anything in Cholon. Everything from live chickens to incense to pictures of Ho Chi Minh.

We stopped walking. I remembered this place too. It was the vegetable vendor's stall. The old man had told the taxi driver to stop here. I thought back to that night. The old man had jumped out of the cab. Stood right here for a long time. He'd spoken to the vegetable seller. I looked and could see the guy inside his shop. I wondered if it was him we'd come to see. But no, it couldn't be — the old man had talked about a woman when he spoke to Mrs. Soon.

We went on past the stall — in the direction the vegetable merchant had pointed that first night. We walked, not far, then turned into a little street, actually more of an alley than a real street. Mrs. Soon pointed ahead.

"It is just there," she said. We walked a little further, stopped in front of a place that looked more like a shack built onto the back of some kind of shop.

Mrs. Soon went to the door, but the old man stopped her. He turned to me. "Nate, you remember I told you about the Tet Offensive, when the VC ... the Viet Cong attacked cities and towns all through the south."

"You said it was pretty bad in Saigon."

He nodded. "I was here because it was right after the fight on 453. I'd been wounded in the hand, was put on light duty until my tour was over and it was time to go home. I helped load a few trucks with supplies, but I spent most of my time doing bugger all. Then Tet happened. There were VC everywhere. Lots of fighting in the streets. Stuff blowing up all around us. No one knew who the bad guys were. Everybody was scared, spooked —"

Mrs. Soon interrupted. "Americans were everywhere too."

"Yes." The old man nodded. "Americans were everywhere too."

He turned back to me. "You asked about My Lai. I told you then that I killed people. We were brought here to kill people, and I did what I was supposed to do. I believed at the time that the people I killed were the enemy, all of them. I *believed* it. But I didn't know. Not for sure."

He nodded to Mrs. Soon. She knocked on the door of the shack. When no one came, she knocked again. Called something in Vietnamese.

The door opened. A woman stood looking at us. Small, bent over a little. Poor, I'd say, but she was clean; her clothes were old and well-used but neat. I tried to guess at her age. Not as old as the old man maybe, but quite a bit older than Mrs. Soon.

Mrs. Soon spoke to her for a couple of minutes. The woman didn't say anything at first but looked back and forth between Mrs. Soon and the old man. She spoke a few words to Mrs. Soon, who turned then to the old man.

"She is Ba Li." (I found out later that "Ba" was a term of respect that people called older women. It was sort of like "aunt" but it wasn't just for relatives.)

The old man dipped his head toward Ba Li. "Have you told her I was a soldier?"

"Yes."

"Tell her I was in Saigon during the Tet Offensive, January, 1968."

"I don't have to tell her when Tet was. Our people know that. We celebrate it."

"Tell her I was here. In Saigon."

Mrs. Soon spoke again to Ba Li. She nodded. She was looking at the old man.

"Ask her how old she was then."

"She might not tell you that."

"Ask her."

Mrs. Soon said something to the woman who said something back. Madame Soon looked surprised. "She was eight years old."

About the same age as An Tien.

"Was her brother older or younger?"

Mrs. Soon translated, and then, after the lady spoke, said, "She wants to know why you ask about her brother."

"Was he older or younger?"

Mrs. Soon shrugged, and as near as I could tell, repeated the question. Got an answer. "Her brother was twelve years old."

The old man nodded, seemed to think about what he wanted to say next. "The day her brother died, they were on the street, that street." The old man pointed to the street we'd come from, the one where the vegetable vendor's shop was. "There was a curfew. Why were they on the street after curfew?"

Mrs. Soon spoke again to Ba Li. The answer was short. "Why do you want to know this?"

"Ask her again."

She did, got the same response.

"Ask her again."

This time Mrs. Soon did not translate. "Why do you want to know?"

The old man was sweating, and his voice seemed higher. If I was looking for a word to describe him right then, I'd say desperate.

"Ask her again. Why were they on the street after curfew?" He almost screamed the words.

Mrs. Soon turned slowly back to Ba Li. Her voice sounded like a whisper after the old man's yell.

Ba Li said more this time, and Mrs. Soon interpreted without looking at the old man. "They were hungry … looking for food. Their father had been killed two days before, their mother was missing. They were on the street after curfew because they were trying to steal food."

The old man's voice was more normal as he said, "Soldiers came. They saw you and your brother. Your brother threw something at the soldiers. They shot him. Tell her that. Then ask her if her brother was VC."

Mrs. Soon didn't say anything. She was looking at Ba Li. "Say it," the old man told her. "Ask her if her brother was VC."

Mrs. Soon said something. Ba Li looked down at her hands, then up at the old man. She said something. Mrs. Soon translated. "She wants to know if you killed her brother."

"Was he Viet Cong?"

Mrs. Soon turned to the old man again. "He was twelve years old."

"I saw people killed and maimed from grenades thrown by kids ten years old. I saw one of our officers die a bad death when he ate a piece of fruit that a little girl, maybe seven years old, had given him. Poison. I saw soldiers die because they believed what they were told by

194

old people, by women with babies in their arms, by pretty girls on bicycles, by children. They believed and then walked into booby traps and ambushes."

He took a step closer to the woman. "Please … it's important. Was your brother VC?"

The woman spoke, then Mrs. Soon. "She wants to know if you killed her brother."

I looked at the old man. I saw his face go all distorted, and I saw tears on his face. He hadn't cried when he was telling me what happened on Hill 453, but he was crying now. When some people cry, it seems more than sad.… Looking at him, it was like watching him die.

He wiped a hand across his eyes, and he spoke in a voice I hadn't heard ever before … not from him. Not from anyone. "I killed your brother," he said. "I killed your brother on that street. We … I thought he was VC. He threw something. I thought it was something that would explode. I was afraid … and I shot him. I came here to tell you I'm sorry. I never wanted to kill children. I'm sorry."

Mrs. Soon translated and no one spoke after that. The only sound was the old man's breathing. Loud breathing. He wiped his face again with his arm. It felt like a minute passed. Maybe two.

"Please tell me if your brother was VC. Please … I need to know that."

Ba Li spat. The spittle struck the old man in the face. He didn't wipe it away.

"I … I would like to do something for you. If there is something I can do for you. Money, get you some food, some clothes … "

When Ba Li spoke, it was in a voice so full of anger, so full of hate. Then she turned, went back into her house and closed the door.

The old man stepped back. He pulled a handkerchief out of his pocket and wiped his face. Mrs. Soon turned away from the house and looked at us. Her eyes were very much like the woman's had been.

The old man looked at her. "Was he Viet Cong?"

"She didn't answer that."

"What did she say?"

"First she said that she would like to kill your son. So you would know."

The old man's face didn't change, but he lowered his head a little. Maybe a couple of centimetres or so. "What else? What else did she say?"

"She said her brother threw an onion at the soldiers. You killed him for throwing an onion." Mrs. Soon walked away without saying anymore. The old man never got the chance to pay her for her translating. She disappeared out onto the street and into the hundreds of people there.

We didn't move for a while. The old man stared at the door of the shack where Ba Li lived. I never knew what he was thinking about right then.

I didn't know if I should do something, take his arm and lead him away or maybe say something. I didn't do anything. I'm not sure how long we stood there before he turned and walked slowly away. I walked with him, but we didn't speak any more that night. I'm not sure he knew I was there.

3

The next morning when I woke up, he was dressed and getting ready to go out.

"What's up?"

"I'm going up to the roof to have some coffee. Maybe some breakfast. Looks like a nice morning. You can come up there when you're up and dressed if you want to."

"Yeah, okay."

"We'll be leaving tomorrow to go home." He went out and closed the door behind him.

On my way up to the roof of the Rex, I sent Jen another text.

I miss you. R U back? Going back to Canada tomorrow. Call or text me. N.

I remember reading that signing an email or a text with just an initial was supposed to mean something special. I wasn't sure what, but I figured, now that I was on the clock with Jen. I'd better pull out all the stops.

I ordered French toast and tried to keep an eye on my phone and the old man at the same time. He was drinking coffee, and there was an order of toast in front of him, but he didn't seem all that interested. He was sitting sideways to the table and had the paper in his hands. It gave me a chance to study him. I noticed something. He seemed thinner than the day he'd picked me up at the house.

And something else. I couldn't believe I hadn't noticed this before. There was a scar along the back of his left hand and two of the fingers, the index and middle finger didn't sit quite right. They were at an angle that you don't usually see fingers going. Bent, not like totally backwards or anything, but just not right. And it didn't look like he used them the normal way either. Or maybe at all. He was holding the newspaper with both hands, but it didn't look like those fingers were helping his left hand all that much. How long had we been together, and I'd just noticed that now. So much for my career as a detective.

I wanted to say something. I wanted to ask him about the fingers even though I already knew. Most of all, I wanted to take away some of what had happened the night before. Mom had told me to take care of him. I wished right then that I could. But I didn't have the words. I ate French toast, checked out the back of the paper like I had that other time. Different news but the same.

My phone rang, and I almost knocked my breakfast off the table getting at it. Then tried to sound cool when I answered.

"Hello. Oh, hey, Jen, how you doing?" Like she was the last person I expected to hear from.

The old man turned his head and looked at me. Smiling. Okay, so cool didn't work.

We didn't talk long. She suggested we meet about four o'clock at the Black Cat. I said that was great, I'd see her then.

The Black Cat. *Our place.*

The old man asked me if I wanted to do anything for a few hours before "my big date." I said sure, but I didn't know what.

"How about a walk?"

So we walked. The Rex is on Nguyen Hue. One block over is Dong Khoi, kind of like Main Street. We walked the one block to Dong Khoi and turned down it. Lots of shops, expensive stuff.

We didn't go very fast, and it looked to me like the last few days had been hard on him. On his illness. He didn't say anything and he wasn't grimacing or anything, but it didn't look to me like he was a hundred percent. Which I guess made sense.

"So would you think it was a dumb idea for a guy like me to come back here in a few years, maybe teach English to people?"

He stopped and looked at me, I think to see if I was kidding. Then when we started walking again, he said, "You like it here?"

"I don't mind it," I said. "I mean there's stuff I don't like too much, but there's other stuff that I guess I like okay."

"With an answer like that you could have run the Five O'Clock Follies."

"What's the Five O'Clock Follies?"

"The lobby of the Rex, during the war, all the war correspondents would come there every morning for the latest briefing on the progress of the war. Fifty percent of the briefing was all about saying nothing and the other fifty percent was bullshit."

That pissed me off. "You think I'm bullshitting about coming back here."

"No," he shook his head. "No, I don't think that, Nate. I just meant your answer didn't tell me much about how you feel about this place. I think it would be very cool if you came back here someday."

"Even if you, you know, hate it?"

"Before we came here, you and me, I thought I hated Vietnam. I wanted to see it again to try to remember some things I thought I should remember, but I hated the place. But since we got here, I figured out that I hate the war, and I hate what the war did to me. And I hate that I saw friends die for reasons I'll never understand. And I really hated that fake cowboy with the plastic guns...."

We stopped walking, laughed a little at the joke.

"I don't hate this country, Nate. And I don't hate these people."

"I walked by this place where they teach English to Vietnamese people. There was a little girl there, and she had an English book. I talked to her, it was cool, and I taught her a couple of new words."

"I hope they were appropriate ones. I've heard some of your words."

"They were appropriate. And anyway, I've heard a couple of things come out of your mouth that they probably don't teach at that school."

We both laughed again, a little harder this time.

"I guess you're right. Sorry."

I wanted to ask him if he was okay after what had happened the night before. But I figured if he wanted to talk about it, he'd bring it up. We stopped and had a coffee at a place on Dong Khoi.

"You hungry? You want something to eat?"

I shook my head. "I'm saving up. Jen and I are meeting at the Black Cat. They've got amazing burgers there."

"How's that going, you and Jen?"

He wasn't asking like he was trying to pry into anything. It was kind of like one of your friends would ask you at school.

"Well, let's see, her old man doesn't really like me because he thinks I'm related to a lunatic, and she didn't text or phone me the whole time she was in Hanoi, and we're going home tomorrow, and she's going back to Australia pretty soon, which is about a gazillion miles from my house, but other than that I'd say everything's perfect."

"Good. Glad to hear it."

He stood up. "If it's okay with you, I wouldn't mind heading back to the hotel. I might lie down for a while. That way I'll be able to pace the floor tonight worrying about when you're going to get home."

We went back to the hotel, and I jumped in the shower. When I came out, he was lying down reading.

"You ... uh ... wouldn't be able to spare a little aftershave, would you? I notice you have some in there."

"Go ahead, but I'd use it sparingly. My experience is that girls don't like it if you marinate yourself in the stuff."

"Right."

I went back in the bathroom and did all the good smell stuff. Deodorant, toothpaste, aftershave. When I came out, the old man sniffed the air.

I said, "I might suck at this date stuff, but I'm not going to stink at it." He smiled at that, then closed his eyes.

By the time I got dressed, he was sleeping. I eased my way out the door. Three twenty. Just about right to be at the Black Cat at four.

4

I walked in at about five minutes to. Jen was already there, drinking a Coke. She stood up and stepped around the table, gave me a hug. There are hugs, and there are hugs. This wasn't the hug of a girl who had been missing the hell out of a guy and was overjoyed to see him. This was more of a *so-did-you-bear-that-the-groundhog-saw-his-shadow-and-there's-six-more-weeks-of-winter* hug. But maybe I was reading too much into it.

She went back around the table and sat down. I sat down opposite her. She looked good. Smelled good too. *But so do I, right?*

"How was Hanoi?"

"Boring. Mom and I shopped while Dad went to all these meetings with people he wanted to talk to for his book. There's this prison, I can't remember the name, but a lot of pilots who got shot down ended up there. They called it the Hanoi Hilton. And some of the actual pilots who had been prisoners there went through the place with him. So he was all excited.

"Then we went to everything to do with Ho Chi Minh — his house, where he's buried, plus I think we saw every portrait and photo of the guy. If I never see Uncle Ho again, that will be just fine."

She took a drink of her Coke. "How about you. Been having fun?"

"Not really. Went horseback riding and stuff. It was okay. I spent most of my time missing you."

She didn't get a chance to answer because a girl came to our table to take our order.

I shook my head when the girl offered a menu. "I'm thinking of having another one of those burgers. How about you?"

Jen took the menu but didn't give it much of a look.

"Sure, a burger's okay, I guess. And another Coke." *Coke, not beer . . . another bad sign?*

When the girl had gone from our table, I leaned forward. "So how come you didn't text or call me?" I tried to keep my voice light, like it wasn't a big deal, like I was just teasing her.

"Listen, Nate, I'm really sorry about the other night."

So that's it — she's feeling guilty that we went that far that fast.

"Hey, listen, it was me too. I wanted you just as much as you wanted me. And anyway, we didn't do anything I'd call bad."

"That's not it."

"What then?"

The serving person came back to our table. "I forgot to ask you if you wanted a drink."

"Yeah, sure, a Coke's fine." *And if you come back to this table one more time, I'll kill you right here.*

She left again. I wanted to reach across the table and take Jen's hand, let her know that everything was fine. But I didn't think that was quite the right thing to do. Turns out I was right.

She put her arms on the table and leaned forward. *Closer to me. Good.*

"I have a boyfriend."

If she'd leaned across the table and gouged out one of my eyes, it wouldn't have surprised me any more than those four words, five syllables.

But in times of trouble I've always been able to come up with the right words. "You have a boyfriend?" See what I mean?

I was suddenly filled with the urge to study every picture on every wall of the Black Cat. I spun one way on my chair, then the other, then back again. I must have looked like a pinball on steroids.

I leaned forward on the table. She pulled back again like you do when a crazy person gets too close.

"You have a boyfriend?" I think I was very loud.

She nodded. "I'm so sorry. I should never have —"

She stopped. The burgers had arrived. Why is it when you want the service to be slow, they set a Guinness record for getting the food to your table?

"Did you want ketchup or anything?"

I looked up at the server. "She has a boyfriend."

"I know," she answered. "Everyone in the restaurant knows."

I spun around again, this time looking at the people. A lot of them were looking at us. Others were pretending not to. Okay, so apparently my reaction to Jen's announcement had been a little over the top.

"No, thank you. No ketchup," I whispered.

I knew I wasn't handling this well, but I hadn't had much practice.

"So ... so what was the other night all about?"

A sip of Coke. "Nate, I like you. I really do. And the other night we were having fun and I ... kind of got carried away. We ... my boyfriend and I had this huge fight just before I left to come here. And I guess I thought we were done … or at least I thought I could see other guys, or … I don't know what I thought."

I didn't know what to do with my face. Pissed off? Devastated? Shocked? Some combination of all of those?

"Anyway, the day after you and I went out, he called me and we sort of got back together. Well, not right away, but he called and texted when I was in Hanoi, and I guess the bottom line is Roger and I, we're back togeth —"

"Roger? Your boyfriend's name is Roger?"

"And I told him —"

"Nobody has a boyfriend named Roger."

"You are being a total jerk about this. I told him that there was this guy who tried to make it with me and —"

"I tried to make it with you?" Okay, for a while I'd been trying to keep it together, but I have to admit I kind of lost it right there.

The server came hustling over. "Sir, you must keep your voice down, please."

I held my hands out in front of me. "Sorry." I looked around the room at the other diners. "I'm sorry. Really."

"Thank you, sir," the server said.

"Excuse me…" I looked at her nametag. It read Lo. "Lo, do you have a boyfriend?"

She stepped back. I knew I was being rude asking a stranger a personal question like that. But I kind of didn't care about manners right at that moment. "Seriously, Lo, do you have a boyfriend?"

The girl looked down at the floor, then back up at me and smiled. "Yes," she said.

"And what is his name?"

She hesitated but finally said, "Van Loc. Loc."

"Loc," I repeated. "Not Roger." I turned to Jen. "See, not Roger."

Jen stood up. "I'm leaving."

I took her hand, pulled her back down into her chair. "Okay, listen, I'm sorry. I guess I've never been dumped before. Mostly because I've never had a girlfriend before. And I definitely have never had a girlfriend who already had a boyfriend before."

She looked at me and smiled. "You'll have lots of girlfriends, Nate." If that was her attempt at making me feel better, it didn't work.

"What I said before …" Jen looked at me. "That night was my fault. I shouldn't have led you on. And I shouldn't have —"

I held up a hand to stop her. "It doesn't matter. Really, it doesn't matter. It's not like we were going to see each other. Probably in a few weeks we wouldn't have even kept texting. Or sending emails."

"Probably."

"Anyway, eat your burger. I promise I won't be a jerk anymore."

We ate our burgers — actually, she ate hers, I only had a couple of bites of mine. We talked about what we'd do when we got home; I made a joke about Aussie Rules Football. I can't remember it, but I don't think it was that funny, and that was it. We went outside, had a friends hug (totally boring), and then we walked off in opposite directions.

After I'd gone a little ways, I turned back and yelled,

"Give my best to Roger," but I think she was too far away to hear me. If she did, she didn't turn around.

I took quite a while getting to the Rex. I walked slowly and took a long route back. I went up to the room. The old man wasn't there, but he'd left a note that he was up on the roof. I decided that it wouldn't be a bad way to spend my last night in Saigon.

When I got up there, he was sitting with a drink in his hand staring out at the sunset.

"Hi," I said as I sat down.

"Hey, how did it go? I didn't think I'd see you until late."

"Yeah."

He looked back at the sunset, and I watched too for a few minutes.

"You want something to eat?"

I thought about it. "I want a steak, and I want a beer."

He looked at me. "You're either celebrating, or she dumped you. That isn't the face of a man who is celebrating."

"She's got a boyfriend. Roger."

"Roger."

"That's what I said when I heard it too."

He waved to the waiter who starred toward our table.

"How do you like your steak?"

"I don't know. Sort of well-done, I guess."

When the waiter got there, the old man ordered a steak, medium well, another of whatever it was he was drinking, and a beer. No questions asked. By him or the waiter.

We sat with our drinks looking at the sunset. My steak came, and I worked away at it. I wasn't used to going to restaurants for steak, but if this was what it was like, I could do it a lot more.

Neither of us said much for a while. I was almost finished eating when he turned to me and said, "Whoever it was who said 'all's fair in love and war' was full of crap on both counts."

The sun dropped lower in the sky to the west. I set my knife and fork down. "Can I ask you something?"

The old man turned to look at me. "Sure."

"What if you'd never been in the war? I mean there were lots of guys who weren't. Some of them even went to Canada, so they wouldn't have to fight. And you were already *in* Canada and went anyway."

"Yeah, that's about how it was."

"Do you ever wish you'd never been in the war? I mean it's not like World War Two, where the whole world had to stop the Nazis or it was all over. I mean in this war … you said yourself you didn't really know what you were fighting for … and you guys lost."

He set his drink down and seemed to think about what I'd asked him.

"Nate, Vietnam was a bad deal. It shouldn't have happened. Like a lot of wars shouldn't happen. But one thing I learned. Once you're in a firefight or on a search and destroy or getting the shit kicked out of you on a hill with a number for a name, you aren't fighting for your country or to make the world a better place. You fight for the guys around you. You ever hear that expression about the guys in the trenches?"

I nodded.

"When you're in those trenches, the only people who matter to you are the people beside you. They're trying to stay alive; you're trying to stay alive. And you're trying to keep each other alive. That's what I was doing in Vietnam. I didn't know that's the way it would be when I enlisted. I thought I'd be fighting for my country and my family and my officers and my uniform — stuff like that. But that isn't how it turned out."

I thought about that. Took a sip of beer. "Yeah, I can see how that would be what matters."

"Nate, I went to war and did the best I could. It wasn't good enough, but I couldn't do more than that."

I looked at him, but he wasn't looking at me. He was still staring up at the night sky. He moved his shoulders up and down. "You asked me what if I hadn't come here to fight. I don't know. Maybe I'd have been an accountant or taught school. Or gone ranching sooner than I did.

"I know this. I'd be a different person than the one I am. I know things about me that I wouldn't have known if I hadn't been a soldier in Vietnam. I know that no matter how scared I am, I can still fight. I know that the men next to me on the battlefield can count on me. I know I can see death coming and fight like a son of a bitch to keep it away. That's going to be kind of important for the next while."

We sat for quite a long time. The sun had almost disappeared.

"And if I hadn't come here the first time, I wouldn't be sitting here now with my kid in a restaurant in Saigon, having a drink and a conversation. I told you, it's like a buddy movie."

I smiled for the first time at the joke. This wasn't a buddy movie, and we both knew it, but it was okay to think about it in that way.

"Yeah, buddy," I said. "Do me one favour. Tell me we don't have to get up at oh-six-hundred hours tomorrow."

"That is affirmative. Tomorrow it's feet on the floor at oh-five-hundred hours."

"Shit."

"Yeah."

5

The next morning we flew home from Vietnam

1

There isn't much more to tell. When I got home some of the kids asked about where I'd been and what I'd been doing so far that summer. I kind of dodged around it, didn't really tell them much.

You're probably wondering about the five point plan I started the summer with, remember The Summer of the Huffman? In case you've forgotten, here they are again:

1. Win the War against Acne.
2. Gain five pounds of muscle.
3. Read two novels, good ones, one each month. I figured I'd start with *Catch-22*, then decide on the second novel a little closer to August.
4. Work three nights a week at the Grocery Plaza. Maybe Saturdays too if I can stand my boss Helen "Bitch" Boyes that many times a week.
5. This is the big one. Take out Jen Wertz.

I'm doing pretty good with the acne. I don't know if it's all those products I use or the noodles diet in southeast Asia, but my skin is better than it's been in the last couple of years. And I haven't had a headache since I got back.

I'm not sure why that is, but I'm not complaining.

I have gained the five pounds, actually six, which is weird because when I got home from Vietnam, I'd actually lost a couple of pounds.

I'm reading *Catch-22*. I didn't like it at first, but I'm into it now. It's pretty funny, but I haven't decided yet who's crazy and who isn't.

I decided against the job at the Grocery Plaza. I don't know if they'd have hired me anyway after I missed some of the summer. Anyway, I'm not missing Helen "Bitch" Boyes. I got a job at a florist shop. Four hours, four mornings a week loading the truck that makes deliveries to the other stores and some individual buyers too. I start work at 8.00 a.m., which means that Monday through Thursday I have to get up at oh-seven-hundred hours.

Jen Wertz has a boyfriend. The bad news is it isn't me. The good news is his name's not Roger. I haven't taken anybody out since I got back, but I'm not as worried about it as I used to be.

2

The old man phoned me a few times after we got back. It felt like the conversations were more normal, not like before when they seemed like duty calls. We just talked about … stuff. Sports, music, movies, girls … sometimes Mom. I never asked him how he was feeling. I didn't think he'd want me to do that.

Then the phone calls stopped. I thought about phoning him, even dialled the number on my cellphone once. But I didn't hit send.

A few weeks after I got home, an envelope came to the house addressed to Mom and me. In it was a deed to the old man's ranch in Arizona. The deed had my name on it. The old man also sent along a note that said he had sold thirty acres of the Cactus West Land and Cattle Company and set the proceeds of the sale aside to pay for Colleen Huffman to pursue her nursing education and for Nate Huffman to go to university. The note also said that he had given 160 acres to Gilbert Ruiz in return for his agreeing to look after the ranch until his retirement — and to send Nate Huffman an annual report of the ranch operations along with fifty percent of the proceeds from the yearly sale of longhorn calves and quarter horse foals.

Mom is enjoying those nursing classes. Well, I think she is. It's a lot of work and she keeps saying how hard it is to study and stuff when you've been out of school as long as she has. I told her I have trouble with that whole studying thing too, and I've never *not* been in school.

Some nights we sit at the kitchen table together and do homework. At first I thought that would feel weird, but actually it's pretty cool. And quite often we finish off the study session with a bowl of popcorn or a dish of ice cream. Not bad.

A couple of times I've told her I'm too sick to go to school, and she should practise her nursing skills on me that day. So far she hasn't bought it. Last time I tried it, she said not to let the door hit me in the ass on my way out. Terrible bedside manner if you ask me.

I haven't been to the 7-Eleven store even once. That's not true. I've been a few times to buy stuff but not to hang

out. I guess Vietnam made me different too. Or something did.

You want to know something weird. There's this Vietnamese restaurant a few blocks from our house. I go there
every once in a while, just by myself. The strange part is
that most of the time I have the noodle bowl.

I got a package in the mail. It was from Tal Ledbetter. There was a letter with the package. It was handwritten but very neat. It read:

Dear Nathan Huffman,

Your daddy died on November 21. We had a very fine day that day. It was real warm for November so we sat outside in the morning and looked out over my moat. We watched those two cows of mine. We ate some toast and honey. Your daddy wasn't eating much at the end but he seemed to enjoy the toast and honey that day. We talked about some things and he said he thought you were a fine young man. I told him I thought so too. After a while he said he'd like to go in and lie down. I took him inside and put him on top of his bed. He said he didn't want to be covered up so I left him like that for a while. He asked me if I'd read to him a bit. I don't have much to read around the place but I read to him *from a* Popular Mechanics *magazine. It was an article about a new BMW motorcycle called the Motorrad. We both thought it was a very cool bike. I read some more and then when I looked up he had passed away. Real peaceful.*

I spread some of his ashes around this place but I know he wanted me to send some to you. I guess you'll have an idea what to do with them.

Your daddy was a good son of a bitch.
Tal Ledbetter

There was a small urn in the package. I didn't know what to do at first. I told Mom that the old man had died, and she cried some that night and was really quiet for the next couple of days.

I decided what I wanted to do. There's a place just outside of town that rents horses. I went there one day and rented a horse and rode out over these hills that look back on the town.

I got out there a ways and got down off my horse. I took the urn and as I walked along, leading my horse with one hand, I spread the old man's ashes out into the wind. They settled on a real nice hillside with grass and a stand of poplar trees near the top.

As near as I can remember, this is what I said as I spread the ashes, even though no one was there to hear me: "In Dalat you said you wished you'd really been a dad for me. I just want you to know I'm not mad anymore that you weren't. I would have liked to have a dad who was around more, but I'm doing okay. I'm real glad we had some time last summer to do stuff. Dads make their kids laugh. You made me laugh. Dads do stuff with their kids. You rode elephants with me and took me to a crazy house and walked through the jungle with me. I guess some dads even give their kids condoms. I've still got mine, by the way. And dads teach their kids stuff. You taught me a lot in Vietnam. I won't forget that. And I won't forget you … Dad."

Acknowledgements

A number of people helped make this book possible. I am indebted to Glen Huser and Susan Juby, both wonderful writers, for their support and insights. I am grateful to all of my Japanese and Korean friends for their hospitality and especially to Mary, Yoshi, Harumi, and Yuko at St. Mary's International School in Tokyo for their help with my research and for their encouragement. My agent, Arnold Gosewich, and editor, Sylvia McConnell, have again been wonderful to work with. Most of all, I have been fortunate to have Barb as (what Stephen King calls) my Ideal Reader. And finally, to all of those, on both sides, who sacrificed so much in the Vietnam War, you were very much in my thoughts as I wrote this book.

Also by David A. Poulsen

Billy and the Bearman
978-0929141480

$7.95

A dramatic turn of events unites twelve-year-old Billy Gavin and seventeen-year-old John "Bearman" Redell, two boys from seemingly different backgrounds who discover that they in fact have a great deal in common — they are both runaways. Together, alone against nature in the rugged Alberta wilderness, they begin to deal with the demons of their pasts. When the news of a downed plane and a missing rodeo cowboy in the woods and mountains nearby reaches them, Bearman, an expert tracker who knows the woods like the back of his hand, becomes obsessed with the thought of finding the lost man. The boys find themselves faced with the greatest challenge of their lives. Do they have the courage to find the missing man? More importantly, will this adventure give them the self-confidence they need both to outrun the past and to embrace the future?

Available from your favourite Bookseller.

DUNDURN
www.dundurn.com

Visit us at
Dundurn.com
Definingcanada.ca
@dundurnpress
Facebook.com/dundurnpress

teacher resources
www.dundurn.com/teachers

Free, downloadable Teacher Resource Guides

Robin tossed and turned,
puzzling over Ambrose's riddle, wondering
where all the clues would lead them, and
thinking back over the events of the past day.
She was just about to get up and get a drink
of water when she heard a strange, scratching
sound. She pulled the bedcovers up to her
chin and looked around. There was nothing
to see in the blackness of the room.

"There are no such things as ghosts," she
told herself firmly.

All of a sudden, a wild burst of light flashed
upon her and something white flitted through
the room. The light veered crazily, hitting
Robin and then Jo full in the face, blinding
them, and then sliding away to reveal a
shapeless white form without a face that
screeched like an owl. . . .

The Bridges
in Edinburgh

MICHELE SOBEL SPIRN

FOUR CORNERS PUBLISHING CO.

NEW YORK

Four Corners Publishing Company
45 West 10th Street, Suite 4J
New York, NY 10011
www.fourcornersbooks.com

Printed in U.S.A.

Map © 2004 Mapping Solutions, Anchorage, AK
Cover illustration by Bill Farnsworth.
Design by Kris Waldherr Art and Words.

07 06 05 04   5 4 3 2 1

Library of Congress Cataloging-in-Publication Data

Spirn, Michele.
    The bridges in Edinburgh / Michele Sobel Spirn.– 1st ed.
        p. cm. – (Going to)
    Summary: Fourteen-year-old Robin and twelve-year-old Jo Bridge
accompany their parents to visit a newly-discovered Scottish cousin,
only to get mixed up in an old rivalry and a series of clues that must
be solved to learn who will inherit the family mansion.
    ISBN 1-893577-11-2
    [1. Inheritance and succession–Fiction. 2. Sisters–Fiction. 3.
Cousins–Fiction. 4. Edinburgh (Scotland)–Fiction. 5.
Scotland–Fiction. 6. Mystery and detective stories.] I. Title. II.
Series.
    PZ7.S757Bm 2004
    [Fic]–dc22

                                                    2003026173

                        1-893577-11-2

FOR STEVE,

the best traveling companion,
and for Josh and Kirsten, Ryan, Emily, Jack, and Chloe,
whose travels have just begun.

PUBLISHER'S NOTE

On September 11th, 2001, our country was attacked. The World Trade Center in New York was destroyed and the Pentagon in Washington, DC was partially destroyed. People of different lands and cultures lost their lives in these attacks. So now, more than ever, we must learn about other people in other places, because for the children of today, understanding will mean everything.

CONTENTS

CHAPTER ONE

The Mysterious Mansion

 The old house in Edinburgh settled in the night with protesting creaks and squeaks. For fourteen-year-old Robin Bridge, tossing and turning in a soft feather bed, it seemed as if sleep would never come. Ideas raced through her head. In the bed next to hers, her twelve-year-old sister, Jo, snored softly. Robin closed her eyes, then opened them and stared into the darkness, remembering how the Bridges had ended up in this Scottish mansion, trying to solve the mystery of Uncle Ambrose's missing will.

Just the day before, the Bridges had been in Paris and she had studied the map of Europe for an interesting place to visit.

"Spain would be fun," she said. "I always wanted to go there."

"How about Italy?" asked Jo. "Then we could have lots of pizza."

"You're always thinking about your stomach," said Robin.

"If I don't think about it, nobody else does," replied Jo.

"Let's wait for your father, girls," said their mother, pushing back her thick red hair. "I'm sure he'll have some ideas about where we spend the last week of our vacation."

The Bridges had started the summer in London, and then Robin and Jo had gone to Paris on an educational tour while their parents had attended conferences in Rome. With a week of vacation left, the Bridges were together again in Paris. They were determined to travel to a new place for the week.

"Jo and I could go back to London," suggested Robin.

"You just want to see Vic again," said Jo, making kissing noises. Robin had met her pen pal, Vic, in London, and the two of them and Jo had had many adventures together.

"Don't be such a brat," said Robin, throwing a pillow at her sister. "Vic is my pen pal, nothing else."

Jo heaved the pillow back. "Pen pal! That's for sure! You two write a lot of letters—like every day."

Robin was about to leap on Jo, when her mother held up her hand. "Stop!"

"Stop what?" asked Mr. Bridge, coming into the room.

"Nothing," muttered Robin and Jo, while Mrs. Bridge rolled her eyes.

"Let's go to Italy, Dad!" cried Jo.

"No! We're not going to Italy!" exclaimed Robin. "We're going somewhere else."

"That's right, Robin," said Mr. Bridge, "we are going somewhere else." He smiled at Mrs. Bridge and his brown eyes sparkled.

"I can't imagine where," she said.

"I'll give you a hint," Mr. Bridge announced. "It's someplace where they speak English."

"London!" cried Robin. "Wait 'til I tell Vic!"

"No, it's not London," Mr. Bridge said.

Robin frowned. "Then I don't know where we're going."

"We're going to Edinburgh, in Scotland," he said.

"Why?" asked Robin, gloomily.

"We have a cousin there, Angus McDougall," answered Mr. Bridge.

"I never heard of him," said Jo. "I thought I knew all our relatives."

"None of us has ever met him. He's sort of a distant cousin," Mr. Bridge explained. "When I knew we were going to be in Europe, I sent him a note. Now he's invited us to his house for the week."

"Does he have any children?" Jo asked.

"No, he's single and still quite young," said Mr. Bridge. "He's in his early thirties and just inherited an old mansion in town. He said it's very comfortable with lots of room for us."

"It doesn't sound very exciting," Robin remarked. "What's there to do in Edinburgh?"

"It's rich in history," said Mrs. Bridge. "There's a wonderful castle and lots of writers come from Scotland, including Robert Louis Stevenson."

"The one who wrote *Treasure Island*?" Robin asked.

"Yes, plus Sir Walter Scott and Robert Burns . . . "

Robin listened to the ticking of the grandfather clock in the hall and thought about how they had scurried to pack for the short plane ride. She remembered the drive into town. They had all craned their necks looking at the countryside.

"It doesn't look very different from home," Jo commented.

"Wait until we get to town," said Mrs. Bridge. "I hope Cousin Angus will show us around."

"He said he had to see his solicitor today," Mr. Bridge noted. "We'll meet him at the house."

But when they got to the house, a big, dignified white stone building with sparkling glass panes at the top of the front door, Cousin Angus wasn't there.

"Ah, yes, sir, he told me you were coming," said the young woman of about twenty with short red hair who greeted them. Her green wool skirt matched her sweater and she wore a strand of pearls around her neck.

"He'll be back soon. I'm Nelly, the housekeeper and cook. I'll show you to your rooms."

"Thank you, Nelly." Mr. Bridge began to lift their bulging

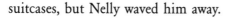

suitcases, but Nelly waved him away.

"Munro will see to those," she said.

A skinny boy who looked as if he was just out of high school sidled in. His rosy cheeks got redder when he saw the girls, but he grabbed the bags and lightly ran up the steps.

Nelly led them up the stairs to the first landing. "This is your room," she said to Mr. and Mrs. Bridge. "Please let me know if you need anything."

Mrs. Bridge gasped. The room was painted a soft cream color and trimmed with dark wood. It had a four-poster bed hung with cream-and-pale-blue curtains, and the same curtains framed windows that sparkled with tiny, diamond-shaped glass panes. A fireplace was decorated with glossy blue tiles, and a luxurious blue-and-gold Persian rug covered the floor. Rich, dark oil paintings highlighted the pale walls, and beside the bed was a glass lamp resting on a gleaming old chest.

"What a beautiful room," Mrs. Bridge said.

"Thank you, madam. And now I'll show the girls their wee room."

"Wee?" muttered Jo. "Must be really tiny."

But when Nelly threw open the dark wood door, Jo shrieked. Then she sighed and said, "This is the bedroom I always wanted." She jumped on one of the twin beds, covered with pink frilly bedspreads, which flanked one wall, their headboards almost hidden behind piles of white, lace-trimmed pillows.

 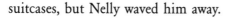

Robin saw that under a bay window of the same tiny, diamond-shaped panes that she'd seen in her parents' room, green silk pillows lined a window seat. As if in a dream, she walked over to a dressing table with a white lace skirt and a heart-shaped mirror. She was about to sit down when something jumped from the white chair and nearly attacked her.

"Aaagh!" she cried.

"Ah, that's just Lorna Doone," said Nelly. "Naughty cat! She's always sneaking in here for a nap." She made a shooing gesture towards the white tabby, who put up her tail and stalked out of the room.

"Lorna Doone?" asked Robin. "Isn't that the name of a book?"

"I suppose so," remarked Nelly. "I'm not much for reading, but Mr. Ambrose was very fond of books. Shall I help with your unpacking?"

"Oh, no, we can unpack ourselves," Robin said. "We don't have that much."

"Very well. Dinner's in half an hour." Nelly turned and left.

"When she said 'wee room,' I thought this would be small," Jo said. "It's lots bigger than our room at home."

"I think she meant it was smaller than Mom and Dad's." Robin began unpacking her books, putting them on a small white table near her bed.

Jo quickly finished hanging up her clothes and started thumbing through Robin's books.

"*The Mystery of the Old Clock, The Purloined Letter, Secret Codes of World War II* . . . you've got a lot of mysteries here. Are they any good?"

"They're great," said Robin, enthusiastically. "I love to see if I can figure out the mystery before the end."

"Well, here's a mystery. What do you think they'll give us for dinner?" Jo asked.

"Take a look in the guidebook. It talks about Scottish food," Robin said, handing her their guide to Scotland. She picked up one of her mysteries and began to read.

"Scotland's most famous dish, haggis, is an ancient folk recipe for using up the cheapest cuts of meat," Jo read aloud. She put down the book and wrinkled her nose. "It sounds awful."

The girls jumped at a sharp knock on the door.

"Here are some extra blankets," said Nelly. "It can get very cold at night. Are you sure you don't need a hand?"

"No thank you," answered Robin politely, "we're fine."

"Nelly, what's haggis?" asked Jo.

"It's kind of hard to explain," said Nelly. "You start with a sheep's stomach . . ." She broke off, grinning, when she saw Jo's face.

"Sheep's stomach!" shrieked Jo. "I'm not going to eat sheep's stomach!"

"Do you eat it all the time?" Robin asked hesitantly.

"It's a special dish. Some people wait all year to eat it,

particularly on holidays," Nelly said. "It always gives me indigestion and keeps me up. I wouldn't want that—particularly if I were sleeping in this room."

"What's wrong with this room?" Robin asked.

"There's some that say that McDougall's wife haunts it. That's her picture there. You see, a wee bairn was born to them, but it died when it was a day old. After McDougall's wife passed on, some have claimed they saw her come back to this room to search for the babe. This was the nursery, you know," Nelly said, smugly. "I wouldn't sleep here for anything."

"I'm sure it will be fine," Mrs. Bridge reassured them, coming in at the end of the conversation.

"To each his own." Nelly tossed her head and left the room.

"I came to see if you girls are ready to go downstairs for dinner," said Mrs. Bridge. Robin had already picked up her book and was eagerly reading. "Robin . . . Robin," her mother called.

"Earth to Robin," Jo said. "Wake up. Brring! Brring!"

Robin jumped as Jo danced around her.

"It's not necessary to be annoying," Robin said, putting her book down. "I heard you."

Mr. Bridge joined them in the hall and the family walked down the thickly carpeted stairs. Bouncing from step to step, Jo glanced at the family portraits that were hung on the wall.

"Nobody looks very happy here," she said. "Well, maybe he does." She pointed to a more modern portrait at the end of the staircase.

Munro was waiting for the Bridges at the bottom of the stairs. "That's Mr. Ambrose McDougall, the late owner of the house," he whispered, shyly hanging his head. "Please follow me to the dining room."

"Here you are! Welcome to McDougall House." A tall, thin man with thick black hair stood in the doorway of the dining room, waiting for them. He wore a beige sweater and tweed pants and his green eyes twinkled as he looked them over.

"Cousin Angus, it's good to meet you at last," said Mr. Bridge, extending his hand.

"Cousin Robert, my pleasure," boomed the man in a deep voice. "And I gather this is your fine family?"

Mr. Bridge introduced him to Mrs. Bridge and the girls. Angus shook hands with all of them.

"You're just what this gloomy old house needs," Angus said to Robin and Jo.

Robin looked around at the dining room, paneled in dark wood. Several antlered deers' heads were mounted on the walls. Silently she agreed with Cousin Angus. The dining room was creepy.

But Mrs. Bridge said, "The upstairs is charming. Our rooms are lovely."

"Oh, that's the influence of Uncle Ambrose's wife, Mary. After she died, he kept everything the same, and never allowed anyone to change it. But the downstairs has always been dreary," Angus said. "Well, enough about the house. How do you like Scotland so far?"

"I'm kind of disappointed," Jo said.

Robin gasped and Mrs. Bridge frowned at Jo.

"And why is that?" Angus asked.

"Well, Cousin Angus, we've been in Scotland for half a day now and I haven't seen one person wearing a kilt and I haven't heard any bagpipes!"

Angus threw back his head and laughed. "And a right lot of idiots we'd look if we marched around in our kilts playing bagpipes at the bank or the greengrocer's. We save those for special occasions."

Jo looked thoughtfully at Angus. "You don't look a lot like Dad," she said. "He's short and you're tall. He's got brown hair and yours is black and your eyes aren't the same color. But you laugh the same way."

"I'm very glad to claim you as relations," Angus said. "My parents died a few years ago and I've no brothers or sisters. So I was happy to hear I had more family." As they took their places around the large mahogany dining table, he smiled at Jo and Robin and said, "We'll have to think about how to give you a real taste of Edinburgh. You're staying the week, right?" He looked at Mr. Bridge.

"If that's all right with you," Mrs. Bridge said. "We don't want to impose."

"Oh, you're not imposing," stated Angus, suddenly looking grim. "A week is fine. But I can't offer you more. I'm afraid we're all going to be thrown out of here at the end of the week."

CHAPTER TWO

The Mysterious Clues

 "What do you mean?" Mr. Bridge asked. "Who would throw you out of the house? Isn't it yours?"

"I thought so," said Angus. "Uncle Ambrose told me dozens of times that he promised it to me. I was very close to him, and when he was dying I moved in to take care of him. Poor man. He was never the same after his wife passed away. That's Aunt Mary's portrait in the girls' bedroom, by the way."

Robin remembered that Nelly had pointed out the oil painting of Ambrose McDougall's wife. She had soft brown hair and blue eyes and wore a pink ball gown and a sparkling tiara. Robin had thought the woman looked gentle and sweet tempered.

"I don't believe she's the kind of person who'd come back to haunt people," she thought to herself. "And, of course, I don't believe in ghosts!"

"But what happened?" Jo insisted. "Why will you be thrown out?"

Just then Nelly entered. She had put on a white apron over her skirt and sweater and held a big gold and white soup tureen. "Cock-a-leekie soup, sir," she announced, ladling out portions into the deep white and gold bowls.

Jo sniffed it. "It's not made from anything like sheep, is it?" she asked fearfully.

"Of course not. Have you never had cock-a-leekie soup before?" Angus asked.

"Of course you have," Mrs. Bridge said. "It's just chicken soup."

Reassured, Jo took a big spoonful.

"You were telling us about the house," Robin reminded Angus. Nelly glanced at her, smiled, and left the room.

"Ah, yes, well, I simply stayed on after the funeral being that Uncle Ambrose had said a number of times that I should. At any rate, today I went to see Uncle Ambrose's solicitor about the formalities and he told me something shocking. Uncle Ambrose never gave him his will."

"How could that be?" asked Robin.

"Oh, he kept asking Uncle Ambrose for it, and Uncle Ambrose kept putting him off. First, he was too young a man to make a will. Then, he was too old and tired. Finally, he was too sick. The upshot of it is that whatever Uncle Ambrose said to me won't hold up in court."

"But surely the lawyer knows your cousin meant for you to have the house?" asked Mrs. Bridge.

"Oh, yes," said Angus, gloomily, "but there is another person with a claim to the house."

"Who is that?" Mr. Bridge asked.

"Cousin Tammie McDougall," Angus spat out.

"Won't she understand that Uncle Ambrose promised it to you?" asked Robin.

"Ah, Tammie's not a woman, he's a man, a black-hearted sort of fellow. And he's a solicitor, as well, so he's up to all the tricks," Angus said.

"At home, Tami is a girl's name," explained Jo.

"Tammie's a nickname here for Thomas," said Angus.

"Oh, like Tommy," Robin said. "Now I understand."

"How is Tammie related?" asked Mr. Bridge. "Is he a cousin of mine, too?"

"Perhaps," said Angus. "He's a more distant relative of Uncle Ambrose than I am."

"Doesn't that work in your favor?" Mr. Bridge asked. "In the U.S. it's generally the person who's the closest relation to the deceased that inherits."

"Yes, that would be the way of it," Angus explained, "except Uncle Ambrose was a very playful man. He liked his little joke. You see he's set up a competition. He didn't leave a will. Instead, he left a set of clues with the lawyer. The first one to figure them out gets the house. He set a time limit, too. One week from today."

"That's great!" Robin exclaimed.

"What's so great about it?" Angus asked.

"We'll help you figure them out!"

"Robin loves mysteries," Jo said. "And she's good at solving them."

"I don't think Cousin Angus needs our help," said Mrs. Bridge. "We're just guests here."

"But I do need your help," said Angus. "I'm totally hopeless at puzzles, always was."

"And always will be, Cousin," another voice drawled.

Robin looked up from her soup to see a tall, thin man in his thirties, dressed in a black suit, step into the dining room with Munro following him. He would have been handsome except that he glared at them through black-rimmed eyeglasses.

"I told him the family was at dinner, sir," Munro said, wringing his hands, "but he insisted on coming in."

"Cousin Tammie, I presume." Mr. Bridge nodded to him.

"Got it in one," said Tammie, running his hand through his short blond hair. "I don't believe I have the pleasure . . ."

"These are my cousins, the Bridges," said Angus. " They're from America. As you can see, we're in the middle of dinner. Perhaps another time . . ."

"Oh, yes, Cousin," Tammie said, mockingly. "Perhaps when I'm sitting at the head of this table in my house."

"You will excuse us," said Angus, throwing down his napkin and standing up from the table.

"I'll be off to my own supper," Tammie said, "but I just wanted to tell you I've solved the first clue. It won't be long before I'll be moving in. Just to give you fair notice and enough time to pack up your bits and pieces."

"I wouldn't be in such a hurry," Robin chimed in, indignantly. "Cousin Angus may surprise you yet."

Tammie looked down at Robin and smiled. "If he does, I hope he doesn't have to rely on a schoolroom miss from the States to help him."

Robin turned red and started to say something, but Mrs. Bridge spoke up. "I had heard that Scots were the souls of hospitality and courtesy, but perhaps you aren't Scottish by birth?"

"Well said, madam. But I believe it's my cousin who's been remiss as to hospitality and courtesy. He hasn't even offered me a drop of soup or even a chair. Perhaps when I take possession, you and your family will visit me and I'll show you real Scottish hospitality." Tammie bowed and swept out of the room.

"As if," Jo declared and turned back to her soup.

"What a very unpleasant man!" exclaimed Mrs. Bridge.

"Ever since we were children together, he's had it in for me," said Angus. "If I won something, he wouldn't rest until he got the better of me. When we were little, he used to thrash me. But when I got older and stronger, he resorted to trickery. One time we were both entered in a horse show. My horse and I won the blue ribbon and Tammie went to the judges and claimed I had doped my horse and that he really deserved the prize. I managed to convince the judges but by the time I was done, the thrill of winning was gone. Another time we were both sitting exams and he left a crib sheet on my chair when we were done. Again, I got into a lot of trouble but my teachers swore I had never cheated before and I was allowed to take the exams again, alone. I hate to think of him living here."

"Don't worry," Robin reassured him. "We have a whole week to figure the clues out."

"We'll be glad to help," Mrs. Bridge said. "But I don't understand why your cousin would include him in the will if he's so horrible."

"Oh, Tammie was always able to fool Uncle Ambrose," Angus said. "He can be quite charming when he wants to be. I'm one of the few people who know him for what he really is."

Just then Nelly entered with a large roast beef on a silver platter.

"The joint, sir."

"Is that what they call roast beef in Scotland?" asked Jo.

"Yes, any roast is called a joint," Angus said. He busied himself carving the meat into slices and passing them around. Nelly helped Robin and the others to potatoes, applesauce, and peas.

"Yum," said Jo. "This is good."

"Wonderful," said Mr. Bridge. "I guess we won't hear any more about pizza tonight."

"I haven't forgotten about it," said Jo, "but this is okay. It's almost like home here."

"But Edinburgh is much, much older, isn't it?" asked Mr. Bridge.

"Yes. The rock on which the castle was built dates from the last Ice Age. There was an archeological dig in the 1990s to find out how long ago people lived on that rock. They found some chewed herring bones that dated back to 800 BC."

"Cool. That's so far back!" Robin exclaimed.

"There were people in Edinburgh even before that. We know that the rock was a stronghold of the Saxon King Edwin in the Dark Ages," Angus explained.

"When was that?" asked Jo.

"In the 600s," Angus said. "But it wasn't until the 1100s that Edinburgh became the capital. Queen Margaret married King Malcolm and persuaded him to move the capital from Dunfermline, which is north of here."

"Pudding, sir," Nelly interrupted. She carried a big bowl of something topped with cream.

"That doesn't look like chocolate pudding," Jo said.

"Pudding here is another name for dessert," Mrs. Bridge said. "Remember, we learned that in London."

"Everything is so confusing when you travel," Jo said, yawning.

"Let's have some dessert," suggested Mrs. Bridge. "Then I think it's time for bed."

Nelly walked around the table, spooning out portions.

"What is it?" asked Robin.

"Tipsy Laird," said Nelly. "Haven't you ever had it?"

"Hush, Nelly," Angus said. "I'm sure there are all kind of American foods we've never had. Tipsy Laird is a trifle made from cake and custard and fruit. It's quite delicious. Try some."

Nelly laughed quietly as she spooned some of the trifle onto Robin's plate and Robin blushed. She tried to change the subject.

"Cousin Angus, you started to tell us the problem about the clues," Robin reminded him.

"Oh, yes," Angus said. He reached into his jacket pocket and brought out a folded sheet of paper. He passed it to Robin.

She looked at it front and back.

"But this is blank," she said.

"That's the problem," declared Angus.

CHAPTER THREE

Mysterious Things in the Night

 Robin smiled in the darkness as she remembered how the others had all gasped when they saw the empty sheet of paper.

"But . . . but . . ." sputtered Mrs. Bridge.

"It must be some sort of joke," Mr. Bridge said. "Maybe the clues are somewhere else."

"No, I'm afraid not." Angus shook his head slowly. "The solicitor said that Uncle Ambrose had written that all the clues we needed were on this sheet. He gave one to me and one to Tammie."

"I can't believe that Tammie has figured this out already," said Jo. "He's just trying to fool you. Don't you think so, Robin?" She turned to her sister, but got no response.

"Robin? Earth to Robin . . . Mom, Dad, she's spacing out again," Jo complained.

"Robin," her father said, "come back to us." He shook her shoulder gently.

"What? There's something I have to get," Robin said, the vacant look leaving her face. "I'll be right back."

She raced up the stairs and into her room. Hastily, she rummaged through her books. Finally, she found the one she wanted and hurriedly thumbed through it. A triumphant look spread over her face and she pumped her arm in the air. "Got it!" she yelled, and ran back down the stairs.

"Robin, where did you go?" her mother asked.

"Never mind," groaned her father. "It's those mystery books again. When are you going to start reading something good? It's so annoying," he said to Angus. "Both my wife and I are academics and our daughter does nothing but read this junk. It's not as if she's not bright, but she won't even look at the classics unless it's Sherlock Holmes!"

"You're going to apologize to me, Dad, when you see what I've learned from mysteries," Robin announced with a smile. She turned to Angus. "Do you have a lighter or a match and a candle?"

"Of course," said Angus. "Nelly, could you bring us some matches and a candle?"

Nelly was back in a minute with a slender white taper and several long kitchen matches. Robin took them from her, lit the candle, and held it up.

"Now give me the paper, please, Cousin Angus," she said. "If I'm right, the clues should appear soon."

Robin held the candle to the paper so that the flame heated it but was not close enough to burn it.

"Be careful," warned Mrs. Bridge. "Don't set the paper on fire."

As they all stared, brown, spidery-looking writing started appearing on the page. Nelly gasped and put her hand to her mouth while Jo applauded wildly.

"You did it, Robin. You found the clues!" she shouted.

"How did you know they were there?" Mr. Bridge asked.

"Simple. I read it in one of my Agatha Christie books. It's called sympathetic writing. Uncle Ambrose wrote the clues on the paper with lemon juice. When you hold it to a flame, the writing appears," answered Robin.

"Well done, Cousin Robin. I'm in your debt," Angus said. "I never would have figured it out."

Robin smiled at her father. "Dad?" she asked.

"All right," he said. "Maybe there is some merit in those mysteries, but I'd like you to read other books as well."

As Nelly cleared the dishes, they pored over what Uncle Ambrose had written. Robin read it aloud:

"Congratulations, Nephew. You've jumped the first hurdle. Now on to the race and may the winner take all. Anyone who lives in McDougall House must love my city as much I do, so let's see how much you know about Edinburgh. Here is the first clue:

Picture this: I am the eye that sees Edinburgh's style
From Castle Rock to Royal Mile
I live up high, and out of sight,
And have the gift of blinding light.

Once you decipher the first clue, go to the place and another clue will be waiting for you. There are five clues in all. Good luck to you!"

Robin moved as Nelly leaned over to take her plate. "Do you know the place he's talking about here?" she asked.

"He's talking about an eye," Angus said. "I'm really not sure. It must be someplace high to see the castle and the Royal Mile."

"What's the Royal Mile?" Robin asked.

"It's the long cobblestoned walk that runs between the castle and the Palace of Holyroodhouse," Angus explained.

"What's the highest point there?" Mr. Bridge asked.

"It would be the castle so I don't really understand his clue," Angus said. He looked at his watch just as the grandfather clock struck eleven.

"It's getting late and you must be dog tired. We'll talk again tomorrow." He turned to Nelly, who was moving slowly around the table.

"You're a bit slow tonight, aren't you Nelly?" he asked.

"More dishes than usual," she said brightly. "But I'll be done soon."

"I can give you a hand," offered Mrs. Bridge.

"Thank you, madam, but it's not necessary."

"We'd better hurry and figure this out tomorrow," said Mr. Bridge, grimly. "Sounds like Tammie's got a head start."

"I'm not so sure about that," Mrs. Bridge said. "Maybe Jo

is right and Tammie was just trying to scare us off."

She roused Jo, whose head was drooping over the trifle, and the Bridges got up from the table.

"Sleep well," Angus said to them, his head still bent over the paper.

Nelly paused in her clearing up.

> *"From ghoulies and ghosties and long-leggety beasties,*
> *And things that go bump in the night,*
> *Good Lord, deliver us!"*

she quoted and grinned at Robin.

"What's that mean?" Robin asked, as Jo shivered.

"It's an old Scottish prayer," said Mr. Bridge. "Thanks, Nelly. I had forgotten that."

The Bridges filed slowly back upstairs. Jo was so tired that Mrs. Bridge had to help her take off her clothes. In a minute, without brushing her teeth or washing her face, the twelve-year-old was asleep.

"She's really worn out," Mrs. Bridge said. "Get a good night's sleep, both of you." She kissed Robin good night.

Robin finished cleaning her face and brushing her hair. Then she slipped into bed with one of her favorite mysteries, Agatha Christie's *They Do It With Mirrors*. Even though she had read it before and knew who the murderer was, she liked to reread it.

Finally she heard Angus walking up the stairs and calling good night to Nelly. Then the house, creaking and squeaking, settled into the night. Robin felt tired enough to try to sleep. She glanced over at Jo, who slept on. Robin was tempted to look under the bed and in the closet, but then she felt foolish.

"Just because Nelly said this room was haunted, I'm not going to be scared. There are no such things as ghosts," she murmured to herself. She closed her eyes and tried to will herself to sleep. She dozed off. Later, she felt herself awaken. The grandfather clock in the hall was striking three. Bong, bong, bong! Robin felt she'd never be able to fall back to sleep.

She tossed and turned, puzzling over Ambrose's riddle, wondering where all the clues would lead them, and thinking back over the events of the past day. She was just about to get up and get a drink of water when she heard a strange, scratching sound. Robin pulled the bedcovers up to her chin and looked around. There was nothing to see in the blackness of the room.

"There are no such things as ghosts," she told herself firmly.

All of a sudden, a wild burst of light flashed upon her and something white flitted through the room. The light veered crazily, hitting Robin and then Jo full in the face, blinding them, and then sliding away to reveal a shapeless white form without a face that screeched like an owl.

"Aaah!" screamed Robin.

"What! What!" yelled Jo, shaken from a sound sleep. She saw

the white thing and leaped from her bed into Robin's. She huddled, shivering, against her sister and stared, transfixed, at the pale shape.

"Help!" she shrieked. "Mom! Dad!"

Instantly, the light went off, something went clunk, and the white thing disappeared in the darkness, but Jo continued to scream over and over.

"What's the matter? What happened?" yelled Mr. and Mrs. Bridge, racing into the room.

"A ghost!" cried Jo.

"Jo, dear, you had a nightmare," Mrs. Bridge said, hugging Jo and smoothing back her tangled brown hair. She took the younger girl back to her bed.

"There was something there," Robin said. "I saw it, too."

"Not you, too, Robin," Mr. Bridge scoffed. "There's no scientific proof that ghosts exist. You know that."

"You girls are just over tired," Mrs. Bridge said. "Sleep late tomorrow."

"Stay here," moaned Jo.

"Now, Jo, you're a big girl." Then, seeing that Jo was really upset, Mrs. Bridge sighed and said, "Move over."

"I'm going back to sleep," Mr. Bridge said.

Mrs. Bridge lay down with Jo. "Turn the light off, Robin, please."

"Just a minute, Mom. I want to get some water," Robin replied.

Her mother and Jo closed their eyes. Robin slipped out of bed and walked over to the closet. She carefully examined its door and walls and then its floor. Finally, she took a black sweater out of the dresser and wrapped something up in it.

"Robin, what's taking you so long?" asked her mother. "I want to get some sleep."

"Okay, Mom. I'm just about done," Robin called. She carefully put the sweater in her bureau drawer and shut it tight. Then she got a drink of water, turned out the light, and got back into bed.

"Dad was right. There *are* no such things as ghosts!" she said to her mother, smiling in the darkness.

CHAPTER FOUR

Mysterious Things at Breakfast

 Mrs. Bridge drew back the drapes and let the sunshine flood the room.

"Robin, time to get up," she said. "It's almost nine o'clock!"

Robin sat up in bed and rubbed her eyes. "I can't believe I slept so late," she mumbled. Her mother was dressed for the day in slacks and a sweater. Robin jumped out of bed.

"I'll be ready in a minute. Where's Jo?" She looked around for her sister.

"Surprisingly enough, she woke up early this morning," her mother said. "I was worried about her, but she seems fine. She's forgotten whatever nightmare she had last night—or at least she's not talking about it. Do you know what happened?"

"Mom, there was something or somebody in the room," Robin said. "I saw it myself."

"Impossible! Now hurry up. Breakfast is waiting."

Before Robin washed her face or brushed her teeth, she looked in the drawer where she had put her sweater. There it was, covered with white cat hair, wrapped around a small, hard object.

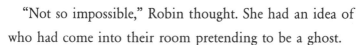

"Not so impossible," Robin thought. She had an idea of who had come into their room pretending to be a ghost.

Quickly, she washed up, dressed, and ran down the stairs. There were her parents, Jo, and Cousin Angus at the breakfast table.

"Ah, good morning, Robin," Angus said. "I understand you and Jo didn't sleep too well last night. We'll have to do better tonight."

He poured her a glass of milk and passed the toast to her.

"It's not that we didn't sleep well, Cousin Angus, but—" Robin began.

"Is there any marmalade, Angus?" Mrs. Bridge interrupted.

"Certainly," answered Angus. "And there's porridge coming up."

While Angus passed the marmalade, Mrs. Bridge whispered to Robin, "Please don't bother Cousin Angus."

Munro, the boy who had taken their luggage up the day before, appeared with a steaming tureen of oatmeal. He walked around the table and ladled it out into bowls.

When he came to Robin, she said, "Hello," but he only mumbled, turned bright red, and retreated into the kitchen.

"You mustn't mind Munro," explained Angus. "He's quite shy. He's Nelly's brother and helps out from time to time during the school holidays and when she's away."

"Is Nelly away now?" Robin asked.

"Yes, she didn't feel well last night after dinner so she asked if

 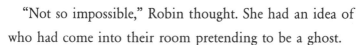

she could go home early. Of course, I said yes," Angus said. "Munro is perfectly capable of making breakfast."

Robin dropped the oatmeal spoon she was holding and bent down under the table to pick it up.

"I waited till you were all here to tell you my good news." Angus beamed. "I've figured out what the first clue is."

"That's wonderful, Cousin Angus!" cried Jo. "Let's go." She leaped out of her seat and was almost to the door.

"I thought you might want to finish your breakfast and meet me there," Angus said.

"Nothing doing," replied Jo. The rest of the family agreed and Mr. and Mrs. Bridge got up from the table.

"What is it?" Mr. Bridge asked.

"It's the Camera Obscura," Angus said. "It's a tall building that overlooks the Royal Mile. Once you're upstairs, they use mirrors to show you a panoramic view of Edinburgh."

"I can hardly wait." Jo danced impatiently. "Come on, Robin!"

"I'll just slip upstairs and get my camera," said Mr. Bridge. "I'd like to take a picture of our whole family together."

Excited to get to the first clue, Robin gulped her milk and crunched her toast. A few spoonfuls of oatmeal and she was done.

"How did you think of it?" she asked Angus, who was pacing up and down.

"I don't know. Usually I'm not very good at these things, but I racked my brains last night. This morning, when I woke up, it came to me," he said.

"Kate, have you seen my camera?" Mr. Bridge called to Mrs. Bridge from the top of the stairs.

"I'd better go up and help Bob look," Mrs. Bridge remarked to Angus.

"Fine," he said. "I'll just tell Munro we're going and not to expect us back for lunch."

Robin and Jo sat at the table. Jo played with the oatmeal left in her bowl while Robin took sips of her milk.

"About last night . . ." they both said at once.

Robin laughed and Jo continued, hanging her head.

"I'm sorry I was such a baby. I thought once I was twelve I wouldn't have nightmares anymore," she mumbled.

"It wasn't a nightmare," Robin said. Her eyes snapped as she realized how bad her sister felt. "Someone tried to spook us on purpose."

"But Mom said?"

"Mom wasn't there when it happened. I looked in the closet afterwards, when she got into bed with you. There were white cat hairs there," Robin stated.

"Oh, you think it was Lorna Doone, that cat," Jo said, her voice sounding stronger.

"I found something else, too," Robin said.

"What?" asked Jo, leaning forward.

"I found—"

"Well, it can't just have disappeared," Mrs. Bridge declared, as she and her husband came back into the dining room.

"I'm sure I put it right on the mantel in the room," Mr. Bridge said. "I can't believe it's gone. This is impossible."

"Seems like a lot of impossible things are happening," Robin remarked.

"Never mind, Robin," Mrs. Bridge said. "Are we ready to go?"

"But I was looking forward to taking that family snapshot," Mr. Bridge complained.

"Please don't tell Angus, Bob. He's got enough to worry about now. We can buy one of those cheap disposable cameras." Mrs. Bridge took her husband's arm and they walked to the front door.

"I know, but it's not the same, Kate. That was an expensive camera . . ." His voice trailed off as Cousin Angus came towards them.

"Where's your camera, Bob?" he asked.

"I must have forgotten to pack it," Mr. Bridge said. "We'll buy one. We have to have a record of this family."

Cousin Angus opened the front door of McDougall House and followed Mr. and Mrs. Bridge out. Hearing the door open and shut, Robin and Jo raced outside to catch up with the adults. The sun shone brightly but the wind was brisk.

"It almost feels like fall," Robin observed.

"Yes, it can get quite chilly up here," Angus said. "Don't forget you're farther north than you are at home."

They passed a few streets that were crammed with shops.

"Look!" cried Jo. "There's a Gap!"

Then they came to Princes Street. On one side the street was lined with stores, on the other with a garden, a green lawn, and benches. People sat on the benches eating ice cream or strolled in the parklike setting.

"How pretty," said Mrs. Bridge.

"There's the railway station," Angus pointed out, "and over here is a statue of Sir Walter Scott, the famous novelist and poet."

The girls gazed at the statue of the writer enclosed in a pavilion.

"I knew that Scott wrote *Ivanhoe*," said Mrs. Bridge, "but I don't know his poetry."

Cousin Angus looked at her and his mouth dropped open.

"Ah, but you must know this one!" He struck a pose and declaimed:

> *"Breathes there the man, with soul so dead,*
> *Who never to himself hath said,*
> *This is my own, my native land!*
> *Whose heart hath ne'er within him burn'd*
> *As home his footsteps he hath turned,*
> *From wandering on a foreign strand?"*

Angus stopped to take a deep breath and the girls rolled their eyes at each other. Meanwhile, passers-by stared as Angus began to recite again:

> *"If such there breathe, go, mark him well;*
> *For him no minstrel raptures swell;*
> *High though his titles, proud his name,*
> *Boundless his wealth as wish can claim,—"*

Angus threw out his arms and his voice rose. Jo tried to slink away but her mother caught her.

> *"Despite those titles, power and pelf,*
> *The wretch, concentered all in self,*
> *Living, shall forfeit fair renown,"—*

Robin looked down at the ground, wishing Angus would hurry up.

> *"And, doubly dying, shall go down*
> *To the vile dust, from whence he sprung,*
> *Unwept, unhonour'd, and unsung."*

During the last lines, Angus's voice boomed and people around them stopped to listen. Jo and Robin tried to hide behind their parents. When he stopped reciting, people clapped and Angus bowed.

"Well said, Cousin," Mr. Bridge remarked, applauding with the rest.

"Of course I've heard that before," Mrs. Bridge said. "Now I remember. It's from *The Lay of the Last Minstrel.*"

"That's right," Angus said. He and Mr. and Mrs. Bridge walked on while Robin and Jo slunk behind, trying to pretend they weren't together.

"That was sooooo embarrassing," Jo whispered to Robin.

"I can't believe he did that." Robin's cheeks were bright red.

The girls continued to walk behind the adults, glancing now and then at the scenery.

"Look!" Robin pointed to a spot high above them. There, a dark shape seemed to brood over the landscape. Carved out of rock, it towered over them.

"What's that, Angus?" Jo asked, forgetting her embarrassment.

"That's the castle," he said. "We'll be up there soon."

"But how will we ever get up there?" Robin asked.

"It's a walk, but we'll make it."

Turning a corner, Robin saw a bridge ahead. She and Jo ran up to look over the railing. The wind tore at their hair and sweaters, but the view was riveting.

"Look at the hills and that old, ruined mansion," Robin said.

"And look, on this side you can see the railroad," Jo answered her.

The grown-ups caught up with them and Cousin Angus said,

"Just a little more up this hill, turn right, and we'll be on the Royal Mile."

They stepped onto the cobblestoned road and started the climb to the castle. As they walked, Robin and Jo fell behind, gazing curiously at the shops that lined the way.

"Look! There's a police shop!" Jo exclaimed.

They peered in the window and saw T-shirts and other paraphernalia with police symbols on them.

Jo looked around and saw that the adults were far ahead of them now. She turned to Robin and said, "What else were you going to tell me about last night?"

"Someone was there with the cat," Robin murmured. They started walking up the hill again.

"How do you know?" whispered Jo.

"Simple. I found something on the floor after the ruckus was over," Robin whispered back.

"What was it?" Jo asked.

"It was a small flashlight," Robin said. "I think what happened is the cat was struggling with the person holding it, and the person dropped it. Remember, everything went dark quickly."

Jo shuddered. "I remember. Why would someone play such a trick on us?"

"The way I see it there are only two possibilities. Either there's something in that room that someone wants and we're in the way or we know something and someone wants to get rid of us," Robin said.

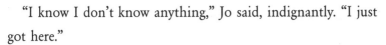

"I know I don't know anything," Jo said, indignantly. "I just got here."

"I think we'd better search the room when we get back," Robin said.

"Okay," said Jo, "but I don't like this. I don't like this at all."

CHAPTER FIVE

The Mysterious Closing

 When the girls got to the top of the Royal Mile, they saw their mother and father and Cousin Angus standing in front of a building.

"Is this it?" Jo asked.

"Yes, but it seems to be shut," Angus answered. He pointed to a sign that said "Closed Until Further Notice."

"Is the Camera Obscura usually closed during August?" Mrs. Bridge asked.

"I've never known it to be," Cousin Angus said.

"How will you find the clue now?" Robin asked. "There must be a way in."

"I'll try the door," Cousin Angus said. It opened when he turned the knob.

"Hello," he called, "anyone there?"

There was no answer. Jo and Robin peered in and saw winding stairs that seemed to circle to the top of the building.

"Why don't we climb up and see if anyone's there?" Robin asked. "There must be someone because the door's unlocked. Maybe they'll let us look around and we'll find the clue."

"I don't know," said Angus, but Jo ran up the stairs.

"Jo," called Mrs. Bridge, "come back."

"I'll get her, Cousin Kate," said Angus.

"This is a good time to buy that camera," Mr. Bridge said. "We'll meet you back here."

He and Mrs. Bridge left while Angus and Robin trudged up the stairs, which seemed to go on forever. Before they reached the top, Jo popped her head over the bannister and called, "Hurry! I've found something!"

At the top, Robin and Angus stopped for a moment to catch their breath, but Jo came over with a young man dressed in jeans and a T-shirt. He had a mop of brown hair that he kept pushing back from his forehead.

"This is Charlie. He runs the Camera Obscura. Tell them what you told me," she demanded.

Charlie ran a hand through his hair and complained, "I told her we weren't closed. We never close in August. There are too many tourists then. I don't know where she got the idea we were closed!"

"I told you—there's a sign downstairs that says you're closed. Come down and I'll show you," Jo insisted, trying to drag Charlie towards the stairs.

Charlie started to protest again, but Angus moved Jo aside gently and asked him, "Tell me, was a tall blond man here today?"

"There are so many people who come in and out of here. How am I supposed to remember?" Charlie whined.

"He might have asked you for something or wanted to search the Camera Obscura," Angus said.

"Oh, you mean that daftie who wanted me to turn the whole place upside down looking for a letter for him. I told him fair that this wasn't the post and to go down the road if he wanted a letter," Charlie muttered, indignantly.

"Not a letter," Angus said, almost to himself. "What could it be? Do you mind if I take a look around?"

"No problem. Just don't touch the machines," Charlie said.

"How does the Camera Obscura work?" Robin asked.

"It's all done with mirrors. Come and I'll show you." Charlie sat the girls down in a round room. After he adjusted the mirrors, he told the girls to look at the circle in the center of the room, where images were projected onto the mirrors.

"It's the Royal Mile," cried Robin. There in miniature were the buildings they had passed on their way up.

"The people look like ants," Jo squealed, clapping her hands.

"Watch," said Charlie, with a mischievous grin. Using an open book, he held a page into the circle so that it seemed as if the ant people were crawling up the page.

"That's so much fun!" Jo exclaimed. Charlie turned the mirrors a few times so they saw several different views. Then he moved them back.

"I'd better go down and take that sign away," Charlie explained. "I wouldn't want my boss to think I was chasing customers away."

"Thanks for the show," Robin said.

"It was great," Jo added, smiling at him.

As Charlie went to put the book away, Robin asked, "Could I see the book for a minute?"

Jo craned to look at the title. "It's *Treasure Island*," she said. "That's the one about the pirates and Long John Silver, right, Robin?"

Robin didn't answer.

"Robin . . . Hello, Robin . . ."

"I think I've found it," Robin said, slowly. "Jo, get Cousin Angus."

Jo ran to find Angus and they both hurried back to Robin.

"I think I've found it," Robin repeated, gazing at the book in her hands. All of a sudden, she looked up at Angus and smiled. "I opened the book and I saw there was a little slip of paper near the end," she said. She showed it to him and Jo.

On the slip of paper was written:

Well done, Nephew. Now on to Puzzle Two:

> *I was an author of such acclaim,*
> *Honoured and feted in my fame.*
> *To find the clue, look in this town,*
> *Remember I was of great renown.*
> *A lady gave me this space,*
> *For RLS, one last resting place.*

"I don't understand," said Jo. "What does it mean?"

"It means that for once I'm ahead of Tammie!" Angus crowed. "And it's all thanks to you girls." He hugged both of them and slipped the paper into his pocket.

"Now let's go find your parents and I'll think about this next clue," he said. They clattered down the stairs to find Mr. and Mrs. Bridge outside, taking snapshots of the Royal Mile.

"We found it! We found it!" Jo shouted to her parents.

While Jo and Mr. and Mrs. Bridge crowded around Angus, Robin looked around the street. She saw a tall blond man slip into a store as she watched. Robin rubbed her eyes. Was it Tammie? She couldn't be sure.

"Do you know where to go next?" Mrs. Bridge asked.

"I'm at sea again." Angus scratched his head. "I don't understand this clue."

"The initials RLS are about Robert Louis Stevenson, who wrote *Treasure Island*, aren't they?" Mr. Bridge asked.

"And *Kidnapped* and *Dr. Jekyll and Mr. Hyde*, among others," Angus replied.

"It talks about his final resting place," Mr. Bridge continued. "Where is Stevenson buried?"

"That's just what I don't understand," said Angus. "Stevenson was buried halfway around the world—in Samoa."

"Is there any place you think we should look?" Mrs. Bridge asked.

"Not that I can think of right now. Why don't we walk up

to the castle, and you can look around, and I can think."

As they walked the final steps to the castle, Angus pointed out a spot on the cobblestoned walk.

"This is where they used to burn witches," he announced. "There's another spot, too, in the Lawnmarket."

"Really burn them?" Jo asked, her eyes wide.

"Oh, yes," Angus said. "Edinburgh was the main center for witchcraft. Between 1479 and 1722 more than three hundred women were burned to death on this spot after being found guilty of 'working for the devil.'"

"It sounds gruesome," Robin commented.

"There were also hangings. Life was rough then. But there was one hanging that had a happy ending," Angus said.

"What was that?" asked Mr. Bridge.

"A woman named Margaret Dickson was being hanged for a crime in 1724. She was very popular and thousands turned out for her execution."

"Yuck!" said Jo.

"People came to hangings all the time," said Angus. "It was a break from the hard grind of their daily life. But to continue, Maggie's friends brought a cart and a coffin so they could give her a decent burial. As the body was cut down, they got into a fight with some medical students who wanted to take Maggie's corpse for their laboratory. The crowd was furious and gave the students a good beating. Meanwhile, her friends put Maggie in the coffin. But imagine their surprise when they got to the graveyard a few miles away and heard groans coming from inside the coffin. They opened it and found Maggie alive!"

"What happened to her?" Robin asked. "Was she hanged again?"

"The solicitors argued about it and discussed it, but finally everybody agreed that Maggie would have to go free because she had been pronounced dead by the authorities. Maggie lived for another forty years, but she never got into trouble with the law again. And forever after she was known as 'Half Hangit Maggie Dickson'!"

By the time Angus had finished his story, they had reached the castle. Robin could see that what, from a distance, seemed like a dark, brooding shape, up close was a huge group of buildings that looked as if they had been hacked out of rock. The sides of the castle were black and rough.

"It sure doesn't look like a fairy tale castle," she remarked.

"No, this was a place for battles, not royal luxury," Angus said. He looked at his watch. "Come, we just have time to meet Mons Meg. Then something special will happen at one o'clock."

"Who is Mons Meg?" Jo asked. "Was she a witch?"

Angus chuckled as he led them to the rear of the castle and up to a cavelike structure.

"In here," he gestured to them.

The Bridges walked into a dark, dank stone room. There was a huge black cannon in the middle.

"Introducing Mons Meg." Angus bowed to them and then the cannon.

"Wow," said Jo. "This is huge."

"And it could fire a three-hundred-and-thirty-pound cannonball at a target two-and-a-half miles away," Mr. Bridge read from his guidebook.

"Why is it inside?" Robin asked.

"To protect it from the weather," Angus said. "Mons Meg dates back to the fifteenth century. But there are lots of other things to see here, too."

As they walked out of the room, Jo ran out into the open courtyard and towards the ramparts of the castle.

BOOM!

"What was that?" she yelled.

"It's the One O'Clock Gun," Angus said. "All over Edinburgh, people set their clocks and watches by that gun. They know that it's fired every day except Sunday at exactly one o'clock."

As Robin turned away from the guns and looked back towards the castle, she thought she caught a glimpse of someone who looked familiar.

"Am I seeing things?" she thought. Now the person she thought she saw wasn't Tammie, it was Nelly, Angus's cook.

CHAPTER SIX

The Mysterious Deacon

 After inspecting the Crown Jewels and the Stone of Destiny, Robin and Jo were ready to leave the castle.

"I'm starved," grumbled Jo. "I'm so hungry my stomach is rumbling."

"I'm so sorry," apologized Angus. "We'll stop for lunch immediately."

Encouraged by Angus's attitude, Jo clutched her stomach and moaned and groaned.

"Take no notice of her, Angus," said Mr. Bridge. "She's hungry all the time, but only for pizza."

Jo brightened. "Do they have pizza in Scotland?" she asked.

"Of course," replied Angus, "but there's no place near here. I thought perhaps we'd have lunch with the Deacon. You might like that."

"With the Deacon?" Mrs. Bridge asked, raising her eyebrows.

"Oh, not a real deacon," added Angus, hastily. "I meant Deacon Brodie. Do you know about him?"

"Was he a church official?" Robin asked.

"No, a deacon in those days was a public figure like a

politician," Angus said. "Any road, William Brodie came from a well-respected family. He was a carpenter and sat on the town council and was a wealthy man. But he was a terrible gambler and he would drink all night in the taverns. To support his bad habits, he began stealing from people. He would make clay impressions of their keys during the day when he was working for them, and at night he robbed their houses."

"Did they ever catch him?" Jo asked.

"Yes. He took on three men to help him, and they stole a huge amount of silk from a merchant. The authorities put it out that anyone informing on the criminals would not be arrested for the crime. One of Brodie's men testified against him and he was caught before he could escape to America. You almost wound up with one of Edinburgh's most famous criminals."

"What a story!" Mr. Bridge stared at Angus.

"Yes, it inspired Robert Louis Stevenson. Respected man by day, robber by night. That's how Stevenson thought up Dr. Jekyll and Mr. Hyde," Angus remarked, as they walked through a small entryway into a courtyard marked "Brodie's Close."

"And here's Deacon Brodie's Tavern," said Angus. He opened the door to a small restaurant lined with dark wooden beams on the ceiling and filled with tables and benches.

While they ate their sandwiches, Robin and Jo speculated about the clue they had found at the Camera Obscura.

"Do you think the next clue could be here?" Robin asked. "After all, Stevenson wrote about Deacon Brodie."

"Stevenson wrote about many places in Edinburgh. If we tried to track them all down, we'd never find the will in time," Angus informed them. "Besides, it said something about his final resting place. Stevenson never stayed here."

"Do you think it's a graveyard?" Jo asked. "That's so spooky." She shivered and Mrs. Bridge put her arm around Jo's shoulders.

"I think you've heard too many ghost stories today," she said.

"Oh, Mom, you don't have to treat me like a baby. I like ghost stories. I'm not scared!" Jo retorted shrilly.

"Maybe you'd like the ghost tour they have here at night," said Angus.

Mrs. Bridge frowned but Mr. Bridge said, "That sounds like fun."

"It really is quite silly but the girls would probably enjoy it. They tell ghost stories associated with this part of Edinburgh, and they're very interesting."

"Mom, can we go?" Jo begged.

"I'd love that," Robin said, at the same time.

"We'll all go," announced Mr. Bridge, firmly.

"You have to sign up at the Witchery," said Angus. "We can go there when we've finished."

"What's the Witchery?" asked Jo, eagerly. "Is it a school for witches?"

Angus laughed. "No, it's a restaurant and a very nice one, too. I'll take you there now if you've finished."

"We'll meet you there." Jo jumped up and tugged at Angus, pulling him towards the door.

Robin went to the ladies' room. When she came out, she overheard her parents arguing.

"I don't think it's a good idea," Mrs. Bridge said angrily. "After all, she had another nightmare last night . . . "

"You can't baby her forever," Mr. Bridge replied. "We shouldn't encourage her to be afraid of things."

"I don't baby her. I'm her mother. I'm trying to take care of her." Mrs. Bridge walked out of the restaurant, leaving Mr. Bridge staring after her.

"Dad . . . Dad," Robin said, "let's go."

Her father turned to her and smiled.

"Sorry, Robin, I was thinking about something else," he said.

"I know. You were worrying about Jo, but there really was someone in the room last night," Robin insisted.

"Don't you start, too, Robin," her father said, sternly. "I refuse to talk about this now. Let's have a pleasant afternoon."

Robin sighed and answered, "Yes, Dad."

Outside a stone building near the castle, Angus, Jo, and Mrs. Bridge were waiting for them.

Mr. Bridge got out his guidebook.

"Where would you like to go now?" he asked Mrs. Bridge. "We're near Gladstone's Land."

"What's that?" Jo asked.

"It's a museum," Mr. Bridge replied.

Jo wrinkled her nose. "Do we have to?"

"I think I'll leave you now and rack my brains about the clue," Angus said.

"Where will you go?" Jo asked.

"Back to the house and have some tea," he responded.

"Robin and I could go with you," Jo said. "I don't want to go to any old museum."

Meanwhile, Mr. and Mrs. Bridge thumbed through the guidebook.

"Here." They both spoke at once. "The girls might like this. It's just what we were talking about."

"What's that?" asked Robin.

"The Writers' Museum," said Mrs. Bridge. "Let's go, girls."

"Another old museum," grumbled Jo. "I'm sick of museums. I want to go with Cousin Angus."

"Let's go, Jo," ordered her father. "We'll see you back at the house, Angus."

"I'll leave you a message if I go out," said Angus. "We'll have dinner at six and then go on to the ghost tour together."

Dragging her heels on the cobblestones, Jo walked with Robin behind their parents.

"I thought if we went back with Cousin Angus, we could search our room," Jo whispered.

"Nice try, but I don't think they'll leave us alone until we get back," Robin hissed back.

As they walked, Robin looked over her shoulder.

"Why do you keep looking back?" Jo asked.

"Before I had the feeling someone was watching us," Robin said. "I still have that feeling."

"It's creepy," said Jo. She began turning every second to see if she could catch someone behind them. As they walked into yet another courtyard, she ran smack into two men with swords.

"Ods bodkins, what kind of creatures are these?" one man asked, as he put his sword down.

"I can't tell. Are they boys or girls? Or bodies from another land?" the other man remarked, pulling down his green velvet doublet. "This one's got short hair so it can't be a girl."

"At your service, creatures." The first man gestured gracefully.

Then the two men began a sword fight. They moved back and forth, parrying and lunging swiftly across the brick courtyard. Finally, they stopped, bowed, and wiped the sweat from their foreheads.

"Who are you?" Jo asked, as her parents applauded.

"We're actors from the theater around the corner," answered one man. "Sorry for teasing you, but we just couldn't resist."

"That's all right," said Robin. "At first I thought I had stepped into another century."

"When is your play?" Mr. Bridge asked.

"In three weeks. We're in rehearsals now," said the first man. "Come see us."

"I'm afraid we'll be home by then," responded Mr. Bridge. "But break a leg."

"Thank you, kind sir," the first man replied, and the men walked back through the courtyard.

"Why did you tell them to break a leg, Dad?" Jo asked.

"That's a way of wishing people in the theater good luck," her father said.

Jo became lost in thought as they walked on to the museum.

"Look up, girls!" Mr. Bridge pointed to an old brick building with a tower. "According to my guidebook, this house was built in 1622 for William Grey. He had the words 'Feare The Lord and Depart From Evil' carved above the door along with his initials."

"There they are," Robin pointed out. "But what do the initials G. S. stand for?"

Mr. Bridge turned the page of his guidebook. "They're the initials of his wife, Geida Smith."

"What's inside the museum, Dad?" Jo asked.

"It's dedicated to three famous writers of Scotland, Sir Walter Scott, Robert Burns, and Robert Louis Stevenson," he replied.

As they entered the museum, Robin glanced around.

"Not many people here today," she commented.

"No, we don't get that many visitors," agreed a woman who was sitting at the front desk. She tore off four tickets from a roll and handed them to Mr. Bridge. "Certainly not as many as they get at the castle or the palace. Now where are you from, loves?" she asked Robin and Jo.

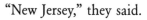

"New Jersey," they said.

"The Isle of Jersey?" the woman asked.

"No," said Mrs. Bridge. "The state of New Jersey in the United States."

"Ah, now I see." The woman wrote something in a black, leather-covered book. "We like to keep track of where our visitors come from. Well, welcome to Lady Stair's house."

"I'm Jo and this is my sister, Robin," Jo said.

"Pleased to meet you, dear. I'm Mrs. Dundee," the woman answered.

Jo walked over to a narrow staircase on the side of the room.

"Let's start here," she said.

"Just be careful going up and down the stairs," Mrs. Dundee warned. "When Mr. Grey had this place built, he installed an early form of protection against burglars. He made the height of each step different, so it's hard to run up and down the staircase—and easy to trip and fall!"

"Why did you say 'welcome to Lady Stair's house?'" Robin asked.

"Just a manner of speaking. Lady Stair bought this house in 1719 and it's been called by her name ever since," said Mrs. Dundee.

Robin slowly followed Jo up the narrow, winding, brick stairs, with their parents behind them. They came to an exhibit of pictures of Robert Burns and Sir Walter Scott and their books

 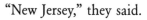

and letters, and as the others looked around, Robin stared off into space.

"What's the matter with you, Robin?" her mother asked. "I thought you'd be interested in this."

"I'm going to go downstairs to the Robert Louis Stevenson exhibit, Mom," she said. "I'll take Jo with me."

"You won't take Jo anyplace," retorted Jo. "But I will go with you."

"Just be careful going down those stairs," Mrs. Bridge warned. "Oh, look at this, Bob." Both she and Mr. Bridge were intent on examining the writers' letters.

Robin was silent as they walked down the twisting stairs, back to the main floor, and then down another set of narrow stairs to the basement and the Robert Louis Stevenson exhibit.

"Good. No one's here. Help me look around," Robin said.

"Look around for what?" Jo asked.

"The clue. It all adds up. Remember, the clue Cousin Angus found? It talked about a lady giving Stevenson a resting place. Well, this is Lady Stair's house, and this is a resting place for lots of Stevenson's things, like his books and his letters. I think the clue is here," Robin stated.

"If it is, how come Cousin Angus didn't think of it?" Jo asked.

"I don't know. He seems to have a mental block about this," Robin replied. "It's almost as if he expects Tammie to beat him."

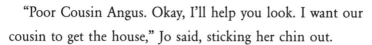

"Poor Cousin Angus. Okay, I'll help you look. I want our cousin to get the house," Jo said, sticking her chin out.

But after ten minutes of looking, the girls hadn't found anything.

"It's not as if this was a huge room," Jo said.

"Yes, it's pretty small, about as big as our bedroom at home," Robin agreed. "We've looked in all the display cases and under them. We even looked on the floor. Where could he have hidden it?"

The girls scanned the room, trying to find something, anything, that could be the clue.

Robin directed Jo. "You take this side of the room. I'll take the other. Maybe we missed something."

Robin moved carefully around her part of the exhibit. Here were the same letters in the glass cases she had examined carefully, the same pens that Stevenson had used, the same pictures on the wall . . .

Robin stood still for a moment. Then she called frantically, "Jo, come here, quickly!"

"What is it?" Jo asked.

"What's that a picture of?"

Jo read the inscription carefully from the bottom of the photo. "The author's final resting place in Samoa."

"But I don't see a clue in the picture," she added.

Robin reached behind the picture. When she removed her hand, she held a piece of white paper.

"You found it! You found it!" Jo danced around her. "Now, Angus is sure to get the house. Hurray! Hurray!"

A shadow fell over them, and the girls looked up.

"I wouldn't be too sure about that," said Tammie, as he stretched out his hand for the clue.

CHAPTER SEVEN

The Mysterious Museum

 The girls shrank back as Tammie approached them, his hand outstretched for the clue Robin had just found.

"Give me that clue," Tammie demanded, his green eyes glaring at Robin.

Stubbornly, Robin shook her head. "I found it," she insisted, "and I'm giving it to Cousin Angus."

Tammie's thin lips curled up in an evil-looking smile.

"You don't think that I'm going to let two little girls stand in my way, do you?" He grabbed Robin roughly by the shoulder and tried to snatch the piece of paper out of her hand. Jo dodged out from behind Robin's back.

"I'm going to get Dad," she yelled, and tore off up the stairs. Robin heard a thud and then Jo's wail.

"Not very good stairs to race up," Tammie sneered. "Well, she'll be occupied for a while. Now give me that paper."

His hands dug fiercely into Robin's shoulders and they started to ache. He was strong and Robin wondered if she'd be able to withstand the pressure.

"My father will be here any minute." Robin gritted her teeth and clutched the paper so hard it crumpled in her hand.

"And what will he do?" Tammie snarled, shaking her hard. "He has no claim to this paper. It's mine and I would have gotten it if you hadn't found it first."

"If Cousin Angus were here, I would have given it to him," Robin groaned.

"But he wasn't smart enough to follow you." Tammie snickered. "You seem to be a very clever miss. I knew I was right to track you down and see where you'd go. That dunder-head cousin of mine never would have figured this out."

Tammie laughed and relaxed his hands for a minute. Taking advantage of his lack of pressure, Robin slithered out of his grasp, but he grabbed her again as she tried to slip past him. She strained her ears, hoping to hear her father's footsteps, but all she heard were the muffled sounds of people moving around downstairs.

"It would be a shame to break your arm," Tammie remarked, in a matter-of-fact way, "but really, you're giving me no choice."

He bent her arm behind her back and started twisting.

"Dad!" yelped Robin. "Help!" She screamed as loud as she could, but no one came.

Finally, she could bear the pain no longer.

"All right," she screamed. "Let me go and I'll give it to you."

Tammie dropped her arm, and Robin kicked him hard in the knee.

"Ow!" he yelled. He bent over for a minute to rub his knee, and in a flash she was out of the room. Moving as fast as she could, she ran up the uneven staircase. She could hear Tammie behind her, breathing hard and cursing.

Robin rounded the stairs with Tammie hard on her heels. She was almost at the main floor now, and she bounded up a little faster. Trying to avoid the rough places on the bricks, Robin had only one thought—to reach her father and mother and safety.

"Stop that girl!" Tammie yelled. "She's stolen something from the exhibit!"

Robin jumped the last set of steps and reached the main floor, only to barrel into Mrs. Dundee, the woman who had given them their tickets. A second later, Tammie smacked into Robin from behind.

"What's all this fuss, now?" she scolded. "I've got one child with a skinned knee being patched up. Now another comes running in here like Deacon Brodie's ghost was after her. This is a nice, quiet museum, not one of those discos you Americans are used to."

Tammie immediately turned to the woman and in his most polite manner said, "This young Sassenach took something from the Stevenson exhibit. I was just trying to get it back."

"No, you weren't," retorted Robin. "You were trying to break my arm." She launched into an explanation of Uncle Ambrose's will and the competition between Angus and Tammie and tried to explain the clue she had found. The woman held up her hand.

"I'm not understanding a bit of this," she said, peering at Robin as if she were an alien.

"Robin! What's going on here?" Mr. Bridge surveyed the scene as he came through the hall. "We just got Jo bandaged up. She took quite a tumble on the stairs, and she told us something about you and Tammie. Mom's with her now in the ladies' room."

"Tammie tried to break my arm!" Robin shouted.

Mr. Bridge glared at Tammie and put his arm around Robin.

"Stay away from my daughter!" He glared at the tall blond man.

"I'll be happy to," Tammie replied calmly. "I'll just take what belongs to me—the clue."

"I thought you said the wee lass took something from the exhibit," Mrs. Dundee said. She looked at Tammie suspiciously.

"She did," Tammie muttered.

"No, I just took this piece of paper that Uncle Ambrose hid there," Robin said. She showed the woman the piece of paper.

"I'd better look at it to see if it's part of the exhibit." Mrs.

Dundee slipped on a pair of gold-rimmed spectacles she took from her sweater pocket.

"Hmm! This doesn't sound like anything Stevenson wrote," she remarked, chuckling. She read aloud what was written on the paper:

> *"This friend was a friend for all his life*
> *Through rain and snow, trouble and strife.*
> *Now water commemorates his name*
> *And informs us all of this little one's fame."*

She turned to look at Tammie, but he pushed past Robin, nearly knocking her over, as soon as he heard the clue. Then he vanished.

"Oh, no, now he's gone and he'll find the next clue before Cousin Angus will," Robin wailed. "And I was so excited when I found it."

Tears came to her eyes and her father hugged her.

"Don't fash yourself, lass," Mrs. Dundee said, with a little smile. "I saw him as he went past you. He was repeating the little rhyme over and over so he wouldn't forget it, the fule. I don't think he has a clue what it means. But I do."

"You do?" Robin turned eagerly to the older woman.

"Robin! Are you all right? Is Tammie still here?" Jo hobbled over to Robin, a white bandage gleaming on her knee. Mrs.

Bridge followed her, pushing back her thick red hair.

"I tried to get Mom and Dad, but then I fell," Jo said, looking down at her knee.

"It's all right," Robin reassured her. "He tried to break my arm, but I got away from him."

Mrs. Bridge looked grim and started talking to her husband, while Robin filled Jo in on what had happened.

"I don't like this at all," Mrs. Bridge declared. "I think we should move to a hotel and leave Angus and Tammie to figure these clues out on their own."

"I feel sorry for Angus," Mr. Bridge said, "but of course the girls' safety comes first."

"Oh, no, Mom," Robin cried, "we've done so well. We'll be safe. Please, we have to help Cousin Angus. He'll never get it on his own. We can't let Tammie win the house."

"Your father and I will discuss this, Robin," Mrs. Bridge said firmly. "I'm sorry you girls ever got involved."

"We'll talk about it on the way back to the house." Mr. Bridge took Mrs. Bridge's hand and they walked out of the museum.

Jo and Robin started to follow slowly.

"Pssst . . . lassie . . ."

Robin turned to see who had called to her. It was Mrs. Dundee. She was waving the note.

"Don't you want your clue? After all that fuss, I'm thinking you don't want to be leaving without it," she said.

Robin went to get it, but her thoughts were centered on her parents. Would they make her and Jo stop following the clues? Would they move out of Angus's house and into a hotel? It occurred to her that if they did, Tammie would get his way without any problem. She and Jo were Angus's best hope of solving the mystery of Uncle Ambrose's clues.

Mrs. Dundee held out the note.

"Here 'tis. The one who wrote this had a way with words, even though he's no Robert Louis Stevenson."

"No, it was written by my Uncle Ambrose. It's a competition," Robin tried to explain again.

"And that black-hearted fellow's trying to win?" Mrs. Dundee asked.

"Oh, yes," Robin said.

"I didn't like the way he stared at you," Mrs. Dundee said, "so I'll give you some help. I know what your cousin was trying to hint at in this clue. It's about a wee doggie."

"A dog?" Robin couldn't believe her ears. "What does a dog have to do with it?"

Jo was fidgeting in the background. "Come on, Robin," she yelled. "Mom and Dad are calling for us."

"Have you never heard of Greyfriars Bobby?" Mrs. Dundee asked.

"No," said Robin.

"Och, that's because you're a Sassenach," Mrs. Dundee said.

"That's what Tammie called me before," Robin said. "What does that mean?"

"It's what we call people who aren't from Scotland. But there's your clue. Greyfriars Bobby. That's what it's about. You look it up." Mrs. Dundee walked back to her desk and sat down and started going through some papers.

Robin would have liked to ask her more, but Jo was waving at her frantically.

"Come on, Robin. Let's go!"

Outside, they joined her parents, who were waiting for them impatiently.

"What took you girls so long?" Mrs. Bridge asked, looking around suspiciously.

"I went to the ladies' room," Robin said. "Where are we going now?"

"Let's have some tea," said Mrs. Bridge. "I think we all need some refreshment."

Jo lagged behind with Robin as they walked down the cobblestoned street.

"Why did you lie? What were you talking with that lady about?" she asked.

Robin's eyes sparkled. "She told me she knew what the next clue meant."

"What did it say?" Jo asked. "Remember, I was in the

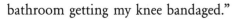

bathroom getting my knee bandaged."

Robin handed her the note and walked slowly while Jo read it.

"What does it mean?" Jo asked.

"She said something about a dog and Greyfriars Bobby."

"Where can we find out about it?" Jo wondered.

"We'll take a look at Dad's guidebook. If it's not there, we'll have to wait until we get back and ask Cousin Angus," Robin answered.

They came to a little cottage with a sign that read "Clarinda's Tea Room." Once inside, Mrs. Bridge relaxed at their table and slipped off her shoes.

"My feet are killing me. I'm going to order a nice pot of hot tea. That'll help revive me," she announced.

Jo and Robin chose lemonade and shortbread cookies, while Mr. Bridge had tea and a scone with raspberry jam.

"Dad, can I take a look at your guidebook?" Robin asked. "I want to figure out what we'd like to see next."

"The next thing we're doing is going back to the house and talking with Cousin Angus," stated Mrs. Bridge. Mr. Bridge nodded and Robin guessed they had discussed it thoroughly while they were walking to the tea room.

"This is supposed to be a vacation," Mr. Bridge said.

While her parents sipped their tea and ate, Robin thumbed furiously through the guidebook. Then she came upon a page and started reading intently.

 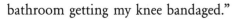

"What are you reading, Robin?" Jo inquired, trying to look over Robin's shoulder.

"This is very interesting," Robin said. "I'll read it to you."

"Greyfriars Kirk is the burial place of John Gray, a policeman who owned the dog Greyfriars Bobby. The dog got his name when Gray died and was buried in the churchyard and the dog refused to leave his master's grave. Eventually, Bobby adopted a local restaurant. Tourists came every day to see the dog arrive each lunchtime. When Bobby died in 1872, a baroness had a fountain put up in the dog's name. It's at the top of Candlemaker Row."

"I think we should go there next," Jo announced. "I'd like to see that."

Mrs. Bridge rubbed her left foot and said, "The only place we're going is back to Cousin Angus's house. Before we see another sight, I'm going to have a talk with him."

The Mysterious Box

 Try as they might, Robin and Jo couldn't persuade their parents to continue sightseeing.

"I even offered to go to another museum," Jo pouted, as they walked back to the house.

"I was afraid to tell Mom that we wanted to see Greyfriars Bobby because of the clue. She's so dead set against the whole thing now. But we'll tell Cousin Angus about it and he can get it," Robin said.

"I hope so," Jo answered. "He's such a slowpoke. I'll bet Tammie's snatched that clue already."

"He can't be that sharp if he had to follow us to discover the clues," Robin said, smiling at the thought.

"Yes, for all his craftiness, he's not that smart," Jo agreed, cheering up.

When they reached the house, Robin and Jo wanted to tell Angus about the clue they had discovered, but Mrs. Bridge was determined to speak to their cousin privately.

"Girls, we want some time alone with Cousin Angus," she said. She began to look for their cousin. He wasn't in the living room.

"Angus!" Mr. Bridge called. There was no answer. Mr. Bridge called again and Nelly came out of the kitchen.

"He's not here. He had to go out. But he left you this wee note." She indicated a piece of paper on the mahogany sideboard, then disappeared back into the kitchen.

Mr. Bridge took the note and began to read it:

> "*Dear Cousins,*
>
> *I had to go out for a bit, but I'll return by dinnertime. Words fail me when I think of how you've helped me so far with the most important contest of my life. I can only let Robert Louis Stevenson speak for me—'So long as we are loved by others, I would almost say that we are indispensable; and no man is useless while he has a friend.' Thank you, dear cousins, for being my friends.—Angus*"

Mr. Bridge groaned.

"Oh dear," sighed Mrs. Bridge. "This is going to be harder than I thought. I'm going to lie down before dinner and get my strength back."

She marched upstairs with Mr. Bridge following her, then turned at the top of the staircase. "Girls," she said, "I want to see you in your room right now. No running around. We have to make sure you're safe."

Jo and Robin trudged up the stairs and stalked into their room.

"Don't you feel just like a baby?" Jo asked. "Now we have to stay in our room."

Robin threw herself on the bed and sulked. Then she straightened up.

"We forgot. We were going to search the room. Remember?" she reminded her sister.

"Why?" asked Jo.

"Because someone wants us out of here," Robin said.

"Do you think it's because we're so good at solving clues?" Jo asked.

"Maybe, but I think there's something hidden in this room that's important," Robin said.

The girls started looking under the rug on the floor, and then moved up to the walls.

"Let's tap them. If it sounds hollow, maybe there's a secret panel," Robin said.

Robin and Jo thumped the walls thoroughly, but found nothing.

"What about in the closet?" Jo asked. "That's where the ghost came from."

"Of course," Robin said.

They opened the door to the large walk-in closet. There were boxes on the floor and on a shelf above the rail where the girls' clothes were hanging.

"Achoo!" sneezed Jo. She sneezed again.

Robin picked up a box and opened it. Inside was a pink hat with a long white plume. She put the lid back on and opened another one. This time, she found a pink silk dress neatly folded in tissue paper.

"I think these are Uncle Ambrose's wife's clothes." Robin took the dress out of the closet and into the bedroom and held it up near the painting.

"Yes, it's the same dress," Jo said. "I wonder where the jewels are."

"Let's look."

They searched through all the boxes until they came to a flat blue velvet box in the back of the closet.

"Maybe this is it. It looks like it would hold jewelry." Robin snapped it open, but the box was empty.

"I wonder why the box is empty," Robin thought aloud. "All the other boxes have something in them. Why would they keep an empty box here?"

"Don't know," said Jo. She was too busy trying on the pink silk dress.

"How do I look?" she asked.

"Silly," Robin said. "That dress is miles too big for you."

"The trouble with you is you have no imagination," sniffed Jo. She lifted the trailing hem of the dress. "Now, just imagine this dress is shorter. What do you think?"

"I still think it looks silly." Robin giggled.

Jo picked up one of the pillows lying on her bed and threw it at her sister. Robin threw it back. Soon all the pillows were flying and Robin was chasing Jo, who kept tripping in the dress.

They were so busy they didn't hear the knock at the door. When Nelly opened it and stuck her head into the room, she gasped.

"You're wearing madam's dress. No one ever is allowed to wear it," she shrilled, staring at Jo.

"I'm sorry," said Jo. "I was just trying it on."

"Where did you find that?" Nelly snapped, her eyes flashing.

"In the closet," Jo answered, meekly.

"Take it off and put it away immediately. In fact, take it off and I'll see it's put away properly. The dress isn't some plaything. It's part of the house's history and Mr. Ambrose is turning over in his grave to see you playing dress up in it," Nelly scolded. She grabbed the dress from Jo's shaking hands and stalked off, saying "Dinner's ready" before she slammed the door shut.

"What was that all about?" Robin wondered.

"I guess I shouldn't have tried the dress on," Jo mumbled.

"She acts like she owns it," Robin said. "Are you okay?"

"Uh-huh. Let's go eat. I just hope she doesn't poison my food," Jo replied.

But there was nothing wrong with their dinner—golden brown roasted chicken and creamy mashed potatoes. Nelly served them calmly. Munro helped her with the vegetables. But Cousin Angus was still missing.

"Where is he?" Jo asked.

"He rang up and said he'd be a while longer. Were you supposed to do something later?" Nelly asked, smoothing her apron over her skirt.

"We're supposed to go on the ghost tour with him," Jo blurted out.

"I expect he'll meet you there," Nelly said.

"It seems strange that he didn't ask to speak to us," Mr. Bridge remarked.

"He was on one of those public phones and the pips were going," Nelly said. When she saw the Bridges looking at her strangely, she said, "The pips! You know, he was running out of coins."

"Oh, you mean his time was up on the phone and it was beeping," Mrs. Bridge said. "We call 'pips' 'beeps.'"

"Yes, that's it," Nelly said, and retreated back to the kitchen.

By the time Nelly served ice cream and shortbread cookies for dessert, the girls were dancing with impatience to be out of the house.

"Ready?" Jo asked. She looked at her mother and father. "You two are such slowpokes."

"I'm not sure we shouldn't wait for Cousin Angus," Mrs. Bridge said slowly.

"You heard Nelly," Robin replied, impatiently. "He'll probably meet us there."

"The girls will be with us," Mr. Bridge said. "Nothing can happen to them."

Reluctantly, Mrs. Bridge agreed and went to get a sweater. Then the four of them set out for the ghost tour.

When they reached the Witchery restaurant, a small crowd had gathered. Most of them seemed to be tourists, but now and then Robin heard a Scottish accent. Then the crowd hushed. A young man, his face white with makeup, appeared suddenly from the restaurant doorway.

He was dressed in a long black cape and he bowed to the crowd and said, "Allow me to introduce myself. I'm Adam Lyal, deceased."

Here and there people laughed, and he went on, "Unfortunately, my name is in the records—on the list of executions. I came to a sad end on the hangman's scaffold on the twenty-seventh of March in 1811. You may well ask why I lost my life. It was a small matter of highway robbery, which the citizens of Edinburgh seemed to take seriously. But now I've returned from the dead to take you on a walk through all the haunted alleyways and ghostly courtyards of this old city."

As he led the group through tiny alleys, Adam talked about the many witches and ghosts who were part of Edinburgh's history, as well as some of the city's customs. In one dark passageway, he stopped and said, "In the 1800s, surgeons were keen to use real bodies to study anatomy. But officially, each medical school was allowed only one body, of a criminal who had been executed, per year. Of course, one body a year was not enough, so body snatchers came into fashion. On a moonlit night like tonight, you'd see dark shapes roaming the graveyards, digging up the bodies for the doctors."

As he spoke, Robin and Jo looked down the alley in horror to see a person lugging something that looked like a body. Dressed in dark clothing, the man raced up the slight hill and threw the body at the crowd. For a minute, they were stunned, then some of them burst out laughing.

"It's a dummy!" one man cried. He held it aloft to show it was a stuffed dummy with a clown's face painted on it.

"But there were many dangers for the living, as well, in those dark, perilous days," Adam continued. "Edinburgh was a disease-ridden place." He held a white handkerchief to his nose daintily. "Let us say that sanitary conditions were not what they should have been."

He walked them through another alley. "Edinburgh's citizens had the quaint custom of throwing out all their filth into the streets. They excused this practice by calling out 'gardyloo' from the French saying '*garde à l'eau*' or 'watch out for the water.'"

He paused for a moment. Just then the figure in the dark clothing raced up again, threw a bucket of water at the crowd, and shouted, "Gardyloo!"

Mr. Bridge wiped his face with his handkerchief and muttered, "I see we're going to be in for a lot of bad jokes on this tour."

Robin and Jo laughed and so did Mrs. Bridge.

Adam moved them on and soon they were on a street below the Royal Mile, being regaled with more stories about ghosts and witches.

Finally he ended with, "For my last story, I'd like to tell you about something a little more pleasant than what we've been discussing. You may not believe this, ladies and gentlemen, but at times Scotland has more than its share of snow and ice. I know that's difficult to imagine, but it's true. And, of course, there are all sorts of things people like to do with snow. My story starts on an icy February morning in 1870. There had been a heavy snowfall and some students began throwing snowballs at people on the South Bridge. It was fun until a large group of policemen came to the site to stop the students. The students had stockpiled a large amount of snowballs and began pelting the police with them until the law enforcers had to retreat. Then the students ran to the university, locked the gate, and waited with more snowballs for the police to come. Deciding on a strategy, some police entered by the main gate, while others went in the back way. They captured thirteen of the students, using their nightsticks. By the time the police marched their prisoners out, onlookers began jeering and throwing snowballs at the officers.

In the end, the students were released by the courts because . . .
after all . . . the sun came out and the evidence . . . well, ladies
and gentlemen . . . it just melted away."

With that, Adam disappeared into the darkness, leaving
Robin and Jo with their mouths open.

"That was great," Jo said, with a broad smile.

"But oh those jokes," Mr. Bridge said, shaking his head.

"Oh, come on, Bob, they weren't that bad," Mrs. Bridge
told him.

Meanwhile, Robin looked around at all the dark courtyards
and alleys. She'd never think of Edinburgh the same way as
before, even in the daylight. As they walked back to the house,
she and Jo chuckled as they remembered some of the funnier
pranks that had been pulled on them during the ghost walk.

Finally, they reached the house. Mr. Bridge looked at
his watch.

"Pretty late," he commented. "I guess we'd better not disturb
Cousin Angus. Can you girls get to your room quietly?"

"Sure, Dad," Robin answered, although Jo started giggling
immediately. The house was dark inside and they all climbed the
stairs as quietly as they could. At the door of their room, Robin
and Jo kissed their parents good night.

"I am so tired," yawned Jo, as Robin turned on the light in
their room.

Then both girls stopped cold in the doorway.

"Wow!" exclaimed Jo.

"Look at this! I can't believe it!" Robin was as appalled as her sister. The room had been turned upside down. Their clothes were thrown on the floor, the sheets and covers had been ripped off the bed, even Robin's books had been tossed around.

"What do we do now?" Jo asked.

CHAPTER NINE

The Mysterious Missing Angus

 "I told you there was something in this room!" Robin cried.

Jo repeated, "What do we do now?"

Robin closed the door swiftly. "I'll tell you what we're going to do. We're going to clean this mess up and not tell Mom and Dad because if we do tell them, we'll never, never get to do anything on our own. We'll be locked up like prisoners."

"But, Robin," whined Jo, "I hate cleaning up even when I've made the mess myself. I absolutely refuse to clean up someone else's." Jo stamped her foot.

"All right, I'll do it myself." Robin started making the bed again, pulling the sheets back tight and stuffing the pillows into their cases.

Jo watched her for a few minutes, her arms folded. Then she sighed.

"Okay, okay, I can't let you do everything by yourself. I'll help. But you owe me."

"For what?" Robin asked. "I didn't do this. But whoever did made a big mistake."

"Why's that?"

Robin smiled smugly. "Because they've let us know there's something here that's valuable."

"How do you know they haven't found it?" Jo asked as she was putting Robin's books back on the nightstand.

"I don't know for sure, but I think we must have interrupted whoever it was. Otherwise, they would have cleaned up," Robin reasoned, "and not left this mess for us."

"Oh, great, now I'm really scared. There are robbers in the house." Jo shivered.

"I'm sure they left when they heard us coming in. Remember, the house was dark. They could have gone out the back way." Robin looked at her sister and added, "I'm absolutely sure they've gone."

"Please go and check," Jo pleaded.

"You really expect me to go downstairs in this dark house and check for robbers?" Robin looked at her sister in disbelief.

Jo folded her arms. "Yes."

"You're such a baby," Robin said. "All right. I'm not scared. If I run into anybody, I can always call for Dad and Mom. But you have to finish cleaning up."

"Okay." Jo started attacking the pile of clothes on the floor vigorously.

Reluctantly, Robin left the room. She told Jo to leave the door open, and the bright light streaming from the open doorway lit the dark passage down the stairs. Robin crept down slowly and softly, trying not to disturb her parents. At the bottom of the stairs, she flicked the light switch but the light didn't go on. Then Robin was walking almost blindly through the darkened dining room.

"Ouch!" She had bumped into the dining table. She felt for a light switch on the wall, but her hands only slid over a smooth surface. There was no reassuring switch that meant light. Stillness blanketed the house, and suddenly Robin felt cold. She heard a muffled thump, and her heart stopped for a minute. Then she realized that it was cold enough in the early morning hours for the house's heating system to go on. She sniffed the air and smelled the toasty, wooly smell of the heat coming up in the register. Meanwhile, nothing stirred.

"I'll try the kitchen," she thought. She felt along the wall for the swinging doors that led to the kitchen. Finally she found them and pushed her way into the large room. Her feet felt the difference between the soft rugs in the dining room and the slippery linoleum. Now she heard faint clawing sounds. It seemed as if someone were scratching at the kitchen door which led to the alley outside, trying to pick the lock.

Desperately, Robin searched for the light in the kitchen. She stumbled over chairs and knocked into a table trying to find it. It should have been by the door, but it wasn't. Finally, she managed to touch the stove in the darkness. Maybe Nelly kept matches on the stove to light it. Her hands scrambled over the top of the range, feeling nothing but its even warmth. The scratching sound got louder.

"I have to find out who's at the door," Robin thought. "I can't just run away and let robbers get in here while everyone's sleeping."

Finally, her scrabbling fingers felt a small box on a ledge over the stove. Robin's hands shook as she slid the matchbox open and grabbed at the matches, and they all fell out onto the floor. Robin got down on her hands and knees as the mysterious scratching got louder. Surely they would have been able to pick the lock by now! Finally, she managed to get a match and find the box. She struck the match and it flared for a minute. Then she held the light as she got to her feet. Quickly, she ran with the lighted match in her hand to the kitchen door. But in the rush of air, the light went out.

Robin almost screamed with frustration, but she kept quiet, retraced her steps, and found the matches again. This time, she picked up the box and as many matches as she could manage. She lit one and walked slowly to the door. As she held the match up, Robin peered out into the darkness, ready to run if she saw a face. Slowly she looked out and saw . . . her own reflection. Shading the glass, she peered out again and saw nothing but darkness. Yet the scratching continued. Was the burglar crouched down on his knees? She tried to look down, but the lower half of the door was wood. The glass wouldn't allow her to see what was happening below it.

Cautiously, ready to run at the slightest movement, Robin slid the bolt on the kitchen door. Crack! It sounded like a shot, and she heard a loud, squealing sound. She opened the door quickly and saw a white ball flash past her and run into the house. It was Lorna Doone!

Robin collapsed on the floor. Tricked by the cat again! Then she heard soft footsteps in the distance. Swiftly, she bolted the door and tried to hide in the corner behind the stove.

The footsteps came closer and closer. Robin tried to breathe. Her heart was racing. The doors from the dining room swung open. Then she heard a voice whisper, "Robin? Robin? Where are you?"

She lit a match and saw her sister's face.

"Jo, you nearly scared me to death!" Robin cried. "What are you doing here?"

"You were taking so long I thought I'd better come down," her sister admitted. "I was worried about you."

"Thanks, but everything's fine. The cat was outside, scratching at the door, but there's no sign of the burglars," Robin announced.

"What was the cat doing outside?" Jo asked.

"Maybe they put her out at night?" Robin guessed. "Let's find out tomorrow."

She lit another match and easily found the light switch for

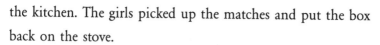

the kitchen. The girls picked up the matches and put the box back on the stove.

"Let's go to sleep." Jo yawned and Robin yawned back.

"And let's sleep late," Jo added.

"We can't sleep too late," Robin reminded her. "We have to find Greyfriars Bobby."

"Well, as late as we can," Jo said, feeling her way through the dark dining room and up the stairs. "Don't forget, we still have to get there without Mom and Dad finding out."

The girls snuggled down into their beds but after a few hours of sleep their rest was interrupted by a series of knocks on their bedroom door.

"Girls! Girls! Wake up!" their father called.

Robin threw on her bathrobe and struggled to the door while Jo slept on.

"What's the matter, Dad?" she asked.

"We went to Cousin Angus's room this morning to see if he was there and his bed hadn't been slept in. We've received no message from him so we think we ought to go to the police," he said.

Robin ran a hand through her tousled hair. "I'll wake Jo and we'll be dressed in a few minutes."

"No, you girls stay here," their father ordered. "Your mother and I will be back as soon as possible. You can catch up on your sleep and it might take a while before we finish at the

 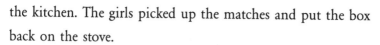

police station. It's a very complicated situation to explain, and we're foreigners."

"But, Dad—" Robin started to protest.

"No buts about it, Robin. We'll be back as soon as we can." Robin watched as her father marched down the stairs to where her mother was waiting. Looking up, her mother saw Robin and waved to her. Then her parents walked out the front door.

Robin closed the door to her bedroom and pounced on her sister's bed.

"Jo, wake up! Come on!" She shook her sister, who looked up at her with one eye open.

"Whassa matter?" Jo mumbled.

"Mom and Dad have left to go to the police station because Cousin Angus seems to have disappeared. Now's our chance to go to Greyfriars Bobby and get the next clue."

Jo sprang up and the two sisters washed and dressed hastily.

Nelly greeted them at the bottom of the stairs.

"Breakfast will be ready in half a tick," she announced.

"Oh, we don't want any breakfast," Jo blurted out.

"Och, you have to have breakfast, and besides, your mam and dad told me to make sure you stayed put," Nelly said, her arms folded across her chest.

Jo started to protest, but Robin dug her in the ribs.

"Ouch!" Jo yelled, but Robin smoothly interrupted by saying, "Of course, Nelly. We hadn't planned on going anywhere. We're

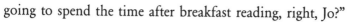

going to spend the time after breakfast reading, right, Jo?"

Jo looked at Robin as if she were demented, but when Robin poked her again answered, "Yeah, sure."

Nelly smiled and went into the kitchen. Jo turned to Robin and snarled, "Well, you can spend your day reading your stupid mystery books, Miss Perfect, but I'm going out to hunt for the clue."

"Shhh! Of course we're going to Greyfriars Bobby," Robin whispered. "I just don't want her to know."

"Why?" Jo asked.

"Because Mom and Dad told her to stop us from going out," Robin said, softly. "We can sneak out later when she's busy in the kitchen."

"Pooh!" Jo sniffed. "I'd like to see her try and stop me."

Nelly brought in the steaming tureen of oatmeal, and the girls got busy spooning it into their bowls and loading it with sugar and milk. They ate it as quickly as they could and when Nelly brought in the toast, she was surprised to see how much they had eaten.

"I couldn't eat another thing," Robin groaned.

"Me neither," Jo moaned, clutching her stomach.

"Very well," Nelly said. She started clearing the table.

"Let's go upstairs, Jo, and I'll give you my Agatha Christie book," Robin said, brightly.

"Great, I've been dying to read it," Jo answered.

They made a show of clumping up the steps and closed their bedroom door. Then Robin and Jo sat on their beds and waited.

"How long before we can sneak out?" Jo asked.

"I'm just waiting for her to go out," Robin said. "I noticed that after breakfast yesterday she left to do the day's shopping for dinner. Maybe she'll go out again today."

Robin cracked their door open and soon they were rewarded by hearing the front door slam.

"Let's go," Jo said.

"Let's wait a minute," Robin said. "Just in case she forgot something and comes back."

Jo danced in place while they waited. Finally, Robin gave the sign for both of them to go. Robin grabbed the guidebook and they walked down the stairs quietly.

"Oops!" Jo bumped into Munro at the bottom of the stairs.

"Good morning, lassies!" He smiled at them, his cheeks flushing pink.

"Good morning," Robin answered. She started to walk to the front door, but Munro stopped her.

"Nelly asked me to make sure you girls stay in until your parents come back," he stated.

"Really?" Robin looked down her nose at him. "Then we're prisoners?"

"Och, no, we just want to make sure you're safe," Munro said.

"Safe from what?" Jo asked. "Is Edinburgh so dangerous? It

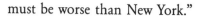

must be worse than New York."

"No, no, Edinburgh's safe as houses," Munro said.

"Then why do we have to stay in?" Jo asked.

Munro scratched his head. "I don't rightly know," he answered. "Nelly told me so."

"Do you always do what your sister tells you?" Jo asked.

"Mostly," Munro admitted. "I cannot thole her when she's unpleasant."

"Listen, Munro," Robin confided, "we just want to go out for a bit. We'll be back in an hour. Nelly won't be back before then, will she?"

"I don't think so. She said she would be awhile."

"Then be a good guy and let us go. After all, we have very little time left to see Edinburgh before we go back to the U.S."

"I see what you mean. It must be terrible to live with all those criminals there, people shooting each other every day. Is it safe to go out on the streets at all?" he asked.

Robin looked at Jo. "Not very," she said. "At home we travel with bodyguards all the time. They're armed with machine guns to protect us. Our house is surrounded by a huge electric fence. That way if burglars try to get in, we can electrocute them. You can see why we just want to walk around on our own here. Everything's so nice and peaceful. It's a wonderful change."

"If it's so terrible in the States, why do you stay there?" Munro asked.

 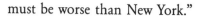

"Our parents make us. They don't really care for our safety. They're just selfish," Jo said. "Please, Mr. Munro, please let us go."

"Aw, go on with you," he said. "I'm that sorry for you. It's a braw day. Enjoy it." He opened the door wide for them and they walked out, trying not to laugh out loud, into the clear, sunny day.

CHAPTER TEN

The Mysterious Statue

 Freed from the house, Robin and Jo raced down the street, laughing. They finally stopped when they had gotten far enough away.

"Do you think he believed you about the fence and bodyguards?" Jo asked.

"He must have," answered Robin. "He felt sorry for us and let us go."

"It's hard to believe anyone could think that about the U.S." Jo kicked a stone on the sidewalk. "Do you think everyone believes it's so dangerous?"

"Of course not," soothed Robin. "But some of the people here just know what they see on TV or read in the newspapers. Remember, they've never been to the U.S."

"Which way do we go to get to Greyfriars Bobby?" asked Jo.

Robin pulled a map out of her pocket and the girls pored over it. Finally, they figured out their route.

"It's not that far from the castle," Robin pointed out. The girls walked up the Royal Mile then veered over to the Grassmarket. Robin shuddered as she read the guidebook.

"This was the place where they hung all the criminals," she said. "It was extremely popular because everybody had a good view because the place was shaped like a stadium."

"Never mind," Jo said. "Where's Greyfriars Bobby?"

The girls turned up Candlemaker Row and saw the statue of the little dog sitting on top of a fountain mounted on a column. They raced to the statue, narrowly missing several tourists who were busy snapping photos of the dog.

"Excuse me," a man dressed in jeans protested, "you're blocking my picture."

"We just want to—" Jo started to say, when the man shoved her aside.

"Hey!" yelled Robin. "Don't push my sister."

"You and your sister are rude little girls. Now my family and I came all the way from Ohio and we intend to take our picture with the little dog statue," the man announced. "Come on, honey." He motioned a woman in a pink top with four little children to the statue. Robin and Jo fumed while he posed them for several different shots.

"Oops! Tommy blinked," he said. He took the photo again.

"Jessie pinched me," one of the little girls complained.

"Now you girls stand in front with Mom in the back," the man went on. "Everybody say 'cheese'!"

Robin and Jo shifted from foot to foot while the man snapped away. Finally, he ran out of film.

"You kids stay right there with Mom while I run to the store," he ordered. "There must be a place around here where I can get some film."

Robin inched towards the statue.

"Excuse me," she murmured, "I just want to look at the statue."

While one of the little boys banged her knee with a sticky lollipop, Robin felt under the statue. There was a piece of paper stuck under there. Robin pulled it out and crumpled it in her hand.

"What's that?" the woman in the pink top asked.

"Nothing," Robin mumbled. She turned to Jo and said, "Let's go."

"Wait a minute!" The woman in pink moved in front of them and put out her hand to stop them.

"Why are you trying to stop us?" Jo asked.

"I think you kids are up to something, touching that statue. I think you took something from it or you did something you shouldn't do. You were too eager to get to the statue. Something's fishy here."

"We didn't do anything wrong," Robin protested. The little boy tackled her knee and held on.

"We'll see about that," the woman replied. "You just wait until my husband gets back and we'll get to the bottom of this."

"You're not my mother!" Jo cried. "I don't have to listen to you." She broke off and started to run away. Robin tried to follow her, but the woman held onto Robin's arm and the little boy still grasped her knee and banged even harder with the lollipop.

"Ow! Let go of my arm!" she yelled.

"Not till I find out what's going on!" the woman cried.

Tears came to Robin's eyes, and she wiped them with her free hand. She tried to squirm away but the woman held her tightly. Finally, Robin looked down, realizing the little boy had stopped hitting her knee. She glanced around and smiled.

"You'd better pay attention to your own children. They're running across the street," Robin said.

The woman whipped her head around to see that her children were trying to cross the road. Immediately, she let go of Robin's arm and ran after them, crying, "Tommy! Jessie! Mark! You get back here! Mary! Get back here right now!"

As soon as the woman dropped her arm, Robin raced off after Jo. In the distance she could hear the woman yelling, "Stop that girl!" mixed with shouts for her children. But Robin never looked back. She ran across the bridge and soon turned right onto the Royal Mile.

"Pssst! Robin!"

Robin looked around wildly and saw Jo hiding in the doorway of a museum.

"I thought I lost you," Jo complained. "What took you so long?"

"That woman grabbed my arm, the one that Tammie twisted," Robin said, rubbing it. "I couldn't get loose without hurting myself."

"Do you have the clue?" Jo asked.

Wordlessly, Robin showed her the crumpled paper. Robin opened it up and together they looked at it. It read:

> *My happiest days, forsooth*
> *Were in my youth.*
> *The place where childhood's sweet*
> *Is where my clue you'll meet,*
> *By the toy that's black and red,*
> *Be careful you don't lose your head.*

"Some clue," said Jo. "I don't have the slightest idea of what he's talking about."

"Me neither," said Robin. "I guess we might as well go back."

"Excuse me," said a woman. "Are you going into the museum?"

"I'm sorry," said Robin. "I didn't realize we were standing in the doorway." She moved back from the entrance and let the woman go in. Then she glanced up at the sign over the door.

"Jo," she asked, excitedly, "do you believe in signs from heaven?"

Jo followed Robin's eyes and looked up too, then grinned.

"The Museum of Childhood," she read. "This must be the place where 'childhood's sweet.'"

Robin and Jo hurried into the building.

"There are plenty of black and red toys," Jo said. "I don't see how we're going to figure out which one he means."

Robin was distracted by the exhibits.

"Look, here's one on castor oil. It says they gave castor oil to children like we take vitamins today. It was supposed to have no taste, but the sign says 'that was a black lie.'"

"It must have tasted awful," Jo said, wrinkling her nose. "Look at the teething doll. How weird! It was for teething babies. You tied a human tooth to the doll and it was supposed to take away the pain. They didn't know much about medicine then."

The girls wandered through the exhibit, marveling over the dollhouses and the giant teddy bears.

"If we weren't looking for the clue, this would be such fun," Jo said. "I love the doll made from an old shoe."

"Yes," said Robin, "and the little grocery store is adorable. It's got everything." They oohed and aahed at the little drawers marked "Chocolate," "Pepper," and "Coffee" and the tiny model hams and cheeses.

"Look! There's the Loch Ness monster!" Jo cried. She pointed to a monster made of carved and painted wood. A man in a boat above it was looking for Nessie.

"Here's the haunted house section," Robin said. She glanced at the skeleton and monster toys and moved on. She looked closely at some soldiers in red and black uniforms but saw no clue.

"I'm about to give up," Jo said. "I'm tired and besides, Mom and Dad are probably back now."

"I guess we'd better leave," Robin said, looking at her wristwatch. "It could take ages to find the clue here."

"One more room," Jo said. They walked past rows and rows of marching toy soldiers. The girls peered at each row, but saw nothing.

Then they heard shouts of laughter coming from a group of children clustered around an exhibit. The girls moved over to the group and Robin asked one of them, "What is it? What are you laughing at?"

"It's so funny," a little boy answered. "Here, miss, take a look."

He moved over and a space opened up for Robin to see. The toy was marked "Madame Guillotine." It was a miniature guillotine, and each time the mechanism moved, the blade came down and cut off a little head. The head was attached to a string and after it rolled off, the string pulled it back up ready to be cut off again.

"It's black and red," mumbled Robin.

"Don't lose your head," Jo said at the same time.

Robin and Jo waited for the other children to leave. Finally, they pulled the head one last time and a man came along and herded them into line. Robin raced over to the exhibit and felt under the table.

"Aha!" Triumphantly, she pulled a piece of paper out.

Just then, a guard strolled into the room.

"Let's go," Jo said. "We'd better get back."

Robin and Jo hurried out of the building and down the Royal Mile.

"Do you want to look at the clue now?" Jo asked.

"Let's wait until we get back to the house. I didn't realize we'd been gone so long. It's been four hours since Mom and Dad left," Robin said.

"I hope they're not back yet," Jo said.

They turned a corner and ran into a policeman.

"I'm sorry, Officer, but we're in a hurry to get back—"

"That's all right, lassies," the policeman said. "You wee things didn't hurt me."

"Stop those girls!" a voice cried.

The policeman eyed them with interest.

"It seems that someone wants me to stop you," he said.

"Yes, Officer," Robin said, "but I can explain. We really didn't do anything to the statue. I wouldn't do something like that. That woman was wrong."

"Absolutely," chimed in Jo. "She was just mean. We did nothing."

"I'm very interested to hear about this," the policeman said, "but it's not a woman who wants you. It's that laddie over there."

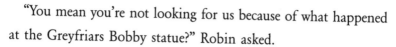

"You mean you're not looking for us because of what happened at the Greyfriars Bobby statue?" Robin asked.

"Och, no!" the policeman said. "I'll be moving on now."

He walked off just as Munro came running up, saying, "You girls fooled me before, but you're not fooling me now. You're coming with me. Let's go."

CHAPTER ELEVEN

The Mysterious Disappearing Girls

"What do you mean scaring us like that?" Robin asked.

"Yeah," said Jo, "we thought you were someone who wanted to get us arrested."

"Never you mind, girls," Munro said. "Nelly's that angry with me that I let you go with all that daft talk about guards and guns. You were fooling me, weren't you?"

Robin blushed. "Well, maybe we exaggerated a little, but it is a lot more dangerous than Scotland."

Munro grabbed their arms and hustled them along.

"Where are we going?" Jo asked.

"I'm taking you back to Nelly where she can keep an eye on you," Munro growled.

"Ouch!" Jo cried. "Ease up a little. You're hurting my arm."

"Very well," he said, "but we have to hurry."

"Are our parents back yet?" Robin asked.

"Not yet. That's why I want you to hurry." And Munro set his jaw grimly and wasted no words as they walked briskly back to the house.

As they climbed the stairs to the front door, Jo whispered

to Robin, "Do you still have the clue?"

Robin nodded.

Nelly opened the door and watched them as they came in.

"Where did you think you were going?" she asked, scornfully. "You were supposed to stay here. Now go up to your room and, Munro, sit outside and make sure they don't leave it. Do you think you can do that?"

Munro looked at her and then escorted the girls up the stairs to their room. Robin slammed the door in his face, and they heard him settle down outside.

By this time, Jo was bright red with rage.

"Who does she think she is, locking us up! Wait till Mom and Dad come back! I'll fix her!" she ranted as she paced around the room.

Robin was busy smoothing out the piece of paper she had crumpled in her hand.

Jo stopped pacing and ran over to her.

"What does it say?" she asked, excitedly.

"Shhh! Let's whisper. I don't want Munro to hear," Robin said. She opened the paper and read:

> "It was Mary, always Mary
> That was the queen of hearts.
> It began with her and ends with her.
> It was Mary from the start."

"That's not much help," Jo grumbled. "Who's Mary?"

"I don't know. Unless . . ." Robin was lost in thought. Then she picked up their guidebook.

"What does it say?" Jo asked.

"It talks about Mary, Queen of Scots, who came here in the 1500s. She lived in the Palace of Holyroodhouse."

"Where's that?"

"At the other end of the Royal Mile. I think we have to go there," Robin said.

"How are we going to get out of here?" Jo asked.

"Let's wait until Mom and Dad get back. They can't be much longer. Then we'll ask them to go with us," Robin said.

"That sounds good," sighed Jo. "I'm tired of doing everything ourselves."

The girls read for a while, then Robin looked at her watch.

"Mom and Dad should have been back by now," she said. "I'm getting worried."

She opened the door and asked Munro, "Are our parents back yet?"

He shook his head, folded his arms, and refused to talk to her.

Just then, Robin heard the downstairs door open. She could hear her father's voice.

Quickly, Munro slammed the bedroom door and held it tight. Robin struggled to get it open, but he was too strong for her.

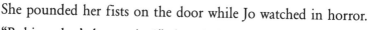

She pounded her fists on the door while Jo watched in horror.

"Robin, what's happening?" she cried.

"Mom and Dad are back and Munro won't let us out."

Jo started kicking the door while Robin pounded on it again, but no one came to their rescue.

"Why don't they hear us?" Jo cried.

"The door is too thick," Robin muttered. "Why won't he let us out? Are they keeping us prisoner here?"

Jo began to cry. "I want to get out. I want to go home. I want Mom."

Robin hugged her sister. "Don't worry, Jo. We'll find a way."

She pounded on the door again and this time Munro opened it.

"There's no use your knocking on the door. You're not getting out," he said smugly.

"Why are you keeping us here?" Jo asked.

"Nelly's orders," he answered.

"We want to see our parents," Robin stated.

"Ah, too bad, they're gone," Munro replied.

"Gone? What do you mean?"

"Nelly told them you've been missing for hours. They went out to look for you," Munro explained.

"But . . . but . . . that's not true," Jo sputtered. "We're here. Why would you do that?"

Robin looked at Munro and then turned to Jo. "Because

 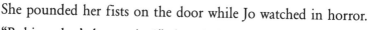

they're in with Tammie. Somehow Tammie must have promised them something if they'd help him."

"Is that so?" Jo asked.

"Aye, your sister's a smart one," Munro said, grudgingly. "Tammie has promised Nelly the moon if she'll help him find the will. And you two seem to be the only ones in her way."

"But we're not in her way," Jo protested. "We don't know anything."

"Don't try to fool me again," Munro said. "We know you've solved the clues. Nelly will be up soon to get the answer from you."

"But we haven't," Robin protested. "We don't know anything more than you do."

"Enough of your lies! Back into the room," Munro said, and he shut the door tightly.

"How are we going to get out of here?" Jo was shaking.

"We'll think of something," Robin said. She sat down on her bed and began to plan.

"I've got it," she announced. She looked out the window and smiled.

"It's perfect," she said to Jo.

Jo looked out, too. She saw what looked like a ten-foot drop from the steep roof outside their window to the bottom of the garden.

"Robin, that's a long way down. We'll never be able to escape that way."

"We won't have to if my plan works," Robin said.

The girls stripped the beds of their sheets and made a long chain, tying the sheets together. They dropped them out of the bedroom window.

"Ready?" Robin asked.

"I guess so," Jo gulped.

Robin made a loud noise and jumped up and down.

When Munro opened the door to see what was happening, the girls were gone. He looked out the window and saw the sheets fluttering in the breeze.

"Nelly! Nelly! They've escaped!"

He ran to the top of the stairs and called again.

"Nelly! Come quickly!"

Soon his sister joined him in the room.

"How did you let them get away this time?" she snapped.

"I guarded the door just like you said," Munro answered. "How was I to know they'd jump out the window?"

"Fool! Go after them. They can't have gotten far!" Nelly ordered.

"What about you?" Munro asked. "If I have to follow these girls around like a hound dog, what are you doing?"

"I've got to go tend to Angus. Tammie wants me to make sure he's fed and locked up tight."

"It seems like this will is more trouble than it's worth," Munro said. "Are you sure this is what you want?"

"What I want? Live like a princess instead of cooking and

cleaning up after other people. Have a house of my own instead of renting a room somewhere. Be able to take care of my no-good brother without worrying that I'll have nothing left. Of course it's what I want, you idiot! Now go. I'll meet you back here in an hour."

When they left the room, it was silent. Robin and Jo waited for ten minutes. Then, sure that Nelly and Munro had gone, they crept out of the closet.

"That was brilliant, Robin," Jo said. "They never even thought of looking in the closet for us."

"Thanks, Jo," Robin replied. "I got the idea from a mystery book. Sometimes if something seems obvious, people don't look elsewhere. Now let's get out of here."

"Where should we go?" Jo asked.

"I say the Palace of Holyroodhouse. At least we'll solve the last clue. Then maybe we'll have something to bargain with. Anyway, we don't know where Mom and Dad are, nor where Tammie's keeping Cousin Angus."

They hurried out of the house, looking both ways to make sure Nelly and Munro weren't lurking.

"All clear," announced Jo, and they ran down the road as fast as they could.

The Mysterious Mary

 Keeping a sharp lookout for Nelly and Munro, Robin and Jo hurried down the Royal Mile. They passed stores displaying red-and-green-tartan kilts and mysterious-looking antiques shops with cloudy windows and dark interiors. Crowds of tourists bumped into them from time to time, but the girls hurried on ahead, murmuring "Excuse me" or "Sorry."

Finally, they saw in the distance the large green hill that loomed over the palace.

"We're almost there," Robin said, puffing. "That's Arthur's Seat."

"Like King Arthur?" Jo inquired.

"No, the guidebook says it probably was called 'Archer's Seat' because people hunted there with bows and arrows, but over the years it became known as 'Arthur's Seat,'" Robin responded.

"Here's the palace," she added, and they walked through a gateway to the great stone castle.

"This is huge," said Jo, gazing up at the building of yellowing stone. "Where do we start?"

Robin bought a guidebook and thumbed through it hastily.

"Here!" she announced. She pointed to a page and read, "Mary, Queen of Scots' bedroom is the most famous room in Scotland. This is where the Queen's bed, of crimson damask bordered with green silk fringes and tassels, rests along with various tables, benches, and chests supposedly used by the Queen."

"Let's go," Jo said, and the girls followed the plan in the guidebook and raced up to the second floor of the palace.

There, they carefully and cautiously examined the tapestries, the furniture, the bed, and the paintings on the wall. Robin moved from her side of the room to Jo's side. Each shook her head. They had found nothing. The guard began looking at them suspiciously.

"Let's go see the gardens," Jo suggested. The girls clattered down the great staircase and out into the late afternoon sunshine.

"Nothing," Robin said.

"Nothing," echoed Jo. "Are you sure this is the place?" she added.

"I don't know any other Mary," Robin said. "Do you?"

"Maybe Uncle Ambrose was making a joke," Jo said. "If he was joking, I don't think it's very funny."

"We've got to find that clue," Robin said. "That's the only way we'll be able to get Angus back."

"You're going to trade them the clue for Angus?" Jo asked in disbelief.

"We have to get them to let him go," Robin said. "Who knows if he's safe or what they've done with him?"

"They'd better not try anything," Jo remarked, grimly. "So what do we do now?"

"I think we should go back to the house and pretend we've found the clue," Robin said. "Mom and Dad will have to come back sometime, and meantime, maybe we can fool Nelly and Munro into letting Angus go."

Jo shuddered, but followed Robin back to the house. Their mother and father were in the hall talking to Nelly.

"Girls, where have you been?" Mrs. Bridge pushed back her hair in her most distracted manner. "We were frantic looking for you."

"Oh, Mom," Jo cried, running into her mother's arms, "they wouldn't let us out of the room. I heard you and they wouldn't let us go to you." She started to sob desperately.

Mr. Bridge looked at Robin with a puzzled expression.

"Just what's been going on here?" he demanded.

"Dad, you wouldn't believe it," Robin said. "First, Nelly kept us locked up. Then we escaped and went to Greyfriars Bobby and—"

"I'm afraid the girls have been very naughty," Nelly interjected smoothly. "They refused to listen to me and I sent Munro after them. I'm sure you didn't want them wandering around on their own." She smiled at the girls smugly.

"But . . . but . . . that's not the way it was!" Robin cried. "Mom, Dad, she's part of the plot. They're keeping Angus prisoner somewhere."

"Och, their heads are full of nonsense, Mr. Bridge," Nelly replied, smoothing her apron. "I've just heard from Mr. Angus. He was called away on business to Glasgow and wants me to give you his apologies. Unfortunately, he won't return until after you leave."

"That's not true!" Robin exclaimed. "I heard you and Munro plotting. You've got Angus locked away somewhere."

"I don't know who to believe," said Mr. Bridge, looking from Robin to Nelly. Jo continued sobbing in her mother's arms.

"Let's go up and calm these girls down," Mrs. Bridge suggested. "We'll call that nice policeman who helped us at the station, and ask him to come here. He can help us find Cousin Angus."

"Yes, that seems a good idea," Nelly agreed.

Robin noticed that Nelly watched them as they all went up to the girls' room.

"I wonder what she's up to," Robin thought to herself.

Finally Jo stopped sobbing and started hiccuping.

"What Robin—hic—said was true," Jo announced. "Hic—they do have—hic—Angus stashed away someplace."

"It seems hard to believe," Mr. Bridge murmured.

"Dad, why would we lie?" Robin cried.

"I'm not saying you're lying, but sometimes you girls do get carried away," he explained.

"Why don't you call that policeman?" Mrs. Bridge asked. "I'll get Jo some water for those hiccups."

Mrs. Bridge opened the door and then backed away. There stood Nelly with a revolver.

"I don't wish to hurt you or your family, but you must stay in the room until we've found the last clue," Nelly announced, waving the gun.

"Nelly, put that gun down!" Mr. Bridge ordered.

"Just get back in there," Nelly replied. "I'm on guard here until Tammie arrives. Do as I say and no one will be hurt."

She stepped into the room and Jo and Robin shrank back when they saw the gun. Nelly smiled at their distress and said, "If you don't want trouble, you'll tell me what the last clue said."

Robin shook her head. "I'm not going to tell you until you let Cousin Angus go."

"That's not up to me," Nelly said. "That's Tammie's decision, but if you help us, I'm sure he'll let Angus go."

"How do I know he'll do that?" Robin asked.

"You don't. You'll have to take that risk," Nelly said. "The clue. Now."

"Give her the clue, Robin," Mr. Bridge said. Mrs. Bridge and Jo watched, their eyes wide, as Robin handed over the crumpled piece of paper.

"Hmm. Mary," Nelly mused. "What do you think it means, Miss Cleverboots?"

"I think it's a clue hidden at the Palace of Holyroodhouse.

I'm sure it has something to do with Queen Mary," Robin answered.

Jo started to protest, but Mrs. Bridge told her to be quiet.

"But Mom, she's giving it away and it's not fair," she whined.

Robin watched Nelly steadily.

"You're probably right," Nelly admitted. "The old fool seemed to be unusually fond of Scottish history." She tapped her foot. "I have to get to Tammie, but I can't leave you here free to call the police. Munro, Munro! Where is that idiot? Munro, I need you!"

Munro came clumping up the stairs and turned pale when he saw the gun in his sister's hand.

"You never said anything about a gun, Nelly," he gulped.

"Never mind that," she snapped. "Help me tie these people up."

"Isn't this going a wee bit far?" Munro asked. "I mean guns and tying people up, seems a bit much."

"Are you a man or a mouse?" Nelly sneered at him. "Come on, you weak-kneed gowk!"

Munro bit his lip, but used the bed sheets to tie the family up.

"Now, tie the pillow slips around their mouths so they can't blub," Nelly ordered impatiently.

Finally, Munro finished and he and Nelly left the room. The girls looked at their parents and Jo began to cry again, while Mrs. Bridge tried to make soothing noises. Then Munro ran back, his finger to his lips. He took the gags off the girls and said, "Hush! Don't say a word. Wait until we're out of the house and then you can yell for help."

"Thank you," whispered Robin.

"House or no house, I don't hold with guns," Munro said, and then disappeared again, calling, "I'm coming, Nelly! Hold your horses, I'm coming!"

"Jo, try to wriggle out of your sheets," Robin said. "Mine aren't that tight. I bet we can get out of them fast and help Mom and Dad."

As she turned to and fro, trying to loosen her bonds, Robin stared at the painting of the sweet-faced woman in the picture, Uncle Ambrose's wife. What was her name? Robin couldn't remember it.

She kept on maneuvering. The sheets felt a bit looser. Soon, she'd get them off. It took another half hour, but finally she was able to slip the sheets off her wrists. Meanwhile, her father and mother had managed to loosen their sheets and Jo had almost gotten hers off. Robin glanced once more at the painting before she turned to help her parents and her sister. Then it hit her.

"Robin, why are you stopping? Come on, help me get loose!" Jo complained.

Robin turned back and helped free her sister and her parents. Mr. and Mrs. Bridge stamped up and down, getting the circulation back in their arms and feet. Jo jumped a few times.

"What are you staring at?" Jo asked, as Robin continued to gaze at the painting.

"What was Uncle Ambrose's wife's name?"

"I don't know," Jo said. "Why would I remember something like that?"

"I think I know," Robin said. "I think it was Mary."

She reached behind the painting and felt the back of it carefully. There was nothing there.

"Dad, help me take the painting down," she ordered.

"All right," Mr. Bridge said, and lifted it onto the bed.

Robin turned it over. Then she scrambled to get her nail scissors.

"Do you really think there's something there?" Mrs. Bridge asked.

"We'll know in a moment," Robin said. She found the scissors and slit the paper backing on the painting. She felt inside the paper and pulled out a white envelope. On the front, it read: "Last Will and Testament of Ambrose McDougall."

"You found it! You found it! Hooray for Robin!" Jo cried, dancing around the room.

"I am impressed," Mr. Bridge said. "I guess reading those mysteries really does pay off."

Mrs. Bridge hugged Robin and said, "Now we have to find Cousin Angus and give it to him before Tammie and his crew can get their hands on it."

"I think the best thing will be to go to the police," Mr. Bridge said.

"Too late for that, Cousin," said a deep voice. "I'll save you the bother. Why don't you just hand that will over." And Tammie entered the room, with Nelly and Munro following him.

CHAPTER THIRTEEN

The Final Clue

 Tammie stalked over to Robin and held out his hand.

"All right, you've had your fun. Now, give me that will," he demanded. Nelly stood by the door, holding the gun, while Munro tried to move away from her. She grabbed him by the wrist.

"Stay here," she muttered. "You've done enough damage. How did they get out of those sheets so fast? Next time, I'll tie them up myself."

Munro stayed by her side but kept his gaze on the floor, careful not to stare at the sisters or their parents.

Mr. Bridge held up his hand. "Robin, give me the will."

"Okay, Dad," she said. She passed him the white envelope.

"Very clever," Tammie declared. "You want to keep your daughter out of danger. But you've only delayed the process. Now, I must insist. Give me that will or I'm afraid that I won't be able to control Nelly and her gun anymore."

"You wouldn't dare shoot us," Mr. Bridge retorted.

"Really?" Tammie sneered at him. "A tourist family visiting

here. No one knows you except Angus. If you went missing, who'd know?"

Jo started to cry again. "My friends! My friends would miss me!"

Tammie smiled scornfully, and didn't bother to answer.

"But you forget that we've been to the police," Mr. Bridge said, clutching the envelope. "They know all about us."

Tammie laughed heartily and Nelly echoed him. "It's tourist season in Edinburgh. Do you know how many tourists the police deal with each day? They'll never remember you. You're just one family out of thousands!"

Robin watched her father turn pale at the thought of putting his family in danger. Her mother stood trembling nearby, stroking the still-sobbing Jo. Robin thought her mother must really be afraid to shake so much. She realized she was wrong when her mother started speaking.

"Very well," she said in a cutting voice. "Take the will and this house, if you can. But first, Nelly must put down that gun and you have to tell us where Angus is. Otherwise, my husband and I will tear up the will before you can get it."

Tammie moved towards Mrs. Bridge but Mr. Bridge got in front of him.

"I wouldn't try it," he said. "You can shoot me, but we can still tear up the will before you're finished."

Robin stared in horror at Tammie and Nelly. Then she

noticed something that made her eyes open even wider.

"Look!" she cried.

Tammie and Nelly didn't move.

"That's the oldest trick in the book," Tammie drawled. "Trying to make believe there's someone behind us." Munro looked where Robin was pointing and moved away from his sister and Tammie quickly.

"It may be old, but it still works, Cousin!" And in walked Angus with four policemen. They quickly subdued Nelly and Tammie.

The Bridges ran to hug Angus, whose hair was standing on end and whose sweater and pants were covered with soot and dust.

"Cousin Angus, we're so happy to see you!" cried Robin, and the rest of the family echoed her. Meanwhile, Tammie stood watching, his green eyes blazing.

"You may have me arrested, Cousin," Tammie spat out, "but there's no charge to hold me on. Nelly had the gun. I didn't threaten anyone. She was crazed for the house and made me go along with her. I still stake my claim to Uncle Ambrose's will."

Nelly shot him a look of anger and said, "He promised me that if I would help him, he'd marry me and I'd never have to wait on anyone again. It's all his fault. He made me play all kinds of tricks on the family and take the gun. I would never have hurt anyone."

"What kind of tricks?" asked Robin.

"Aw, that first night, I was to frighten you out of the house. I grabbed the cat and shone the light in your eyes. Then I used that wee flash camera to blind you. I kept it thinking maybe you wouldn't stay in a house where your valuables went missing, but you just kept on. Then I searched your room for clues, but you came back too soon and I didn't have time to fix it up. I never did find the clues. You were too clever by half, miss," she answered.

"I told you there was someone in the room that night," Robin announced triumphantly to her mother. "But how did you get away so fast?" she asked Nelly.

"That closet has another door to it, hidden behind the clothes. You can pass through it to another guest bedroom. That's why I was so fashed when you were playing with the old lady's pink silk dress."

Jo was staring at Nelly. "You woke me up and scared me like that!"

"You were easy meat," Nelly mocked her. "What a baby!"

Jo clenched her fists. Tammie interrupted smoothly, "You see, officers, the woman is incorrigible. She makes up such amazing lies. I wouldn't marry her if she were the last woman on earth!"

"But you kidnapped Cousin Angus," Robin said.

"Did you ever see me?" Tammie asked Angus.

"No," Angus admitted. "I never saw anyone but Nelly. She

brought me food in that abandoned house you locked me up in."

"How did you get out?" Mr. Bridge asked.

"The last time Nelly was there she was in such a hurry she didn't realize I had jimmied the window open. I waited until she left, then crawled out onto the roof and down the drainpipe. Then I ran as fast as I could to the nearest police station. I was afraid of what might happen to you, cousins," Angus said. He ran his hands through his disheveled hair and tried to brush off his sweater.

"So you can swear to the fact that this woman locked you up, sir?" asked one of the policemen.

"Yes," Angus said.

As one of them led Nelly away, she protested her innocence.

"I never did nothing! Just a few tricks! And all because of that clarty Tammie!"

Robin moved forward as they started to put the handcuffs on Munro.

"He really is innocent," she said. "He tried to help us. Please don't arrest him."

"He'll have to help us with our inquiries," the policeman said, "but we'll probably go easy on him."

"Thank you, miss," Munro said gratefully, as he trudged off. In the distance, they could hear Nelly berating him for not helping her enough.

Robin shook her head. "I'm sorry for him."

The police were still questioning Tammie while the Bridges huddled around Angus. Then Mr. Bridge held his hand to his head.

"I forgot!" he said. "This belongs to you." He handed the envelope containing the will to Angus with a flourish.

"So much has happened since we first started searching for the clues," Angus said. "Where did you find it?"

Robin explained how they had first thought of Mary, Queen of Scots, and then realized that it was Uncle Ambrose's wife.

"After that, it was easy," she said. "I just examined the picture until I found it."

"I am grateful," Angus said. He opened the will and read it. Then he laughed.

"What's so funny?" Mr. Bridge asked.

"Here." Angus passed the will over to Mr. Bridge, who read:

"Greetings! Whichever of you has won the contest, congratulations! You are the sole heir to my house and all the furnishings therein. A detailed will follows but I will spare you the boring details.

"Suffice it to say that I hope the true Scotsman has won! As a final test, this will is valid only if the person possessing it can answer the following question:

"Who wrote: 'To be what we are, and to become what we are capable of becoming, is the only end of life'?

"This is one of the rules by which I've lived, hoping that I have been the best Ambrose McDougall I could be to my wife, my other loved ones, my friends, and my country."

Tammie had stopped talking to the police when Mr. Bridge began reading the will aloud. Now he glared at Angus.

"Well, Cousin, can you answer the question?" he barked.

"Of course," Angus said, smiling. "Can you?"

"Certainly," said Tammie, "but you possess the will so you go first."

Angus stared at him thoughtfully, then took the will from Mr. Bridge. He placed it on a table.

"Officer, in my uncle's library, you'll find a copy of *Bartlett's Quotations*. Would you please bring it up here?" he asked.

Tammie sat down on the bed while the girls lounged on the floor. Mr. and Mrs. Bridge stood near Angus, as if to give him support, while the remaining policeman watched Tammie closely.

"Cousin, I'll give you a sporting chance," Angus said. "If you can name the author of that quotation correctly, I'll split the house with you and drop all charges against you."

"You have no charges against me," Tammie said. "It was all that hag Nelly's fault. But I'll take you up on the offer."

The policeman came into the room holding a green book that looked faded and shabby.

"Is this the one, sir?" he asked.

"That's right. Thank you very much, Officer. Now, Cousin Bob?"

Before he could complete his thought, Tammie interrupted.

"No, not Cousin Bob. He'll favor you and cheat. Give it to the policeman."

"I never cheated in my life!" cried Mr. Bridge.

"Never mind," Mrs. Bridge soothed him. "Let's just see what happens, Bob."

"Very well, Cousin," Tammie said. "I'll go first. As any educated person knows, it was written by Robbie Burns."

Angus grinned. "Call yourself a Scotsman, do you? As any true Scot knows, it was written by Robert Louis Stevenson in *Familiar Studies of Men and Books*. Look it up, please, Officer."

The policeman thumbed through the pages and finally looked up at Angus. "Got it in one, sir."

Before anyone could stop him, Tammie sprang at Angus.

"I've hated you all your life. You always thought you were better than I was, always rubbed it in my face, Uncle Ambrose was always saying how clever you were . . ." he shrieked as he hooked his strong fingers around Angus's neck.

Angus's face turned red as the policemen and Mr. Bridge tried to pry Tammie's hands loose. But the blond man seemed possessed of enormous strength in his anger. Finally, they managed to wrestle him to the floor and subdue him.

"I believe you have grounds for charges now, sir," the

policeman said to Angus, dryly.

"Are you all right, Cousin Angus?" Jo asked.

"Yes, I'm fine," Angus said, a little hoarsely.

Tammie muttered incoherently as the police led him away.

"Poor fellow, I think he snapped," Angus said, shaking his head.

"I don't feel sorry for him or Nelly," Jo announced. "Not after they tried to scare me that night."

"Well, all's well that ends well," said Mr. Bridge. "Just in time, too. We'll be able to see you settled comfortably in the house, Angus, and we'll be able to enjoy a few days in Edinburgh before we go home."

"We'll have to have a party to celebrate before you go back," Angus said. "After all, if Robin hadn't solved the clues, this wouldn't have ended up so happily."

"I helped too!" cried Jo.

"Yes, you did," Angus agreed. "I'm going to plan a real Scottish party for you. Have you ever been to a ceilidh?"

"No, what's that?" Jo asked.

"It's a party where there's dancing and singing and story-telling," Angus answered.

"That sounds like fun." Jo's eyes sparkled. "Will there be anything good to eat?"

"I'll plan some special Scottish treats," Angus promised.

The next night the girls and their parents watched as Angus's friends whirled around the living room doing Scottish dances to the tunes the fiddlers played. After a while, the girls joined in, giggling when they made mistakes and messed up the dancing. But the other dancers helped them and soon they were twirling gracefully.

"Whew!" Jo fanned herself when the music stopped. "That Scottish dancing is hard, and it makes you hungry, too!"

"Ah, I almost forgot!" Angus heard Jo talking. "I have a special treat for you."

"What could it be?" Robin wondered.

"I hope it's Scottish pizza," Jo said.

He ran into the kitchen and brought back a plate filled with gray, mushy stuff.

"What's that?" Jo demanded.

"A special Scottish treat for you, Cousin. It's sheep's stomach—filled with haggis!"

Robin Bridge's Glossary of Scottish Words

Although everyone in Scotland speaks English, Jo and I learned a lot of Scottish words from Cousin Angus and his friends. They are fun to say and some of them sound entirely different from the way they're spelled.

SCOTTISH	AMERICAN
Bairn (pronounced "baren")	Child
Blub	Cry
Bogle	A frightening ghost
Braw	Fine (as in a braw day)
Ceilidh (pronounced "kaylee")	A party with singing, dancing, and storytelling
Clarty	Dirty
Cock-a-leekie soup	Chicken soup with leeks in it
Daft/daftie	Silly/silly person
Fash/fashed	Trouble or upset yourself
Fule	Fool
Gowk	Fool
Greengrocer	Shop that sells vegetables

SCOTTISH	AMERICAN
Haggis	The heart, liver, and lungs of a sheep mixed with fat, oatmeal, and onion, sewn into a sheep's stomach and cooked (YUCK!)
Hangit	Hanged
Joint	Roast (like roast beef)
Lad/laddie	Boy
Lass/lassie	Girl
Och	Oh
Pillow slips	Pillowcases
Pips	Beeps
Porridge	Oatmeal
Post	Mail/post office
Pudding	Dessert
Sassenach	Foreigner
Scone	A sweet cake that looks like a biscuit
Solicitor	Lawyer
Thole	Stand/like/dislike (as in "I can't thole her")
Wee	Small or little

Robin Bridge's Guide to Edinburgh

Remember, opening times and phone numbers change sometimes, and in some cases fees are charged, so you'll probably want to call ahead when you plan to visit these places. If you're calling from the U.S., dial these numbers before the number you want to reach in Edinburgh: 011-44-0131.

① Arthur's Seat

This is a huge, grass-covered hill (actually we found out it's really an extinct volcano) overlooking the **Palace of Holyroodhouse**. Jo and I discovered that it's 822 feet high at its highest point, and it's not as steep as it looks. We climbed it easily one day and had a great view of Edinburgh.

To the right when you are facing the Palace of Holyroodhouse.

② Brodie's Close

This was the home of Deacon Brodie, the model for Robert Louis Stevenson's *Dr. Jekyll and Mr. Hyde*. Deacon Brodie was hanged in 1788, on a gallows he designed himself. Today there is a café, Deacon Brodie's Tavern, inside the close (which is a little courtyard off the **Royal Mile**), where Jo and I had sandwiches, brownies, and soft drinks.

435 Lawnmarket. Open Monday-Saturday 12 p.m.-10 p.m., Sunday 12:30 p.m.-10 p.m. ☎ *225-6531.*

③ Camera Obscura

This really is a cool place. We went back again to see how they use the mirrors to show you a great view of Edinburgh.

594 Castlehill. April-October, open daily 10 a.m.-6 p.m.; November-March, open daily 10 a.m.-5 p.m. ☎ *226-3709.*

④ Clarinda's Tea Room

This is a cozy little place to have a snack. The cakes are delicious, and Jo and I loved the shortbread. Clarinda's is on the way to the **Palace of Holyroodhouse**, so you can stop before or after you tour it.

69 Canongate. Call for hours. ☎ *557-1888.*

⑤ Edinburgh Castle

This is incredible. The castle is huge and there's so much to see. Walking up the **Royal Mile** to the castle, you can imagine what it was like to come here hundreds of years ago. The castle looks like a huge piece of rock that someone hacked out of a mountain. Inside, Jo and I loved the Honours of Scotland, which is what they call the Scottish Crown Jewels. The crown, covered with pearls, diamonds, amethysts, and garnets, is beautiful. We read that the jewels were hidden inside a wall to keep them safe, and they were only discovered after Sir Walter Scott got permission to open the wall. We also liked the Stone of Scone, which looks like any ordinary stone but it's supposed to have supernatural powers. When anyone is crowned under it, they get those powers, too.

Castlehill. April-September, open Monday-Sunday 9:30 a.m.-6 p.m.; October-March, open daily 9:30 a.m.-5 p.m. Closed December 25, 26. Call about the castle opening on New Year's Day. ☎ *225-1012.*

⑥ The Georgian House

If you want to see a house like the one we stayed in that Cousin Angus finally won, go to the Georgian House in the New Town. It's really perfect. We loved the drawing room with its elegant furniture.

7 Charlotte Square. Open April-October, Monday-Saturday 10 a.m.-5 p.m., Sunday 2 p.m.-5 p.m. ☎ *226-3318.*

⑦ The Ghost Tour/The Witchery Restaurant

The **ghost tour** was such fun. As Dad said, the jokes are corny, but when you're listening to spooky stories about Edinburgh, they seem a lot funnier. The guide told Mom that students from the university take turns dressing up as Adam Lyal, the supposedly dead guide. There are lots of good stories, but our favorites were the ones about the Mad Monk and Burke and Hare, the body snatchers.

Contact: The Cadies/Witchery Tours, 352 Castlehill, Royal Mile, Edinburgh, EH12NF. E-mail: info@witcherytours.com.
☎ *225-6745.* Ⓐ *www.witcherytours.com.*

The **Witchery** is a cool restaurant with lots of dark wood and candles. Jo and I ate delicious steak here, but there are many different kinds of things to choose from. We had dinner but it's also open for lunch.

352 Castlehill. Open noon–4 p.m. and 5:30 p.m.–11:30 p.m.
☎ *225-5613.* Ⓐ *www.thewitchery.com.*

⑧ Gladstone's Land

In the early 1600s, Mr. Gledstanes, a wealthy merchant, bought this six-story house. The city has restored it so you can see how people lived in those days. Even though Mr. Gledstanes was rich, Jo and I didn't think the way he lived was so great. The house is kind of dark and cramped. See what you think. And we didn't understand why it's not called Gledstanes's Land, instead of Gladstone's Land.

477 Lawnmarket. Open April–October, Monday–Saturday 10 a.m.–5 p.m., Sunday 2 p.m.–5 p.m. ☎ *226-5856.*

⑨ The Grassmarket

The Grassmarket is the place where lots of people were hanged. Today it's a big, bowl-shaped area that has shops, restaurants, and cafés. They always point it out on the tourist maps, but Jo and I were bored. The shopping is okay, but nothing special.

Walk east from Edinburgh Castle, turn right at George IV Bridge, and the Grassmarket is to the right and near the bridge.

⑩ Greyfriars Bobby

The statue with drinking fountain is on Candlemaker Row. Jo and I think the story is probably better than the drinking fountain, but it's fun to see. Nothing to go out of your way for, though.

Candlemaker Row near Chambers Street and the Grassmarket.

⑪ Lady Stair's House (The Writers' Museum)

There's lots to see at this museum, but you have to be interested in Sir Walter Scott, Robert Louis Stevenson, and Robert Burns. If you are, you can read their letters, see photos of them and their families, and find out more about them as people and as writers. I'm not sure most kids would be interested in these writers. It was special for us because we found a clue there. It is fun to see the uneven steps and find out why they built them that way. If your parents want to spend more time in the museum than you do, there is a big courtyard outside where you can wander around. It's where we saw the actors fencing.

Off Lawnmarket, behind Gladstone's Land. Open Monday-Saturday 10 a.m.-5 p.m. ☎ *529-4901.*

⑫ Museum of Childhood

This was the best! Jo and I could have stayed here all day. There's so much to look at. Make sure to see the little guillotine and the dolls and the tiny grocery store. There are lots of exhibits on what children did hundreds of years ago, and it's fun to compare them with what we do today.

42 High Street. Open Monday-Saturday 10 a.m.-5 p.m. ⓐ *Click on Museum of Childhood under Venues at: www.cac.org.uk/.*

⑬ Palace of Holyroodhouse

This was so different from **Edinburgh Castle**. The castle looks dark and rough. This is a beautiful, elegant palace, filled with luxurious pictures and furniture. I liked the King's bed chamber, where his bed was covered with a canopy and red curtains; Jo liked the Abbey Church, which is in ruins now. It's interesting to see because it was the original building before the palace was built. We both liked the display of things that belonged to Mary, Queen of Scots, like the pomander she carried so she could smell something good (everybody says that Edinburgh was very smelly hundreds of years ago) and the needlework panel she sewed with a picture of a cat.

Canongate, Royal Mile. Open daily November 1-March 31 9:30 a.m.-4:30 p.m. (last admission: 3:45 p.m.); April 1-October 31, 9:30 a.m.-6 p.m. (last admission: 5:15 p.m.). The palace is closed if the Queen is in residence. ☎ *556-1096.*

⑭ Princes Street

Along Princes Street between Waverly Station and Lothian Road is the main shopping area. There are lots of familiar shops like the Gap, and some stores that we don't have at home. It's a good place to go if you like discount bookstores. Jo got the latest Harry Potter at one of them, for half the price it would have cost at home!

⑮ Princes Street Gardens (East and West)

On the south side of the street, there's a long stretch of garden with grass, flowers, and benches. In warm weather, it's a great place to rest, sit, eat ice cream, and relax. We thought it was so pretty.

⑯ The Royal Mile

Most of the attractions in Edinburgh are on the Royal Mile or near it. There's also plenty of shopping on this cobblestoned street, with lots of tourist stuff like tartans, key rings, and T-shirts. Jo and I had fun browsing, but we didn't buy much.

⑰ Sir Walter Scott Monument

It's fun to see this and you can even climb up it. Of course, it's best if you can go with people who don't embarrass you by quoting poetry!

East Princes St. Gardens. March–May and October, open Monday–Saturday 9 a.m.–6 p.m.; June–September, open Monday–Saturday 9 a.m.–8 p.m., Sunday 10 a.m.–6 p.m.; November–February, open Monday–Saturday 9 a.m.–4 p.m., Sunday 10 a.m.–4 p.m. ☎ 529-4068.

⑱ The Writers' Museum

See **Lady Stair's House**.

Web Sites

These Web sites will give you a good idea of what to see in Edinburgh, although we discovered a lot more to see when we were actually there. Still, these sites will tell you the basic information and most of them have special links for kids. Jo and I liked the **www.timeout.com** site because it gives information for kids and it tells you what the local time is while you're at the site. You can get general information from **www.openroads-scotland.co.uk** and **www.aboutbritain.com**. The second site will also tell you about Edinburgh's history. There's also **www.edinburgh.org**. Some of the sites have maps, which are also helpful.

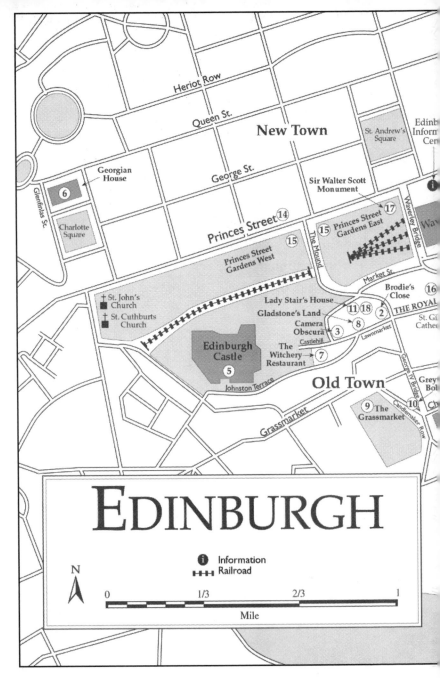

EDINBURGH

ⓘ Information
┣┅┫ Railroad

N

0   1/3   2/3   1

Mile

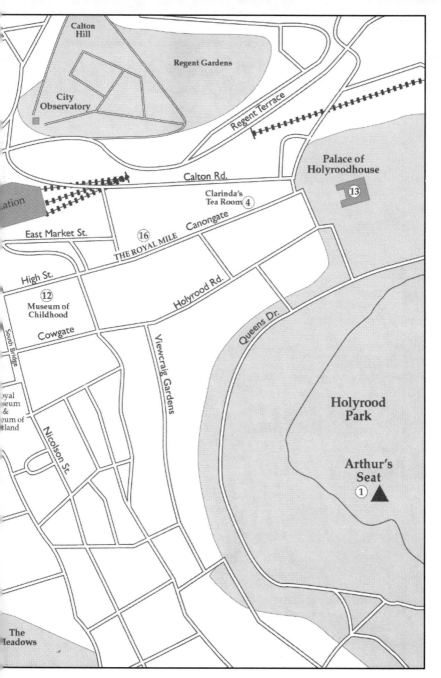

Calton Hill

Regent Gardens

City Observatory

Palace of Holyroodhouse

13

Calton Rd.

Clarinda's Tea Room **4**

ation

East Market St.

16

Canongate

THE ROYAL MILE

High St.

12
Museum of Childhood

Cowgate

Holyrood Rd.

Queens Dr.

Viewcraig Gardens

South Bridge

oyal
seum
&
eum of
tland

Nicolson St.

Holyrood Park

Arthur's Seat
1 ▲

The
Meadows

Also in the Going To series:

This image of a monarch butterfly was chosen as a symbol
for the Going To series because monarchs are strong flyers geared
for travel. They migrate between warmer and colder climates,
often ranging over several thousand miles in a single trip.